# THE
# GRIEF
## OF
# STONES

BY KATHERINE ADDISON

KATHERINE ADDISON

# THE
# GRIEF
## OF
# STONES

**TOR**

A TOM DOHERTY ASSOCIATES BOOK
NEW YORK

THE GRIEF OF STONES

Copyright © 2022 by Sarah Monette

All rights reserved.

A Tor Book
Published by Tom Doherty Associates
120 Broadway
New York, NY 10271

www.tor-forge.com

Tor® is a registered trademark of Macmillan Publishing Group, LLC.

The Library of Congress Cataloging-in-Publication Data is available upon request.

ISBN 978-1-250-81389-3 (hardcover)
ISBN 978-1-250-81390-9 (ebook)

Our books may be purchased in bulk for promotional, educational, or business use. Please contact your local bookseller or the Macmillan Corporate and Premium Sales Department at 1-800-221-7945, extension 5442, or by email at MacmillanSpecialMarkets@macmillan.com.

First Edition: 2022

Printed in the United States of America

0  9  8  7  6  5  4  3  2  1

*to my parents-in-law,*
*Bill & Elizabeth,*
*with much love*
*and many thanks*

On a cloudy autumn day, I attended the execution of Broset Sheveldar.

Anora tried to talk me out of it. He said, "Thou'rt punishing thyself, and it is pointless."

"It's not a punishment," I said. "I don't feel *guilty* about it. I feel *responsible*."

"Thou art splitting hairs," Anora said. "Well, if thou'rt going to insist, dost thou want company?"

"No," I said. "I thank thee, for it is a most kind thought. But I have no qualms about going alone."

"That's not what I asked," Anora said.

"What I *don't* want is to make thee attend this execution."

"I've attended my fair share," Anora said. "Another will not harm me."

"I know that. But . . ."

Anora looked at me over his spectacles. "Truly, thou wishest to go alone?"

"Truly," I said.

"Then I must let thee go," he said, although his ears said he would have preferred to keep arguing.

"I thank thee," I said.

Executions in the city of Amalo took place on the broad plaza in front of the Ulistheileian. They had switched from hanging to beheading in the reign of Prince Orchenis's father, Prince Orchena. Beheading was fast and could be expected to go right the first time, neither of which had been reliably true of hangings, even when the executioner was both competent and sober.

There was always a crowd for a beheading—in this way Amalo

was like every other city I had ever lived in. People seemed to emerge from the flagstones to surround the dais, men and women, elves and goblins, manufactory workers and shop clerks and the idle sons of burghers and nobility, and the vendors, every dozen feet or so, of quickly printed pamphlets about the murderer and his victims and whether or not he had repented of his crimes. Another prelate of Ulis was unremarkable in the crowd, which suited me very well.

They brought him out at noon, the traditional hour for executions. They had cropped his hair and tied his hands behind his back, and the two big goblins from the Vigilant Brotherhood made Sheveldar look almost delicate, breakable. I reminded myself of the women he had murdered, after seducing each one into believing he loved her. There was nothing delicate about Broset Sheveldar.

He stumbled on the steps up to the dais, but the goblins, not breaking stride, kept him upright until he reached the reveth-atha, where they let him fall to his knees.

The executioner was waiting. He didn't give Sheveldar time to think of resisting, whatever resistance he might have been able to make, but shoved his head forward and dropped the stock across the back of his neck. The crowd made a low noise, a sort of moan, and I flinched.

*Thou didst choose to come,* I reminded myself grimly, and then the blade came shining down with a *thwack!,* and the crowd's noise was more of a roar. Sheveldar's head fell into the basket, and that was it. He was dead.

Maybe now I could stop dreaming of his wives.

⟨⟨

It was a few days after Sheveldar's execution that I received a letter asking me to come speak to the Marquess Ulzhavel as soon as was convenient. I gave my black silk coat of office a close scrutiny for frays or dangling threads or other signs of wear, resolutely ignoring how faded it was, for about that I could do nothing. I braided and pinned my hair carefully, and went to visit the marquess that afternoon.

The Marquess Ulzhavel was legendary in Amalo for his stubbornness, he and his father before him. When all the other noble elven families had left the city for their country estates, the Ulzhavada had stayed put. Their property had become a slowly shrinking island amid the Airmen's Quarter and was now down to the original compound walls, which were mortared stone like the walls of the Veren'malo.

There was a liveried servant on duty at the gatehouse, a middle-aged elven man who watched my approach with frank curiosity.

I said, "We are Thara Celehar, a Witness for the Dead. The Marquess Ulzhavel has requested that we attend on him."

"Of course," he said and unlocked the gate.

He could not leave his station, but the way to the main house was unmistakable, broad and straight and lined with elesth trees that had probably been planted when the compound wall was being built. There was a bell rope beside the front door. I pulled it and heard the bell's muffled answer from inside.

It was a few minutes before anyone opened the door, another elven liveried servant, his hair very white and his eyes very pale against the plum-and-crimson-on-black livery of the Ulzhavada. I introduced myself, and he nodded. "The marquess is expecting you. Please come in."

The house was dark inside, great somber brocade hangings on every wall, and the drapes all drawn closed. I followed the servant through a snarl of narrow passageways and small interconnected rooms, wondering if the house had ever been renovated since it was built. Given the candelabrum the servant was carrying, it seemed unlikely that they had gas lighting; if anything, the house was becoming darker as we went. On the other hand, the house did not smell musty at all, and I admired the housekeeper.

We came to a closed door. The servant knocked and called, "The Witness for the Dead is here."

"Let him in," replied a voice from inside the room.

"The Marquess Ulzhavel," the servant said and swung the door open.

Inside, at least there was candlelight, showing a somewhat larger room, though with the same dark brocade hangings on the walls. Against the far wall was a desk, and behind it an old elven man, with a stony face and bright, pale, angry eyes. He was dressed in formal mourning, black-on-black brocade with black lacquer combs and onyx beads in his hair. The emperor's court would call him old-fashioned, but in Amalo, this was no more than was expected.

"We are Thara Celehar," I said. "A Witness for the Dead."

"Yes," said the marquess, in a voice as stony as his face. "We have been expecting you. Please take a seat if you wish."

I sat down, though cautiously, for the chair looked none too sturdy. "How may we be of service, dach'osmer?"

"You come straight to the point. We shall be equally forthright. We wish you to witness for our wife, Tomilo Ulzhavel."

I knew, of course, that the Marquise Ulzhavel was dead. It had been in all the newspapers. It had also been three months ago.

"We beg your pardon," I said, my heart sinking, "but after so long, there is nothing we can do. There is nothing of the spirit left."

"Not *that*," said Ulzhavel. "We meant what we said. We want you to witness for her. For we have discovered evidence that she was murdered."

"*Murdered?*"

"Here," he said and tapped something lying on his desk. "We found it among her papers."

I stood up and came closer. The anger in the marquess's eyes did not become less discomfiting. The thing on his desk was a note, creased as if it had been folded and opened and refolded many times. Printed across the paper in bold letters was the message STOP INTERFERING OR WE WILL MAKE YOU STOP. "We" was plural.

After a dumbfounded pause, I said, "Do you know what this note is about?"

"No. We have no idea. She never mentioned it to us, and she was involved in a number of charitable undertakings that might be construed as 'interfering.'"

That was alarming. I said, "Surely a judicial Witness—"

"No," the marquess said flatly. "We want a proper Witness for the Dead for our wife."

He was well within his rights to insist, though again old-fashioned. "Is there anyone in particular you think we should talk to?"

He shook his head with obvious regret. "We paid little heed to her activities."

"Is there someone we might speak to who *would* know?"

He thought for a moment. "Her closest friend was Dach'osmerrem Cretheno Cambesharan. But Dach'osmerrem Cambesharan does not believe that our wife was murdered, so we do not know if she would speak to you. You can ask Osmin Tativin, our wife's secretary. She kept track of the marquise's engagements."

"Where might we find Osmin Tativin?"

"She is still here. She is a cousin of the marquise, and she has nowhere else to go. We have told her she may stay until she secures another position. She is badly shaken by the marquise's death."

"How did the marquise die?"

"It was very sudden," the marquess said bleakly. "A thunderclap coronary is what our cleric decided."

"Had the marquise any history of heart weakness?"

"None," said the marquess. "We should have been suspicious from the start—but we could not imagine anyone wishing to harm her."

"She had no enemies?"

"None that we knew of. But she did not tell us everything."

"She did not tell you about the note?"

"No. We found it entirely by accident."

"Would she not have told you if she were afraid?"

"She *would* have told us. We can only conclude that she did not think it was serious, but we do not understand, in that case, why she kept it."

"Sometimes people's reasons are unknowable," I said. That was cause to regret that no one had had suspicions at the time of the marquise's death, for it was a question I might have been able to get an answer to. She might even have known from whom the note had come.

"Yes," the marquess said. "There is much about our wife we do not know. But will you witness for her? Not knowing the truth about her death will drive us mad."

"Yes," I said. "We will witness for the Marquise Ulzhavel. Although we must warn you that we may not discover an answer."

"We understand," said the marquess. "Any effort is better than nothing at all. And we have heard of you, Othala Celehar. We think it more likely that you will discover an answer than that you will not."

To which I could only bow and say, "Thank you, Dach'osmer Ulzhavel. We will make our best endeavor."

)(

I found Osmin Tativin where the marquess had predicted I would find her: in the late marquise's solarium, which was possibly the only room in the house into which sunlight was allowed to come.

Osmin Tativin was a middle-aged elven lady, tall, thin, and ferret-faced; she was wearing onyx mourning beads in her hair and hanging from her ears. My knock on the open door startled her; she came bolt upright from where she had been leaning over a secretary-desk. "Oh! Oh, othala, how you frightened us!"

"We beg your pardon," I said. "Are you Osmin Tativin?"

"Yes," she said, frowning in puzzlement. "Were you looking for us?"

"We are Thara Celehar, a Witness for the Dead. The Marquess Ulzhavel has petitioned us to Witness for his wife, Tomilo Ulzhavel."

The formal phrases seemed to alarm her further. "But what reason is there to petition a witness for the marquise? There is no question about how she died."

"The marquess believes she was murdered."

Her knees nearly buckled. I lunged across the room to steady her, but she braced herself on the secretary-desk and said, "We beg your pardon. But *murder*? Who would want to murder the marquise?"

"You don't know of anyone?"

"She was kindness itself," said Osmin Tativin.

"The marquess thinks she could have angered someone with her charitable work."

Osmin Tativin frowned. "The marquess is angry over his wife's death. He wishes there to be someone to blame, but there is not. She died of a coronary. Here in this room. We . . . we saw her die. How could she have been murdered?"

"We do not know," I said, "but the marquess's concerns seem reasonable to us. What charities was the marquise involved with?"

Osmin Tativin bit her lip, her ears dipping, then seemed to decide there was no harm in answering my question. "Education, mainly. She served on the boards of several schools for orphans and foundlings, and she helped start a school for airmen's children. She was also interested in some of the efforts to improve conditions in places like the Marigold Rookeries. And she was very keen to start a school for girls—not a school. More of a university."

"A university for girls?"

She bristled. "Do you disapprove?"

"No. We were just surprised that a lady of the marquise's age would support such a thing."

"She felt very strongly about education," said Osmin Tativin. "*Very* strongly."

"Do you know of anyone she might have angered?"

Osmin Tativin looked horrified. "You don't think it's *true,* do you?"

"We have been asked to witness for the marquise," I said patiently. "This means we must explore the possibility."

"We can think of no one."

I was fairly sure she was lying. "How about disagreements?"

"Well, of course," said Osmin Tativin, who was now wringing her hands. I was relieved that she was not hardening her stance and insisting that the marquise had never disagreed with anyone, either. "But we don't want to accuse anyone of murder."

"We certainly would not take any information you give us as an accusation."

That seemed to reassure her. She said, "It *is* true that the marquise disagreed frequently with Osmer Vobora Bazhevar, and she left the board of the foundling school in Cemchelarna quite suddenly, although we never knew the reason."

"Thank you, Osmin Tativin," I said. "That is very helpful."

"But we truly cannot imagine anyone murdering the marquise," she said. "The marquess *must* be mistaken."

"We will find out," I said and departed.

)(

I emerged from the confines of the Ulzhavadeise compound into the teeth of a bitter wind. I had purchased a shabby overcoat from Mer Estorezh, the secondhand clothes dealer, and I was grateful for it. I walked to the tram stop, debating whether I should try to see Osmer Bazhevar or Dach'osmerrem Cambesharan first. There was enough of the afternoon left for one, but not both—and that was assuming they both kept town residences. I decided as I took the tram north to the Veren'malo that I would try friend before foe.

Most of the city's nobility who kept town residences lived in the neighborhood of the Princess Vodreän Square, where several luxurious blocks of flats had been built on the grounds of the old Brenenada compound. I knew another member of the Cambeshada lived in what had been the opulent main house, so it seemed reasonable to find out if his family was nearby.

On my third attempt, I was lucky. The half-goblin gatekeeper admitted that Dach'osmerrem Cambesharan kept an apartment there, and sent an elven page boy running to see if she was at home to visitors. I didn't think my chances were very good, but the boy came back with an invitation to step inside.

I followed the boy through a tiled atrium and then up a wide spiral staircase with wrought-iron grilles at each landing. Dach'osmerrem Cambesharan lived on the third floor, where the grille was worked in an elaborate pattern of twining roses. The page boy produced a key and let me through the grille, carefully locking it again behind us.

The hallway curved clockwise around the counterclockwise spiral of the stairs until we came to a door with the Cambeshada's crest on it. The boy knocked, and the door opened so quickly that I knew the person on the other side had been waiting for us. She was a skinny part-goblin girl in servant's livery, her hair cropped close to her skull. She said, "This way, please," and I followed her, leaving the page boy to return to his post.

Dach'osmerrem Cambesharan was waiting in her receiving room, which had a series of narrow, arched windows looking out over the building's atrium. She was a diminutive elven woman, her white hair elaborately dressed with combs and tashin sticks and a strand of black pearls, in contrast to her clothes, which were of expensive materials, but very simple. Her eyes, cornflower blue, were full of lively curiosity, and she said, "We do not believe we have ever had a prelate call on us before. We are Cretheno Cambesharan. How do you do?"

"We are Thara Celehar, a Witness for the Dead. The Marquess Ulzhavel has asked us to witness for his wife."

Her mouth tightened. "Is he still insisting on this mad idea that Tomilo was murdered? We grieve for her, too, but that does not mean her death was *murder*."

I said, "We feel that the marquess's concerns are justified. Did he tell you about the note?"

"What note?"

"He found a threatening, unsigned note among the marquise's papers. Did *she* tell you about it?"

"A threatening note? Who in the world would want to threaten Tomilo?"

"That is what we are endeavoring to discover," I said. "Do you know of anyone who was angry at her?"

"Well, there was the Cemchelarna disaster. But that was nothing worth committing murder over."

"People will commit murder for surprisingly trivial reasons. What was the Cemchelarna disaster?"

"Tomilo had been on the board of a foundling school in Cemchelarna for years and years, and then they decided they wanted to economize by lowering the teachers' wages. Tomilo was *outraged*. She argued and argued and finally resigned. She said it was unconscionable and would destroy the school, and two years later, it turned out she was right. The school had to close. Tomilo never forgave any of them."

"Do you think any of them was angry at her?"

"We are sure they must have been, but we cannot imagine they were angry enough to kill. Tomilo did nothing to *cause* the school to close; she was merely correct that that was what was going to happen."

"Some people cannot bear to be proven wrong."

"We have known several such," agreed Dach'osmerrem Cambesharan, "but we still think it an unlikely reason for murder."

"Osmin Tativin mentioned an Osmer Vobora Bazhevar."

"*Him*," said Dach'osmerrem Cambesharan. "We would believe it of him, although you will still have to explain to us how he did it."

"What did he disagree with the marquise about?"

"What *didn't* he, is a better question. Tomilo used to say she was sure he meant well, but we are dubious even of that. He seems to be interested in pursuing only those matters which will allow him to be *seen* to be a great patron of charitable works—not those matters which would make a difference in the lives of the poor. He would rather tear a building down and build a new one than make simple and inexpensive repairs."

"We understand. And the marquise did not agree?"

"Tomilo was a very practical person. She had no patience for Osmer Bazhevar's posturing. And he in turn despised her."

"Would he—did he—describe her as interfering? That is the word the note used."

"We do not remember him ever using that specific word," Dach'osmerrem Cambesharan said carefully, "but it is certainly not contrary to his sentiments."

I would have to talk to Osmer Bazhevar, that much was plain. "Was there anyone else, to your knowledge?"

"No. Tomilo was not a contentious person, othala. She did not make enemies. We still think that Ulzhavel is letting his anger get the better of him. They had been married for fifty years, you know."

"And there were no children?"

"No. Tomilo never conceived. But Ulzhavel refused flatly to divorce her."

"Who is his heir?"

"His great-nephew, Otilis Ulzhavar. If *Ulzhavel* had been murdered, we would tell you to look no further. But Otilis was fond of Tomilo in his own way, and murdering her would avail him nothing." Her ears twitched. "Gracious, how callous we sound."

"You have been very helpful," I said. "Do you remember the name of anyone on the Cemchelarna board?"

"We never served on that board ourself, but just a moment." She crossed the room to where a secretary-desk stood against the wall. She rummaged through its pigeonholes and returned with a red octavo notebook, which she was paging through as she spoke. "We try to keep track of who serves on which educational committee or board. It saves a good deal of heartache when one is looking for someone to fill a seat—or attempting to start a new . . . Here we are!" She scanned the page she'd found. "Most of these people will not speak to you, but Hanaru might. Osmerrem Hanaru Ganatharan. She was *not* one of the people in favor of that idiotic policy."

"Thank you, Dach'osmerrem Cambesharan," I said.

"Well, if Tomilo *was* murdered, we certainly want you to find out who did it," she said. "But we hope you are wrong."

"So do we," I said and bowed.

✕

I took the tram south to the Ulvanensee stop and went to talk to Anora.

I found him preparing for a sundown funeral. As frequently happened, several families whose loved ones were scheduled for burial on the same day had pooled their money to get a funeral at the most auspicious time. Anora disliked conducting multiple simultaneous funerals, but Ulvanensee was ancient and vast and chronically crumbling to bits, and its prelacy needed the money.

"If thou wilt wait, Thara," he said, "we can dine together."

"I would like that," I said, and I spent a peaceful hour wandering among the strange, flat Amaleise gravestones while Anora performed the funeral rites for three old men who'd happened to die within a day of each other. Judging by the clumps of mourners, two had been elven and one goblin. Several of the mourners stayed long enough afterward to thank Anora effusively, to which he merely smiled and said, "We follow our calling."

Then he and I returned to the ulimeire, where I helped him out of his coat of office. He hung it carefully, saying, "There's another day dealt with. Will the Chrysanthemum suit thee for dinner?"

"Admirably," I said.

As we walked, I told him about the Marquess Ulzhavel's petition.

"Dost think he could possibly be correct?" Anora said.

"It seems unlikely," I said, "but not so unlikely that the possibility can be ignored. Tomorrow, I will go ask Dach'othala Ulzhavar if he knows of a poison that looks like a thunderclap coronary."

"It is terrible that someone might have poisoned a benevolent lady like the Marquise Ulzhavel," said Anora.

"Yes," I said. "It does seem possible that she could have angered someone unprincipled enough to resort to murder, although that is still only a theory."

"If the marquess thinks she was murdered, he must have some idea of who would do such a thing."

"He says he does not. He says he didn't know anything about her charitable activities. Of course, he also says that if the note had frightened her, she would have told him about it."

"And thou think'st that untrue?"

"She kept the note, and that's not what anyone does with an unsigned note that doesn't worry them."

"No," Anora said, "although that doesn't mean the note had anything to do with her death."

"True," I said, holding the door of the Chrysanthemum open for him, "but I find the coincidence as suspicious as the marquess does."

The Chrysanthemum was the sort of teahouse where people brought their families. The staff all knew Anora, and we were quickly seated at his favorite table in one of the window bays. It was not the table I would have chosen, but Anora liked to have a lot of light, and although the sun had set, there was a three-globed streetlight directly in front of the window.

We ordered a pot of isevren, which was a good evening tea, and agreed on the chicken pie for dinner. The server, an elven boy who Anora said was the son of the proprietor, brought the tea promptly, and the tea was quickly followed by two wedges of chicken pie, served with a sharp local cheese. Anora and I talked of other things over dinner, but once we had settled the bill and were lingering with the last of the isevren, Anora said, "Thara, truly, why dost thou think the marquise was murdered?"

"I suppose I have been infected by the marquess's certainty," I said. "There was something about that note that frightened me."

"Most of the time, unsigned threats are merely posturing," Anora said. "A coward's bluff."

"Yes," I said. All prelates of Ulis were familiar with unsigned notes not very different from the one the marquise had received. Like Csaiveise clerics, we were frequently blamed for the deaths we attended. A note I had received during my prelacy in Aveio had called me a murderer. The notes I had received when I started my prelacy in Amalo had called me worse, although that was for different reasons. "But this one was . . . I don't know, but I think it was a real threat and that it was carried out."

"But what could the marquise possibly have been 'interfering' in that would necessitate her death?"

"I don't know," I said. "That's what I have to discover."

X

I spent the next morning in my office in the Prince Zhaicava
Building, waiting for petitioners. There were none, and at noon I
was free to find a cheap lunch and take the tram to the Sanctuary of
Csaivo. The goblin novice on duty at the main entrance greeted me
politely and said, "Dach'othala Ulzhavar is in the mortuary, othala,
if that is whom you seek."

"It is, thank you," I said. I descended the spiral stairs, walked
along the gloomy passageway, and found Csenaia Ulzhavar—
middle-aged, elven, wearing worker's boots beneath his robes—
standing over a table in the middle of the mortuary and teaching a
novice—an elven boy, thirteen or fourteen, who looked like he was
about to faint—how to do an autopsy.

"Good afternoon, Othala Celehar," Ulzhavar said.

"Good afternoon, dach'othala," I said. "I have come with a
question."

"Your questions tend to be interesting," said Ulzhavar. "Tera, go
refill our water jug."

The boy fled gratefully with an almost whispered "Yes,
dach'othala."

"It's his first autopsy," said Ulzhavar. "It will get easier for him
with practice."

"Yes," I said, thinking of my own novitiate.

"But what is your question?"

"Is there a poison the effects of which would look like a thunderclap coronary?"

"You aren't asking hypothetically."

"I have a petition," I said.

"Ah. Well, the short answer is, yes, several, although most of
them are quite rare."

"But not all?"

"Hezhelta, which is lovely and grows wild in the Mervarnens, has a flower excellent for dyers and a root that is as poisonous as you could wish. Its effects are indistinguishable from a thunderclap coronary."

"How would you detect its use?"

"There is a quite characteristic scent when you open the abdominal cavity."

"After three months?"

"I have no idea. If you have an exemplar, I'd be happy to find out."

"I don't know if my petitioner would be willing, but if it comes to that, I will certainly remember your offer."

"Of course," said Ulzhavar. The novice returned with the water jug, and I saw the shift in Ulzhavar's attention. "Was there anything else, Celehar?"

"Not at the moment," I said and saw myself out.

✕

After Ulzhavar, I decided I would try to talk to Osmerrem Ganatharan. The Ganathada did not have a town residence, but their estate was near the last tram stop on the Kinreho line. Just as they couldn't afford a second residence, they couldn't afford to live farther out.

Their compound was small compared to others I had visited, small enough that there was no gatehouse, merely a walled approach to the front door. I rang the bell, and the door was opened by a goblin woman in livery of pale blue and gold on black.

"We are Thara Celehar," I said, "a Witness for the Dead. Is Osmerrem Ganatharan at home?"

She looked alarmed and murmured something about going to find out, before shutting the door and leaving me standing on the doorstep. At least it wasn't raining.

When the door opened again, it was Osmerrem Ganatharan herself, an ordinary-looking elven woman probably in her thirties wearing a pale green afternoon dress with dark green embroidery. "We do not understand," she said, almost plaintively. "Why do you wish to speak to *us*?"

I explained my errand. She looked even more bewildered. "But that was *years* ago. Why would anyone . . . ?"

"We do not know," I said. "But do you remember anyone being especially angry at the marquise?"

"They were too pleased with themselves to be angry at her," Osmerrem Ganatharan said tartly. "It was a nine-person board, and there were only three of us who didn't vote yes. The marquise protested the most loudly, but none of them was listening to her. We don't think anyone was angry enough at her to commit murder. And certainly not all these years later."

"Not even when the school failed?"

"They were far too busy trying to find someone to blame," she said, and then looked a little shocked at her own bitterness. "Truly, othala, if the marquise was murdered, it was not by a member of the Cemchelarna Foundling School Board."

"Was there anyone in particular she argued with?"

She shook her head. "Not that we remember. But it was five years ago."

"All right. Thank you for speaking to us."

"There was one thing," she said abruptly as I was turning away.

I turned back.

"It may be nothing, but if you want someone who was *angry* at her . . ."

"Yes?"

"Before all that, she was the one who insisted that Osmin Temin resign from the board, and Osmin Temin was *furious*."

"Why did she make Osmin Temin resign?"

"She said it was either that or she went to the newspapers, and Osmin Temin's reputation would be ruined. Osmin Temin was making the girls pay her to find them positions, and then turning around and making the employers pay her for finding them girls."

"That sounds very lucrative," I said.

"Oh, yes," said Osmerrem Ganatharan. "And it was not illegal! But the marquise said it was grievously unethical, and the rest of us agreed."

"Osmin Temin—what is her given name?"

"Pavalo."

"Thank you. Osmin Temin must have been angry at all of you."

"Yes. But she *blamed* the marquise."

"We understand. Thank you, Osmerrem Ganatharan. You have been very helpful."

"We don't know if we were right to tell you," she said anxiously.

"You were," I said. "If Osmin Temin did not murder the Marquise Ulzhavel, no harm will come to her. If she *did* murder the marquise, you will have helped to catch a particularly calculating murderer."

"All right," she said uncertainly.

"Yes," I said. "Thank you."

She watched me leave, still frowning, her ears low, and I wondered if, when I found Osmin Pavalo Temin, she would prove to be expecting me.

⋊

The next thing to do was to talk to Osmer Bazhevar, but here I hit the problem I had been expecting: Osmer Bazhevar did not want to talk to me. The message was delivered, in those words, by his doorkeeper. There was nothing I could do about it; my office only allowed me to compel cooperation from the dead, not from the living.

I went home, where five cats were waiting for sardines. I worried about them as it got colder, but thus far they showed no signs of distress. The half-blind queen allowed me to pet her when she was done eating, and the great rumble of her purr was soothing. This was the sort of night when I was most tempted to allow the cats inside my room, but I knew better. They were not mine and never would be.

I washed the sardine dishes in my tiny cold-water sink and then, from duty rather than desire, went to the Hanevo Tree and ate dinner. The servers here knew me the same way the servers at the Chrysanthemum knew Anora. They gave me a table against the back wall and brought me a two-cup pot of isevren without my having to ask. I ordered the bean soup, which I knew from past experience was almost as thick as a stew, with onions and carrots and generous chunks of sausage. It would be warming and possibly would induce some sense of comfort.

I drank tea and watched the patrons of the Hanevo Tree go peacefully about their evening. A maza whom I often saw in here was reading a thick book and frowning at it; two partners in a print shop were earnestly discussing their business; the owner had come out and was talking to the othas'ala from the othasmeire two streets over.

The soup came, and although I hadn't been hungry, I was able to eat and even to enjoy. I was almost finished when Subpraeceptor Azhanharad came in.

He saw me and nodded to himself before crossing the room to my table. "Good evening, othala."

"Good evening, Subpraeceptor. Will you sit down?"

He sat, wary as always. Born in the Mervarnens, Azhanharad was almost superstitiously uneasy about my calling—even though he made routine use of my services. He folded his hands on the table and said, "We have a girl. We need you to tell us if it's suicide or not."

"How did she die?"

"Drowning. The body was pulled out of the Mich'maika this afternoon when it got tangled in the ferry ropes."

"Do you need us to come tonight?"

"If you would. The body is . . . not in good condition."

"Of course." I drank the last of my tea, left money on the table, and followed Azhanharad out into the gaslit night.

We did not speak on the way to the Vigilant Brotherhood's Chapterhouse, a vast and ancient stone building on the corner of General Parzhadar Square. In their vault, the girl's mangled body had been hidden beneath a white sheet, and a novice had combed and braided her hair, so that she looked quietly respectable, as she probably would have in life. She was part goblin, her hair an ashy gray that matched her skin. She was very young.

I said the prayer of compassion for the dead and touched her forehead. It was difficult to find anything—the water had washed much of the girl's spirit away—but I finally managed to grip the things Azhanharad most needed to know.

I stepped back. "Her name was Isreän. No family name—she was a foundling. And it was definitely suicide." I shivered a little, remembering the despair that was the most vivid thing about her. "She was pregnant."

Azhanharad sighed in what I knew was anticipation of a weighty task, mixed perhaps with a little compassion. A pregnant woman had to be buried with particular care to be sure the dead child did not rise and go in search of its father.

"Do you know where she came from?" he asked, though not hopefully.

"No. We are sorry."

"Do not be sorry, othala. You have given us valuable information. We merely regret that there is no one to tell about her death."

"She had no one," I said. "She was just a drudge to her employer, and there was simply no one else."

"Clearly she expected nothing from the child's father."

"Her employer."

"Gah," said Azhanharad, pinching the bridge of his nose for a moment. "And that situation is little different from that of hundreds of foundlings across the city."

"Yes," I said. No one envied the foundling's lot.

"The Brotherhood will always accept foundlings," he said. "But we can do nothing for the girls."

"No." There was no comparable organization for women—nothing for female foundlings to look forward to except drudgery or prostitution or a dreary mix of both. Isreän had known she couldn't afford to keep the baby, and she couldn't face the thought of her child growing up in the misery she had known. She had chosen a bad way out, but there were no good ones.

"Thank you, othala," said Azhanharad. "We think that is all. Unless by chance you know her sect."

"No. But you can probably assume she was Ploraneise. There will be no one who can tell you differently."

Azhanharad sighed again. "You are right, othala, as always. Thank you."

"Good night, Subpraeceptor," I said, and left him to the grim task of getting Isreän's body ready for transport to Ulvanensee.

⋇

I slept patchily that night and woke to an overcast dawn; the light was gray and thin. I meditated, went to the public baths, then the Hanevo Tree, then up to the Prince Zhaicava Building and my cold, bare box of an office.

My post at that office, addressed to THE WITNESS FOR THE DEAD, was sporadic but often interesting—although "interesting" was a poor word for the letters I received, sometimes tragic, sometimes blackly comic, sometimes horrifying. There was one man who wrote to me every time someone drowned in the Mich'maika, claiming he had drowned them. I often received letters from people accusing their neighbors of murder, which required a great deal of tedious double-checking to prove wrong. And people wrote to me about ghosts and walking spirits and hauntings, which were almost always nothing of the sort, the exception being the people who wrote to me about the Hill of Werewolves, where the ghosts were genuine.

This morning there was a letter from a scholar of the first rank. That was new, and I opened it warily.

> To Thara Celehar, prelate of Ulis and Witness for the Dead, greetings.
>
> We are writing to ask of you a very peculiar favor. Our area of study is the dissolution of the Anmureise mysteries, and we have heard that the Hill of Werewolves is haunted, if that is the right word, by the purge of the Wolves of Anmura.

> *We are in ill health and cannot go explore the phenom-*
> *enon for ourself, but we understand that you have witnessed*
> *it. Might you be willing to answer a few questions? You will*
> *find us in our workroom at the University most afternoons.*
>
> > *We sign ourself, with great respect,*
> >
> > *Aäthis Rohethar*

I considered this letter, somewhat blankly, for several minutes, before I decided that I had to answer it, for common politeness if nothing else.

I found ink and pen and paper and sealing wax and after some hesitation wrote,

> *To Aäthis Rohethar, scholar of the first rank, greetings.*
> *It is true that we have witnessed the ghosts on the Hill of*
> *Werewolves, and we would be glad to answer any questions*
> *that we can. At the moment we are quite busy, but we will*
> *come to the University on our first free afternoon.*
>
> > *Respectfully,*
> >
> > *Thara Celehar, Witness for the Dead*

I sealed the letter, putting my lighter carefully back in my inner waistcoat pocket. My next step in finding Osmin Pavalo Temin required a visit to the postal service's main office in any event.

I spent the rest of the morning, uninterrupted by petitioners, writing notes about the petition of the Marquess Ulzhavel and my investigation thus far, so that if I was called upon to give a judicial deposition, I would be able to assemble a coherent narrative of my witnessing.

Then I went to the postal service for help in finding Osmin Temin.

The Temada were such a minor house that I had never heard of them. I wondered if they even had an estate, or if they were what was called "town gentry" (something the Marquess Ulzhavel would never be, even though his compound was entirely encapsulated by the city of Amalo). Hence the postal service.

The central office of the Amalo Postal Service was housed in the Prince Thuvenis Building, of which it took up nearly half. It had once been a part of the Cartographers' Guild, but those who wanted to do cartography found that they were spending most of their time on record-keeping and those who were interested in the grand logistical nightmare of delivering the post in a city the size of Amalo found that they were spending most of their time on map-drawing. The split, some twenty years ago, had allegedly been amicable, but the postal service did not use the Guild maps. They had their own, and it was the postal service's maps that would show where the members of the House Temada lived.

The front office in the Prince Thuvenis Building had a young goblin woman at a desk to one side and a row of post collection boxes to the other. After I had put my letter in the appropriate box, I crossed to her desk. It took her a moment to realize that I was actually approaching her.

"Oh! Good morning, othala! May we help you?"

"We are Thara Celehar, a Witness for the Dead. We need to find the House Temada."

"Just a moment." She got up and disappeared through a discreet door among the wall hangings behind her desk. It was longer than "a moment," but not as much as ten minutes before she returned, accompanied by an elderly elven man whom she introduced as a senior clerk of the postal service.

He and I exchanged bows, and he said, "You are looking for the Temada."

"Yes," I said. "Our witnessing requires it."

"The postal service is under no obligation to help you," he said sharply.

"Not at all," I said and wondered if he was going to seek the satisfaction of being disobliging just because he could.

But apparently he had only wanted to make it clear where he stood, for he said, "Their compound is in the Tobazran district. First stop past the Mountain Gate on the Cevoro line. Then you follow the tram line for two blocks, and you'll find the Temada on your right. There is only the one door in that wall."

"You sound as though you've been there," I said.

He smiled slightly. "On your *left*, you'll find Tobazran Post Office Number Three, where we worked for many years."

"Of course," I said. "Thank you."

"The postal service is here to help, othala," he said, and we bowed to each other again.

)(

I walked to the Dachenostro to board the first tram I saw that was taking the Cevoro line. At the first stop after we rattled through the Mountain Gate, I disembarked and found myself in an obviously well-to-do neighborhood of shops and small apartment buildings nothing like the tenement I lived in. I walked north two blocks, following the tram line, and as the clerk had said, there was only one door in the block-long wall on my right.

There was a crest on the door, two swans back-to-back, their necks intertwined. Presumably the Temada's crest—I did not recognize it.

There was a bell rope beside the door. I pulled it firmly and then waited for what seemed like a very long time. Finally, the door was opened by a puzzled-looking elven woman in green-and-gold livery. "Can I help you, othala?"

"I am Thara Celehar, a Witness for the Dead. I am looking for Osmin Pavalo Temin."

"Well, you won't find her here," the woman said. "Osmer Temar won't even have her mentioned."

"Oh dear," I said, with a pang of sympathy for Osmin Temin. "Do you have any idea of where she might be?"

"The last we heard, she'd started some sort of school in Cemchelarna. But that was two years ago. Maybe more. I'm sorry, othala."

Two years ago made it *after* she'd been forced to resign from the foundling school board, so either she had some new venture in Cemchelarna or the woman's information was muddled and out of date. Either seemed plausible.

"Thank you," I said. "That is very helpful."

"Be careful, othala," she said as she closed the door, leaving me unsettled as well as thwarted. But there was nothing for it except to go back the way I had come and try again with the postal service.

)(

The same young goblin woman was still at the desk when I returned. "Did you not find her, othala?"

"No," I said. "We are told she might be in Cemchelarna. Could someone consult the postal registers and look for Pavalo Temin?"

"We will find out," she said and disappeared again through the discreet door in the wall behind her.

I waited.

She was gone for a long time, long enough that I began to worry I had gotten her in some kind of trouble. But she came back as serenely as she had gone and handed me a slip of paper, on which was written in an exquisitely legible hand *Cemchelarna Post Office Number Five, Goshawk Street.*

"That's where she's registered, othala. Mer Aivonezh says that's the most help we can give you."

"This is very helpful indeed."

She smiled and said, "Good luck, othala."

"Thank you," I said. I left, almost clutching the slip of paper, to get the cartography clerks to tell me where Goshawk Street was.

)(

One of the cartographers, a young elven man whose name I had forgotten, was in the front office when I came in, bent over a map with a pair of calipers. He said, "Hello, othala," without straightening. Min Talenin, a good bourgeois elven spinster, turned from her filing cabinets and said, using the plural "we," "Good afternoon, othala. Can we help you?"

"Good afternoon, Min Talenin. Yes, I need to find the post office on Goshawk Street in Cemchelarna."

"A post office!" she said. "Then that is an easy question, for we mark the post offices on our maps. Here." She unrolled a map across her desk, weighting it with an inkwell, a lamp, and two iron pyramids that I recognized as apothecary's weights. "This is the eastern half of Cemchelarna. So Goshawk Street . . . no, not there . . . not there . . . it's in this cluster of bird names. There!" She indicated a line on the map with her forefinger; I saw the tiny blue star representing the post office. "And to get there, you'll want to cross the Abandoned Bridge and keep going on what turns into Lacemaker Street. Follow Lacemaker Street to a cross street called Pigeon Street, turn south, go two blocks, and then an alley on your left will lead to Goshawk Street. The post office should be three blocks south on your left."

"Thank you, Min Talenin," I said, scribbling directions in my notebook. "As always, you are a tremendous help."

She smiled and said, using the plural, "We are always happy to help you, othala."

※

I bought lunch from a street vendor and ate while I walked. Lacemaker Street twisted and turned a good deal, and after a few blocks I had to stop and check every cross street to see if it was Pigeon Street, since I had no good sense of how much real territory was covered by an inch on the cartographers' maps. Many cross streets were not labeled at all, but finally I came to one where the street sign, bolted firmly to the wall of the corner shop, said PIGEON STREET. I turned south and walked two blocks, then scanned the row of houses to my left, looking for an alleyway. At first I didn't see it, but then I realized that the gap between a blue clapboard house and a green clapboard house had to be what Min Talenin had generously described as an alley. It was almost exactly the width of my shoulders and it curved first one way and then the other around the shapes of the houses.

I edged through it, taking almost breath-held care to keep my silk coat of office from snagging on anything. On the other side, hopefully on Goshawk Street, I walked three blocks south and was greeted with a blue sign reading CEMCHELARNA POST OFFICE NO. 5 on a gray brick of a building. Inside, like most post offices, they had a list of registrants on a chalkboard. I skimmed the list and was relieved to find the name Pavalo Temin, and underneath it CEM-CHELARNA SCHOOL FOR FOUNDLING GIRLS.

A part-goblin clerk leaned across the counter and said, "Can I help you, othala?"

"Yes," I said and followed his lead on formality. "I am Thara Celehar, a Witness for the Dead. I'm trying to find the Cemchelarna School for Foundling Girls."

"Couldn't be easier," said the clerk. "One block south, on your right. There's a sign."

"Thank you," I said. Now—after all the seeking back and forth—to find out if this was indeed the Osmin Pavalo Temin who had a reason to hate the Marquise Ulzhavel.

※

The school was a large dormered brick building with a crisp black-on-white sign. I climbed the stairs and pulled open half of the double doors. The inner doors of the narrow foyer were locked, but there was a bell pull. I rang the bell, and after a surprisingly lengthy pause, an elven girl came running down the stairs and unlocked the inner doors.

She was thirteen or fourteen, plain-faced but with strikingly clear blue eyes. She was not all that much younger than Isreän had been, and she seemed scared, her ears almost flat to her head. She was wearing what looked like a uniform, an unbleached linen pinafore over a long-sleeved gray dress. Her hair was in two long plaits, children's plaits although she was old enough to start pinning her hair up.

She bobbed me a curtsy and said, "Please, othala, Osmin Temin says I must ask your name and business."

My formality had to be dictated by my errand. I said, "We are Thara Celehar, a Witness for the Dead, and we must speak to Osmin Temin."

She looked even more scared, but she nodded and said, as she'd obviously been told to say, "If you will wait here, please."

"Of course," I said. She ran back up the stairs, and I looked around. It was a square room with lovely wood paneling; the staircase followed the walls around, with a broad landing just opposite the front doors, and above the landing was a large multipaned window with a pattern in stained glass as a border; it must have cost the building's first owner a small fortune. The carpet was also beautiful, although old and worn.

The elven girl came back down the stairs, sedately this time, and said, "Please, othala, Osmin Temin will see you. If you will follow us?"

I followed her up the stairs. The second floor was two long hallways stretching out from the stairhead; my guide turned left, and we walked about halfway down the hall before she knocked at one of the doors.

"Come in!" called a woman's voice; the girl opened the door and bowed for me to enter.

Osmin Pavalo Temin was a middle-aged elven lady, beautifully dressed and perfectly coiffed, with long tashin sticks like daggers through the bun at the back of her head. There was nothing remarkable about her face, except perhaps for a certain hardness in her eyes. I disliked her instantly and powerfully.

She inclined her head in something that was not quite a bow. "Othala. Your presence is an honor. How may we help you?"

I said, "We are Thara Celehar, a Witness for the Dead. We are witnessing for Tomilo Ulzhavel. We understand that you knew her?"

"*Knew* her?" Osmin Temin looked bewildered, but I could not tell if it was genuine or not. "We served on a foundling school board with her, five years ago, but that is barely more than an acquaintance."

"We understand that you had a serious disagreement with her," I said.

"Oh," she said, her eyes narrowing. "We begin to understand. Someone has a busy tongue."

"We are investigating the possibility she was murdered."

"And what do you expect from us, othala? A confession?"

"If you happen to have killed her, yes, that would save us a good deal of time and bother."

Her laugh was more like a snarl. "We didn't kill her. What good would it have done us? Now, if you don't mind—"

There was a knock at the door.

"Come in!" Osmin Temin said, probably louder than was necessary.

The door opened, and a part-goblin girl came in, wearing the same uniform as the elven girl who had answered the door, with her hair in those two long plaits, although this girl was even older, maybe as old as sixteen, which was old enough to leave school. She, too, looked scared. She came up beside me and curtsied to Osmin Temin. "Please, osmin, Min Tesavin needs you downstairs."

Her foot brushed mine. Glancing down, I saw a piece of paper folded down to almost nothing on the floor between us. I moved the toe of my shoe to cover it. I did not look at the girl.

"Blessed goddesses, what is it *this* time?" Osmin Temin moaned to the ceiling.

The girl said, "I don't know, osmin. Just that it's important."

"It's *always* important with Min Tesavin," Osmin Temin said. "Othala, if you will excuse us, we have a school to run." Her tone indicated she was done with our conversation; I had no reason to argue with her.

"Of course, osmin," I said. "Thank you for your help."

She glared at me in passing; then she was gone, the girl obedient in her wake. I retrieved the paper and tucked it safely in my inside coat pocket, then stepped into the corridor. An elven girl walking alone glanced up and then quickly looked down, hunching her shoulders and speeding up. I found my way back to the stairs and gratefully left.

※

I did not stop to unfold the paper until I was back at the Abandoned Bridge. It read:

*PLEASE HELP US*
*STOP THEM*

I stared at it for a long time, until a passing pedestrian bumped into me and I realized I was standing in the middle of the sidewalk. I put the paper back in my pocket and started walking. A good half of my mind was on that message. *Please help us stop them.* Or *Please help us. Stop them.* Either way it came to the same thing: the pupils at Osmin Temin's school had something they wanted stopped so badly they resorted to passing notes to strangers. But something about which they couldn't simply go to a judicial Witness, meaning perhaps that they wanted it stopped without resorting to the law. I thought of the scared girls I had seen and knew that whatever it was, it was serious, even if it wasn't illegal.

But short of going back to the school and demanding to talk to the girl who had dropped the note—a tactic that seemed guaranteed to fail—what could I do to find out what was going on?

Nothing today, certainly. I had to go ask the Marquess Ulzhavel for permission to exhume his wife's body, and by the time that task was complete—success or failure and I had no idea which—it would be too late to return to Goshawk Street. But perhaps I could do that tomorrow and find out if any of the neighbors were inclined to gossip. Perhaps somebody had seen or heard something that would give me a starting place.

In the meantime, I took the tram from Emperor Belvorsina III Square up to the Dachenostro, the central station, then changed to the Zulnicho line and traveled south to the Ulzhavadeise ostro, where I disembarked and walked to the old compound. The gatekeeper recognized me and let me in.

The elven man in livery said, "Please wait in the hall, othala," and he went to find out whether the marquess would see me.

I waited beside the door, where there was one window with the drapes open, trying not to imagine what it would be like to spend all my time in this gloom, and wondering whether this was a reaction to the marquise's death, or if the marquess had always chosen to live like this.

When the servant returned, the marquess was with him. "Othala Celehar! What have you found?"

"We regret that we cannot report anything conclusive," I said. "We have come to ask if you would consent to an autopsy."

"An autopsy?" He considered the matter. "You hope to find proof that she was murdered?"

"We have spoken to the Master of the Mortuary at the Sanctuary, and he says there is a poison that exactly mimics a thunderclap coronary. He doesn't know if it would still be detectable after three months, but he's willing to find out."

"That's my nephew Otila's younger son. The elder is my heir. Csenaia was always the bright one."

There was no safe answer to that. I waited, and he said, "Yes, all right. If you can prove she was murdered, perhaps it will be easier to get people to talk to you. Everyone loves a scandal."

But no one wanted to be involved in a murder. That, however, was not a discussion I wished to have with the marquess. I said, "Where is the marquise buried?"

"Csenaia will know," he said with a harsh laugh. "Thank you, othala." He turned and started back the way he had come. I bowed to his back and left to walk to the Sanctuary of Csaivo.

〤

I found Ulzhavar again in the mortuary, this time alone and making notes in a massive ledger he had open on the autopsy table. "Celehar," he said in greeting. "What is the word on your potential poisoning victim?"

"Her husband has agreed to an autopsy. He says that you will know where she is buried."

"That *I* will know?" He looked baffled for several seconds, then winced as he understood. "It's Great-Aunt Tomilo."

"Did you know her?"

"Not at all well. My father was rarely on speaking terms with the marquess. My brother isn't on speaking terms with him now. I *do* know where Great-Aunt Tomilo is buried, because I attended the funeral. Otilis did not."

"That's rather . . ."

"The marquess has banned him from the compound, so I'm not entirely sure whether it was pique or common sense."

"I see."

"Otilis is a little too obvious in his belief that the sooner the marquess dies the better. I can't blame the old man for banning him. But no matter. Great-Aunt Tomilo is buried in Ulmavonee."

"*Ulmavonee?*" I said, certain I had misheard. Ulmavonee was the municipal cemetery of Paravi, which was a long way from the Ulzhavadeise compound.

"My grandfather's father had to sell the family cemetery," Csenaia said with a grimace. "It was apparently quite the scandal."

"I should think so," I said, slightly shocked myself. "But why Ulmavonee? Why not Ulvanensee?"

"Ulmavonee was brand new," said Ulzhavar. "It had plenty of room in the catacombs for the ancestors."

"They moved the *whole* cemetery?"

"My great-grandfather was that sort of man. In any event, that's where Great-Aunt Tomilo is, in the Ulzhavadeise quarter of Ulmavonee. I forget the name of the prelate out there."

"Veltanezh," I said. "I do not think he will hinder us."

"No, I remember him now. There's no harm in him."

Which was not something you could say about all the prelates in Amalo, as I was reminded that evening when I got home and checked for my post in the concierge's shabby office. There was a letter from the Ulistheileian, sealed with Dach'othala Vernezar's personal signet.

It couldn't be anything good. Vernezar and I were not enemies, precisely, but the Ulistheileian had washed its collective hands of me, and I had been glad of it.

No cats this evening. Sometimes there were and sometimes there weren't. I went inside and put a five-zashan piece in the gas meter, then turned on the lamp, necessary now as the days got shorter. I took off my coat of office and hung it up carefully and then, reluctantly, opened the letter.

Vernezar's secretary, who had been chosen for his connections rather than his abilities, had at best a semi-legible hand, so that it took me some work to decipher the message.

Then I sat down and read it again.

> TO THARA CELEHAR, WITNESS FOR THE DEAD, GREETINGS.
>   WHEREAS, *you are the only unbeneficed Witness vel ama for the Dead in the city of Amalo, and*
>   WHEREAS, *we have recently welcomed to the city a new prelate, Velhiro Tomasin, who claims she can hear the dead,*
>   THEREFORE, *we wish you to take Othalo Tomasin as your apprentice and train her in your calling.*
>                     WITH ALL GOOD WISHES,
>                     *Aiva Vernezar, Ulisothala of Amalo*

I stared at that letter until the lamp dipped twice, reminding me that I only had five minutes left on the meter. I made my preparations for bed quickly, but still ended up groping my way through my darkened room to the dim shape of the bed against the wall.

I lay in bed wondering if this was Vernezar's revenge for my denying his authority over me or just happenstance. Certainly, he was careful not to say he was *ordering* me to accept Othalo Tomasin, but we both knew all he had to do was bring the matter back to the Amal'othala, and I *would* be ordered to take Othalo Tomasin as my "apprentice"—which was a ridiculous word to use, since no one could be *taught* to hear the dead. Either one could or one couldn't. One had the calling or one didn't. She could learn to be a Witness, but why had she not done so in her novitiate if that was the form her calling took?

I was still wrangling over it when I fell asleep.

〤

W hen I reached my office in the morning, there was a prelate standing by the door, an elven woman in a canon's frock coat and a plain black skirt, her hair in a smooth prelate's braid past her waist, a gray overcoat over one arm and a valise at her feet. Her eyes were pale green. Her ears were low. And she was my age or older.

"Are you Othalo Tomasin?" I said, surprised.

"I'm sorry," she said, blushing and her ears dipping a little lower, "there's been some confusion. It's Tomasaran. I'm a widow."

"I am sorry for your loss," I said.

"It's how I found my calling," she said. "I touched my husband before they closed the coffin and . . ."

"I understand," I said quickly, before she felt obliged to try to describe it to me. "And thus you dedicated yourself to Ulis, and they sent you here."

"Yes."

"Did they give you any training at all?"

"They said I was too old to be a novice. So, no, not very much."

By which she most likely meant *none*. I could follow Vernezar's reasoning, though I did not agree with it: being a Witness *vel ama* for the Dead did not require a prelate's training in ritual and other duties, so why make life difficult for everyone? It was a lazy decision, but I didn't have the authority to change it. "All right," I said. "My name is Thara Celehar."

Her ears lifted a little. "I am Velhiro Tomasaran."

I unlocked the door of my office and waved her in. She put her valise in the corner and stood nervously by the petitioner's chair; I hung my overcoat on the hook on the back of the door, sat down behind my desk, and said, "Please be seated."

She laid her overcoat over the back of the chair and sat, though she still looked nervous. I said, "Othalo Tomasaran, I am not a monster. I certainly don't blame you for the predicament you find yourself in. I will be glad to teach you what I can of being a Witness, but I'm sure you know as well as I do that I can't teach you to hear the dead."

"I don't need you to teach me that," she said. "Although I would be grateful for advice. I don't . . . that is, I've only done it the once."

I was opening my mouth to answer her, though with no good idea of what I was going to say, when a goblin man in his early twenties appeared in the doorway. "Othala Celehar?"

"Yes?" I said.

He looked exhausted and heartbroken. He said, "She hid the money and I don't . . . I don't know where to look."

Showing good instincts, Othalo Tomasaran was already out of the petitioner's chair, and I said, "Please, sit down and tell me what you need of me."

He sat as if all his strings had been cut and leaned forward, elbows on knees, to put his face in his hands. "My wife," he said. "Brenaro. She managed our finances, and I know she kept our money hidden somewhere, but I cannot find it. I have looked and looked . . . othala, it is such a stupid thing to be worrying about when she is—I cannot pay for her funeral." He made a noise, a choked-off sob, and did not raise his head.

"All right," I said. "And you need me to ask her where the money is?"

"Yes," he said. "Please."

"Of course," I said. "Othalo Tomasaran, will you come with us?"

"Yes, of course," she said, surprised.

"There's no better way to learn than to practice," I said, and got up to get my coat.

"My valise? I couldn't leave it at the Ulistheileian, but . . ."

"It will be safe here," I said. "I will lock the door."

"All right," she said and visibly steeled herself for what was to come. "I am ready."

She probably wasn't, but that was another thing one learned with practice.

※

The young man's name was Keila Osthonharad; he had been married for a little less than a year. He was from a tiny village in the Mervarnens and had come to the city to find work. His wife had been Amaleise. They had been, he said, too poor to get married, but they had been desperately in love and had decided they would just somehow make it work.

They lived in the Marigold Rookeries, and Brenaro Osthonharad had very sensibly said that they had to hide their money, or it would be stolen. "She was right," Mer Osthonharad said miserably. "Our apartment was broken into two or three times—maybe four, we were never sure—but they never found the money."

"And she didn't tell you where it was?"

"She said if I trusted her, I didn't need to know. And I *did* trust her. So, no. She didn't."

Merrem Osthonharad had died two days ago, in childbirth. No one was sure if the baby was going to survive. "And I have to pay the midwife," Mer Osthonharad said. "And the wet nurse. They're being very patient, but I can't—" He broke off, looking around the tram car as if looking for his dead wife. "All I have is the money that was in my pockets. I think I've got about ten zashanei left for dinner."

"I will do my best to help you," I said.

"Thank you, othala." He rubbed his eyes with one hand, pinching the bridge of his nose. "I keep hoping I'll wake up and this will all have been an awful dream, and it keeps not happening."

We got off the tram at the Ulvanen'ostro and walked to Ulvanensee, where they were holding Merrem Osthonharad's body in preparation for the funeral. Anora looked relieved to see me. "Othala," he said, "you come in good time." And he raised his eyebrows politely at Othalo Tomasaran.

"This is Othalo Tomasaran. She is a Witness for the Dead."

Anora's eyebrows went higher, but he bowed to her gravely.

"Othalo Tomasaran, I am pleased to make your acquaintance. I am Anora Chanavar."

"Velhiro Tomasaran," she said, bowing in return. Then Anora showed us into the room where they were keeping Merrem Osthon-harad's body. He tactfully stayed outside with Mer Osthonharad.

She had been prepared for burial, wrapped carefully according to the Ploraneise custom, only her face and hands left visible. She had been a goblin woman, heavy jawed, as young as her husband.

There was no point in waiting for something to happen. I said the prayer of compassion for the dead and touched the cool, dead flesh of her forehead.

Brenaro Osthonharad's last thoughts had been of her child. It took some effort to find the answer to Mer Osthonharad's question—*where is the money?*—and when I did, it didn't come in words, or even quite in images, but more in a feeling, the memory of the movements it took to reach the money's hiding place.

I stepped back. "Othalo Tomasaran, would you like to try?"

"Oh!" She hesitated, as if she wasn't sure that I meant it, or as if she suspected a trap.

"You have to start somewhere," I said.

She nodded jerkily and stepped up next to me. She stumbled a little over the words of the prayer of compassion for the dead, but she persevered and reached out with shaking fingers to touch Mer-rem Osthonharad's cheek. She stiffened, and I knew the flood of darkness and emotions and fragments of thought she would be contending with. After a moment, I nudged her gently. She gasped and pulled her hand back.

"Are you all right?"

"Yes, I think . . . yes. Yes, I'm fine. I just . . ."

"It's difficult," I said. "What did you find?"

"Nothing about the money," she said apologetically.

"That's all right. What *did* you find?"

"She was so worried about her baby," said Tomasaran. "She knew . . . she knew she was dying, didn't she?"

"She knew," I said. "She was a brave woman."

"Yes." She gave me a sidelong glance. "Did you find out about the money?"

"Yes, although I'm not quite sure how . . . I think we'll have to go to their apartment."

"All right," said Tomasaran.

"You may not think so when we get there," I said.

Ж

The Marigold Rookeries were one of the worst parts of Amalo—certainly the worst part of the Airmen's Quarter. The tenement that Keila Osthonharad led us to was filthy and dark, and people had put up partitions and knocked out walls seemingly at random, the result being a maze that no outsider could penetrate. Mer Osthonharad led us easily, but I was uncomfortably aware that without him, I had no idea how to get out again.

The apartment was ramshackle but clean, all two rooms of it. Looking around, I understood Mer Osthonharad's desperation; it didn't seem as if there was *anywhere* in this tiny apartment to hide one's savings. But I knew how Merrem Osthonharad had done it, if I could just find the point she had started from.

I moved slowly around the apartment, half listening to Tomasaran and Mer Osthonharad making painful conversation about funeral arrangements. Where had she been standing? I came to a stop in front of the bed, its bare mattress mute testimony to Merrem Osthonharad's death. The sheets would have been burned. *Here.* Yes, she had been standing here. And she stepped up.

There was nowhere else to step up onto; I climbed onto the bed.

"Othala Celehar?" Tomasaran said anxiously.

"Just a moment," I said. From here she had reached up. I looked and saw a gap in the plaster along the edge of the ceiling. I stood on tiptoe on the unpleasantly yielding surface of the mattress and reluctantly slid my hand into the gap.

I was half expecting to be met by a rat's teeth, but there was nothing there. For a horrible moment, I thought I would have to tell Mer

Osthonharad that his money had been stolen after all, but then the last part of the movement—so familiar to Merrem Osthonharad that she didn't have to think of it—came back to my mind. I turned my hand to the right and found that there was a hollow place behind the plaster. It took some difficult maneuvering, and I was nearly up to my elbow in the wall, but finally I touched a leather bag, which I was able, though my fingers were cramping, to drag out.

"I think this is it," I said, stepping down off the bed, and handed the leather bag to Mer Osthonharad.

"Blessed goddesses," he said and quickly opened the bag. "Yes. Yes. Thank you, othala. Now she can be buried properly. *Thank you.*"

"I follow my calling," I said, politely ignoring the tear tracks shining on his face. "But I am afraid you will have to show us the way out."

※

Anora and I took Tomasaran to lunch at the Chrysanthemum, where she and I listened raptly as Anora told stories about his twenty years as a prelate in Ulvanensee. Afterwards, Anora walked back to Ulvanensee to begin preparations for that afternoon's round of funerals, and Tomasaran and I walked to the Sanctuary of Csaivo. Outside its gates, I stopped and said, "I don't know exactly what your instructions from Dach'othala Vernezar are."

"He said you would teach me how to be a Witness for the Dead. There weren't really any instructions involved."

I had been afraid of that. "Then I suppose the best we can do is for you to accompany me. It will certainly show you what being a Witness for the Dead entails."

"I already know more than I did this morning," she said shyly, and I reminded myself to smile at her, no matter how stiff and awkward it was.

"Then the next thing you're going to learn about is exhumations."

"*Exhumations?* But once they're buried, what can you do? Or can you still hear them that long after?"

"No," I said, "you're also going to witness an autopsy."

She stared at me.

I said, "I have been petitioned to witness for a woman who died three months ago. We are exhuming her body to find out if she was murdered, as her husband believes."

"Do you do this kind of thing often?"

"No, this is only the second time. Mer Osthonharad is much more typical of my petitioners."

I led her into the Sanctuary and along the path to the main entrance, where the elven novice on duty smiled at me and said, "Dach'othala Ulzhavar is expecting you, othala."

"Thank you," I said and was grateful she did not ask about Tomasaran.

We went down to the mortuary, where Ulzhavar said, "Good afternoon, Celehar. Who is your companion?"

"Dach'othala Ulzhavar, this is Othalo Tomasaran. She is a Witness for the Dead."

Ulzhavar looked from me to Tomasaran and back again. "A Witness *vel ama*, I gather, for why else would she be dogging *your* heels?"

"You are astute," I said, and he laughed.

"You needn't make that sound like an insult. But come. Othala Veltanezh is waiting for us in Paravi."

Unlike the Amal'othala, who kept a liveried carriage, Ulzhavar traveled by tram. We took the Zulnicho line up to the Dachenostro, then transferred to the Pomadro line for the long trip out to Paravi and Ulmavonee.

Ulzhavar settled himself and his satchel as comfortably as any old grandmother with her shopping and said, "Have you told Othalo Tomasaran the story?"

"No," I said. "We've had a busy morning."

"I know most of it," said Ulzhavar.

"You probably know more than I do," I said. "Tell us about the Marquise Ulzhavel."

"She married my great-uncle when they were both sixteen, and they were married for fifty-eight years. There were no children, which grieved them both greatly, but otherwise they had a remarkably harmonious marriage. The marquess became more and more hermit-like as he aged, but the marquise remained extremely active."

"Charitable works," I said.

"Yes. She always said that she could not donate money—for the Ulzhavada fortune was almost entirely squandered by my great-great-grandfather—but she had all the time anyone could ever need. But then she died. It was very sudden and very unexpected, and I suppose those might be suspicious circumstances, but she was also seventy-four, so that I admit I don't quite understand what makes the marquess so sure she was murdered."

"He found an unsigned, threatening note among her papers," I said.

"Ah," said Ulzhavar. "Yes, that makes sense."

"Do you think she *was* murdered?" said Tomasaran.

"I don't know," I said. "That's part of why we're performing an autopsy. I admit I have not found anyone yet who seems terribly likely to be a murderer, but then, of course, I've only been looking for two days. Who knows what I may find tomorrow?"

⋊

Ulmavonee was new, as municipal cemeteries went, being only about a hundred and twenty years old. Its prelate, Othala Veltanezh, was middle-aged, part goblin, and as pleased to see us as if we had come on a social visit. He was a friend of Anora's—most of the municipal prelates banded together in the endless politicking of Vernezar's Ulistheileian—and seemed quite reflexively to extend that friendship to all three of us.

He showed us out to the Ulzhavadeise quarter of the cemetery, which had a separate staircase down to the catacombs. At ground level, there were only a few graves, almost all of the Amaleise Ulzhavada being now bones in their revethmerai. Thus, the grave of the Marquise Ulzhavel was easy to find, not least because there were two part-goblin sextons with spades standing beside it. "We wanted to be absolutely sure we had the right grave before we started digging," said Veltanezh.

"A sensible policy," said Ulzhavar. "Celehar? It's your petition."

"Yes," I said. The gravestone was beautifully carved and exquisitely legible: TOMILO ULZHAVEL. "This is the correct grave."

The sextons set to work, and Veltanezh said, "I'm afraid you won't think much of our morgue. It's really just a room with a table in it."

"That's all I need," Ulzhavar said cheerfully. "I brought my knives."

"Good, good," said Veltanezh. "In the meantime, while Satha and Kivora are doing their part, may I show you around? Ulmavonee is not very old, but it is quite lovely."

"Yes," I said, struck by an idea. "And will you tell Othalo Tomasaran about your duties? She is a latecomer to the prelacy, and we are trying to catch up her education."

Tomasaran gave me a look compounded of surprise and alarm, but said nothing. Vernezar was wrong to send her out into the world as a Witness with no training at all in the ways of the prelacy, and though I could not change his decision, there was nothing that said I could not remedy it.

"Of course!" said Veltanezh, with what seemed to be genuine enthusiasm. "Let's start in the catacombs." He took us down the Ulzhavada's entrance to the catacombs, a square white marble staircase lit with gas globes. And Ulmavonee's catacombs were white and square and well-lit, too, which had not been my experience in other parts of Amalo. The Ulzhavadeise revethmerai were grouped together around an intersection, where the catacombs of Ulmavonee met the main trunk of the system of tunnels beneath the city. There was a small shrine to Ulis, as clean and new as the rest of Ulmavonee. The passage to the ulimeire was only partly invested with revethmerai, the rest of the space being taken up with an enormous marble high relief of the Five-Fold Harmony, rendered as Anmura, Osreian, Csaivo, Ulis, and Cstheio Czireizhasan in a line holding hands. The sculptor had rendered them as elves and had done exquisitely detailed work on their hair and jewelry.

"Our current stoneworker's grandfather," said Veltanezh, and opened the door to the stairs up to the ulimeire, which were as white and square and well-lit as the stairs at the Ulzhavadeise end. Ulmavonee proved to be well-lit and well-squared throughout, although the costly white marble was used only for the ulimeire and the catacombs. Plaster walls and parquet floors did for the rest: the prelates' house, the archive, the map room.

At first hesitantly, and then with great interest, Othalo Tomasaran asked Veltanezh questions. She was particularly intrigued by the cemetery map and the registers, how Veltanezh and his prelates kept track of who was buried where and for how long. It was, as I knew from my own experience in Lohaiso and Aveio and from watching Anora, an endlessly time-consuming occupation. "The process of tending to death is like a waterwheel," said Veltanezh. "The death itself, then the preparation of the body, the funeral, the burial, the reveth'osrel—the time in the earth—the exhumation, and the transfer to the revethmera, and then when you come up from the catacombs, another body is waiting."

"At many points along the way, a body is waiting," I said.

"True, but injurious to my comparison," said Veltanezh. "My meaning is that the work of a municipal prelate, by which we worship Ulis, is a never-ending cycle, just as in the prayer of compassion for the dead, the last word is also the first word."

"And you have many waterwheels turning at once," I said, grasping what he was trying to say.

"Yes!" said Veltanezh. "Each at a different point in its revolution. It is why we must keep accurate records, lest we fail to keep the wheel spinning."

"Therefore, your worship of Ulis is the water," I said.

He looked at me oddly. "Yes, I suppose it is. I hadn't thought of that."

Tomasaran said, "But how do you keep *track*?"

"With the ledgers," said Veltanezh. "And the map. Here, let me show you."

They bent together over the ledgers, and Ulzhavar said to me, "I looked up 'hezhelta' last night, to refresh my memory, and aside from the smell, there are very few signs we'll be able to detect after three months. It stains the tongue black, and the hands clench violently in the final spasm of the heart. But the junior prelates would have straightened her fingers, and who knows about the condition of the tongue?"

"Perhaps one of the junior prelates might *remember* straightening her fingers?" I said.

"Well, I suppose that's possible," said Ulzhavar. "Othala Veltanezh, are any of your junior prelates here?"

"Yes," Veltanezh said, turning away from the map. "Do you need them for something?"

Ulzhavar said, "We might get some interesting information by talking to the person who prepared the Marquise Ulzhavel's body."

"Oh, well, that's easy," said Veltanezh. "I did."

"*You* did?"

"There's nothing improper in it," Veltanezh said stiffly.

"No, I beg your pardon," Ulzhavar said, "of course not. It was just my understanding that that is part of the duties of the junior prelates."

"It is," said Veltanezh, "but there were particular reasons I wanted to tend to the marquise myself. One of them being to demonstrate to my newest prelate the proper way to do it."

"Yes," said Ulzhavar. "I can certainly see that. But then you probably *do* remember. Were the marquise's hands clenched?"

"Yes," Veltanezh said promptly. "It was quite a job straightening her fingers."

"There you are," Ulzhavar said to me. "It's at least a promising start."

"Yes," I said. "Do you think the sextons are done by now?"

"We can find out," Veltanezh said, and led us back through the elaborate maze of Ulmavonee to the morgue, where the two sextons had brought the body in on a plank and set it on the table. The smell was thick and vile. Beside me, Tomasaran made a choked noise, and I murmured, "Breathe shallowly and steadily. You won't get used to it, exactly, but it will get a little easier."

"Othala," one of the sextons said to Veltanezh, sounding relieved. "We weren't sure if this is what you wanted."

"Yes," Ulzhavar said. "This is exactly what we need. Thank you."

They bowed and left. Veltanezh said, "Is there anything else I can do to help you?"

"Well," Ulzhavar said. "Either we unwrap her or I cut through the windings. Do you have a preference?"

"Cut through the windings," Veltanezh said. "We'll rewrap her with clean windings when you're done."

"That's much easier for me," Ulzhavar said. "All right. All I need now is some time to work."

"Of course," said Veltanezh, and left, probably nearly as grateful as the sextons.

"Celehar, will you help me?" Ulzhavar said. "I need to cut the windings, but I don't want to cut the body."

"What do you need me to do?" I said, coming up beside him. Whatever she had looked like in life, the marquise was unrecognizable now, and the smell was very much like being punched in the face.

"Lift the winding so I can get the scissors between it and the body," Ulzhavar said. I did, and he began the slow, unpleasant process of baring the marquise's torso so that he could open it with one of the sharp knives in his satchel. Step by step, Tomasaran came closer as we worked; by the time Ulzhavar was ready to use the knife, she was standing at the head of the table watching, grim-faced but steady.

"All right?" Ulzhavar said, glancing between us. I nodded. Tomasaran said, "Yes, dach'othala."

"All right," said Ulzhavar, and made the cut.

We all smelled it immediately, incongruous and strong, sweet as attar of roses. The combination with the scent of death nearly made me gag; Tomasaran covered her face with both hands, and Ulzhavar actually took a step back. "That's it," he said. "That's hezhelta."

𝕏

I wanted to apologize to the other tram passengers, who very distinctly left space between us and them, for the smell of the Marquise Ulzhavel's reveth'osrel. Ulzhavar said, "Don't look so worried, Celehar. It's unpleasant, but it's only an odor. It won't harm anyone. Not in a space this size in the time it takes to go from Paravi to the Dachenostro."

"I know," I said. "But it *is* unpleasant."

"It's your petitioner," Ulzhavar said.

"Yes, and I'll have to go tell him that it's certain that his wife was murdered, but I have not the least idea of who the murderer is."

"You must have someone you suspect."

"One person I think extremely unlikely and one person who refuses to talk to me."

"Well, *that's* suspicious."

I shrugged helplessly. "I have no power to compel him, so suspicious or not, that inquiry leads nowhere."

"You may find that he is more willing if you send a note in, telling him that it is not conjecture that the marquise was murdered."

"I will have to try it," I said. "I have no other ideas."

"Tomorrow," Ulzhavar said. "Today, you will come give a deposition about the autopsy of the Marquise Ulzhavel. And then I recommend the public baths."

"I certainly won't be able to sleep otherwise," I said. "What about you, Tomasaran?"

"I can make a deposition if you want me to," she said, a little shyly. "And then I must find a place to stay."

"You don't have one?" Ulzhavar said.

"I spent last night in the novices' dormitory in the Ulistheileian, but I can't keep doing that."

"Certainly not," said Ulzhavar, sounding as horrified as I felt. "As a preferable temporary expedient, you are welcome to stay at the Sanctuary. We have rooms for journeymen. Private rooms."

"You are very kind," Tomasaran said. "If it is not an inconvenience to anyone, I would appreciate it. I do not know my way around the city, and do not know where to look for lodgings, especially as my stipend from the Ulistheileian is . . . not generous."

"No," I said, remembering my first prelacy in Lohaiso. "I can show you a boardinghouse in Cemchelarna tomorrow. I don't know their rates, but the landlady is kind-hearted and might be willing to come to an agreement. And that area of Cemchelarna is safe and inexpensive."

"All right," said Tomasaran. "Yes, thank you."

We changed tramlines at the Dachenostro and took the Zulnicho line, first north a stop to the Amal'theileian so that we could retrieve Tomasaran's valise from my office, then south to the Ulzhavadeise ostro; it was a short walk to the Sanctuary, where Ulzhavar picked the first two clerics he saw to be deposition witnesses and almost literally grabbed a novice who was scurrying past to be the scribe.

He deponed and I deponed, and then we gave Tomasaran a brief lesson in how to make a deposition. Her deposition was very short, but it would corroborate Ulzhavar's and mine should the need arise. Then Ulzhavar took Tomasaran to show her the journeymen's quarters, and I, thankfully, headed for the municipal baths in the Airmen's Quarter so that I could stop smelling of the Marquise Ulzhavel's death.

)(

That night I was restless. Rather than use up my five-zashan coins to read, or lying in the darkness staring at nothing, I decided, recklessly, to go to the Vermilion Opera and find out if Mer Pel-Thenhior would welcome me.

I arrived in an intermission, and the lobby was full of elegant and bejeweled elves, talking in small groups and drinking champagne punch. The newspaper stories about the riot at the premiere of *Zhelsu* had made it sound like the Opera had been gutted, but I saw only a few places where the new vermilion paint did not quite match the rest of the wall.

The audience members didn't notice me, and I made my way to

the auditorium doors, where the two goblin boys on duty recognized me and waved me in. I took the curving hallway around the backs of the boxes to the box nearest the stage, where I opened the door and stepped inside.

At the front of the box Iäna Pel-Thenhior and his assistant were bent together over Pel-Thenhior's notebook. They both turned to look at the door as it closed, and Pel-Thenhior said, "Celehar! What a pleasant surprise!"

My face heated a little, but I said, "You told me I could come."

"Of course, of course!" said Pel-Thenhior. He was half goblin, with golden-yellow eyes and black hair in long Barizheise braids. "I was just beginning to doubt that you would. Come, sit up here. Thoramis has the information he needs."

I looked doubtfully at Thoramis—elven, almost as tall as Pel-Thenhior but on a much skinnier frame, his hair pulled back with a clasp—who gave me a smile and said, "Everything else can wait." He left the box through the second door, the one that led backstage, and I sat down by Pel-Thenhior.

I was being a fool and I knew it.

Pel-Thenhior said, "You've come in good time. The last act of *General Olethazh* is due to start in five minutes."

"How is it faring?"

"Not too badly," Pel-Thenhior said. "I've got *reams* of notes, though. We missed a performance while the Opera was being repaired, and the chorus has become very sloppy. And Nanavo's not singing as well as she should, and I don't know why. The way things are going, I fully expect Shulethis to develop the hiccups."

The audience began reappearing in boxes and filing into the auditorium for the inexpensive seats—although even those inexpensive seats were beyond my budget. Without Pel-Thenhior's kindness, I could not have attended anything performed on the Vermilion Opera's stage.

"You know," Pel-Thenhior said, "you could come every night we perform if you wanted to. It's *my* box, after all."

The echo of my thoughts made me start. "When would I sleep?"

He laughed. "That's right. You can't sleep in the mornings. Or, well, I suppose you *could,* or are you much busier with petitioners than I think you are?"

"Busy enough," I said. I did not add that I knew, from experience, that my office was a miserable place to try to sleep.

"I meant no insult," Pel-Thenhior said, "merely that I did not think that that many people would need to speak to the dead."

"You would be surprised," I said, thinking of Mer Osthonharad. "But I took no insult."

"Good," said Pel-Thenhior, and then the curtain began to rise, and his attention was fixed on the stage.

The third act of *General Olethazh* is the evening of the long day of the opera's duration. The Valet helps the General to bed, the Granddaughter writes a letter of farewell to her suitor, and the General dreams of glory. The appeal of the opera was not in its plot, but in the richness of its score and the depth of characterization it gave its three main characters. Pel-Thenhior might be dissatisfied with Min Rasabin's performance, but I could hear no flaw in it, and Mer Dorenar and Mer Pershar were excellent both together and singly. The chorus sang the final passage, the General's dreams of his ancient triumph, with such beautifully intertwined harmonies that I shivered.

Applause when the curtain lowered was enthusiastic. "Well," Pel-Thenhior said, "no hiccups, anyway." He went backstage, and I hesitated. The reasonable thing to do was to go home and try to go to sleep. Unreasonably, I wanted to stay, to see if Pel-Thenhior would come back and talk to me.

*And what if he does? What then, Celehar?*

I had no answer for myself. I did the reasonable thing and went home.

And did not sleep.

⋈

In the morning, Tomasaran was waiting again in front of my office. She looked less miserable than she had yesterday, which seemed like progress of a sort.

She came in and sat down across from me.

"Were you comfortable last night?" I asked.

"More comfortable than the novices' dormitory," she said. "But the journeymen's quarters are very austere. I suppose the clerics don't want to encourage them to linger."

"We can go to Cemchelarna this afternoon," I said.

"Thank you," she said. "I appreciate your help."

"Of course," I said. "I have business in Cemchelarna anyway."

"Where is Cemchelarna from here?" she said. "Amalo is very confusing."

I was about to answer her when I had a better idea. "Come with me," I said. I risked leaving my office unattended for five minutes and led her to the cartographers' office, which was empty except for Merrem Bechevaran, a young elven widow who preferred clerk's work to remarriage. She was instantly sympathetic to Tomasaran's plight, and I left them standing in front of the biggest wall map and Merrem Bechevaran saying, "The easiest landmark to remember is the Mich'maika, the canal."

*Particularly appreciated among suicides,* I added, and shook the thought away. But it was hard to forget that cold, ashen girl in the Brotherhood's crypt, hard to forget that she was one among probably a dozen who would choose that answer to their problems this year.

I had thought about suicide, after Evru's execution, after my disgrace. Some days I had thought about nothing else. It was probably the emperor who had saved my life, by giving me a purpose, a task, a question to answer. And then Ulis had spoken to me in a dream, and I had known that my calling had not been taken from me. After that there was no question of suicide, not if my god still needed my work. But I remembered what it had felt like.

I sat behind my desk, watching the door, and tried to think of ways I could find out what the girls at Osmin Temin's school went in fear of. Gossiping neighbors were still my surest bet, although I shrank from the prospect of spending the afternoon talking to strangers—especially since this was not official business; this was just my curiosity and the sharp, nasty jolt I felt when I thought of that note, the feeling that if I did not do something, no one would.

Some time later, Tomasaran came back smiling. She said, "Merrem Bechevaran is very kind."

"Do you feel better oriented?"

"Much," she said, "although I am sure I will forget most of it before we leave the building."

"You can go talk to the cartographers whenever you like. I don't expect you to spend the morning cooped up in here with me."

"Why not? Isn't that part of being a Witness for the Dead?"

"Ah," I said. "Actually, no. It's part of an agreement the Archprelate reached with Prince Orchenis. Ordinarily, clerical Witnesses for the Dead have a benefice and speak to the dead as their services are called for. But Prince Orchenis requested the Archprelate assign me here for that purpose and no other."

"Then when you asked Othala Veltanezh to help educate me . . . ?"

"Even if you are not a beneficed prelate yourself, you will find it invaluable to know what beneficed prelates do. Especially if, as seems likely, Dach'othala Vernezar intends this office to persist after I am gone."

"But then why was it Prince Orchenis who asked, and not Dach'othala Vernezar?" she said.

That was a good question. "Dach'othala Vernezar was listening to the faction of prelates who say that speaking to the dead is nonsense."

She gave me a dubious look. "Politics."

"Yes," I said.

"I had hoped to be rid of politics," she said wearily.

"Was your husband in the government?"

"He served on the city council of our town and aspired passionately to be mayor. He thought about little else."

"I know of no endeavor undertaken by elf or goblin that does not have politics saturating it," I said apologetically. "The work of your calling is perhaps the best we can do."

She hesitated; I said, "Ask. Whatever it is."

She still hesitated, then blurted out, "Do you witness for many murders?"

"The Brotherhood come to me first, yes. But murders are not common. I have been here six months and there have only been two. Well, three, although in that case we brought the murderer to the Brotherhood rather than the other way around."

She smiled suddenly. "That sounds like a story that needs to be told."

I explained Broset Sheveldar and his trail of dead wives. She listened wide-eyed and had a flood of questions, which I did my best to answer, although there were still things about Broset Sheveldar I did not know and never would, for he had been cremated and his ashes scattered immediately after the execution.

By the time Tomasaran was done asking questions, the bells of the Amal'theileian's clock were tolling noon. We had lunch at my usual zhoän and then set out for Cemchelarna. Tomasaran looked around eagerly; as we started to cross the Abandoned Bridge, I asked, "How large is the town you come from?"

"Nothing like this," she said. "Oh, goodness!" An elven street acrobat flipped off her goblin partner's shoulders to land on her feet. The people watching applauded, and the girl flashed a brilliant smile before flinging herself at her partner, who caught her, swung her around his body, and somehow she was on his shoulders again, this time with her shoulders against his and her feet uppermost. Her soft, voluminous trousers were gathered at the ankle and preserved what modesty she cared to have.

I tugged gently at Tomasaran's sleeve. "They perform daily."

"Do they?" She followed me, though she craned backwards like a child as the girl revolved around her partner's body again and this time came up standing on his shoulders. "That's the most amazing thing I've ever seen."

"They start training very young," I said. That was another option for foundlings, if they got lucky and had the aptitude the Acrobats' Guild looked for. But very few of them did.

I remembered the way to Merrem Nadaran's boardinghouse;

I was glad to see the green-and-silver flag flying to show that she had rooms available. And Min Nadin was still on the porch, well bundled against the nip in the air, quilting in her steady, tiny stitch.

"Othala!" she said. "I thought we wouldn't see you again. Have you come for a room?"

"Yes, but not for me. This is Othalo Tomasaran. She is new to town."

Min Nadin looked her over, eyes bright and curious. "Is it just you, othalo?"

"Yes," Tomasaran said, and bluntly answered the unasked question, "I am a widow."

Min Nadin nodded. "That's simpler, then. Rooms aren't really big enough for two." She called for her niece, who came out to the porch drying her hands on her apron.

"Aunt Rhadeän? What is— Oh! Hello, Othala Celehar. Can I help you with something?"

"This is Othalo Tomasaran," I said. "She needs a room, and I thought of your establishment."

"Oh, of course!" said Merrem Nadaran. "I am Vinsu Nadaran, and you are welcome to my house. Won't you come inside? I can show you the rooms that are available."

Tomasaran went with her. I sat down beside Min Nadin. She had finished the quilt I had seen the last time I was here and was piecing a new one, carefully choosing scraps from a large basket of rags to get the colors she wanted.

"What an astonishing collection of rags, dachenmaro," I said.

She gave me a sidelong smile. "Vinsu's sister had ten children. Once it's too worn out for them, it comes to me."

"*Ten* children?"

"Oh, I know," Min Nadin said. "Every woman in the Ceverada told her to talk to a cleric, but her husband was raised in a sect that . . . well, Beniro was always such a *biddable* girl. She could never go against him. And then, of course, the eleventh child killed her. Fortunately, at that point her eldest daughter was able to take care of the little ones. But no one in the Ceverada will speak to her husband." She sighed, and her hands neatly finished sewing a blue chintz figured in red to a green chintz figured in yellow. "But here. Let me show you the pattern. It's the Feather Crown, and I'll quilt it in Bright Birds Singing."

She was still talking about her plans for the quilt when Tomasaran came out and said, "It's all settled, and she says I can move in today."

"That's good news," I said, standing up.

"Yes, only now I have to go get my bag, and I don't have any idea of where the Sanctuary is from here."

I said, "I'll go with you. That's easy enough."

"That's very kind of you," she said, "but—"

"I don't think you have another option. Even if you can afford a hack, you can't tell them how to get back here."

"And I can't afford a hack," she agreed dismally.

"I don't mind," I said, which was mostly the truth. It meant I would be unable to go back to Osmin Temin's school today, but I could do that tomorrow. I certainly did not want Tomasaran to become hopelessly lost, which seemed almost inevitably what would happen if she tried to get to the Sanctuary and back on her own.

"Thank you," she said. "Truly. I appreciate . . ." She seemed unsure of how she wanted that sentence to end.

"It's nothing," I said. "Come. We'd better get started."

"Yes—it *is* as far as I think it is, then?"

"Yes," I said. We bade farewell to Min Nadin and started back toward the center of the city.

"I suggest we take the tram," I said. "Unless you need to hoard your zashanei."

"Not so much as that. I would be very glad to take the tram."

We caught the tram at Belvorsina III, changed lines in the bustling chaos of the Dachenostro, and rode south to the Sanctuary, where Tomasaran wasted no time in collecting her valise. We were very shortly on our way back to Merrem Nadaran's boardinghouse.

Belatedly, I asked Tomasaran where she was from.

"A town called Eshvano," she said. "South of Amalo. It took two days to get here, although I traveled with a mule caravan, so we were not very fast. I have never been so far from home before."

"And you said your husband was a councilor."

"Yes. The Tomasada are a very important family in Eshvano. I was born to the Rozhemada, who are not."

I understood instantly what she was saying; my mother's family, the Velverada, were petty gentry, while the Celehada were a family of wealth and rank. It had not been a surprise when I learned my cousin Csoru was to be Varenechibel's fifth empress. "That situation can be uncomfortable." I knew it had been for my mother.

She made a breathy noise that was not quite a laugh. "'Uncomfortable' is a good word for it. Mer Tomasar was most obstinate and almost always got what he wanted. He cared very little for how it affected anyone else."

"Were you unhappy?"

"Oh, I don't know. I married him to please my parents. He married me to please himself. The Tomasada were not *unkind,* but I was an outsider and always would have been."

"'Would have been'?"

This time she did laugh. "The Tomasada have disowned me for pursuing my calling instead of being a dutiful widow."

"The Celehada disowned me long ago," I said, glad to be able to offer some trifle of understanding.

"When you declared your calling?"

"No. It was . . . later." And the crowning irony had been that the only person who had defied my grandmother's edict had been my cousin Csoru, who had always disliked me as much as I disliked her. But she had seen it as a way of showing that no one commanded the empress, and I had been too desperate to resent being used as a piece in her self-important game of bokh.

Tomasaran said, "In any event, if the Tomasada wanted nothing to do with me, the Rozhemada were never going to help me. It took the last of my money to get here."

We reached Belvorsina III (I warned her always to specify *which* Belvorsina, as there was an Emperor Belvorsina II Square in Penchelivor) and were both immediately distracted by a procession, with bells and drums and flutes, heading to the shrine of Esomora, a minor god who was the patron of night watchmen and embroiderists. The music had an infectious rhythm, and the dancers were encouraging the crowd to join them. Tomasaran looked tempted.

I said, "Remember the dignity of your office."

"Yes," she said wistfully, and followed me in the other direction.

We parted for the day on Merrem Nadaran's porch. Tomasaran seemed confident in her ability to find her way to the Prince Zhaicava Building in the morning, and I hoped she was correct.

I decided the best use I could make of the waning afternoon was to attempt again to see Osmer Bazhevar, since he was the only other person I knew of who might have wished the marquise ill. I debated all the way to the gate of his block of flats whether to take the advice of both Ulzhavar and the marquess. Would Osmer Bazhevar be attracted by the lure of scandal or frightened away by the word "murder"? It occurred to me that I had nothing to lose; Osmer Bazhevar had already refused to see me once. All he could do was refuse to see me again.

I tore a page out of my notebook and wrote, *The Marquise Ulzhavel's death was murder.* I asked the elven gatekeeper to have the note delivered to Osmer Bazhevar. I was suspicious that he only agreed because I was a prelate.

The part-goblin page boy came back and said, "Osmer Bazhevar will see you, othala."

ℵ

Osmer Vobora Bazhevar turned out to be a small, middle-aged elven man wearing a modestly elaborate wig.

"Is it true?" he said, not waiting for introductions. "Was the marquise truly murdered?"

"Yes," I said. "She was murdered."

"Then I can tell you who did it." It did not sound like the prelude to a confession.

"Oh?" I said neutrally.

"Yes. We all warned her not to get involved, but she was always headstrong." That was a slightly insulting word to use about a woman old enough to be his mother. I waited, and Osmer Bazhevar leaned forward, lowered his voice, and said, "*The photographers.*"

"The photographers," I said, nonplussed. "What in the world had the Marquise Ulzhavel to do with *photographers?*"

"She was trying to get them banned from the city."

I'd always considered photographers unsavory but essentially harmless. "Why?"

"The marquise found out that several booksellers—I don't know how many, it might be all of them—sell pornographic photographs."

"Then why not attack the booksellers?"

"There are too many of them, she said. And too many people buy books that have nothing to do with pornography. But *photographers.*" He made an expressive, ugly face, apparently indicating that photographers were too depraved for any explanation to be necessary. "She went to the city council, and they said that there was no point in trying to ban photographers. But the marquise wasn't daunted. She was preparing materials to go before the council again the last time I saw her. And I can assure you, from twenty years' experience of her, that she never gave up. Once she'd decided something should be done, she kept working until it happened. Thus, she presented a real threat to the photographers."

"And therefore they poisoned her?"

"Yes!" said Osmer Bazhevar. "It's obvious!"

What was obvious was his desire to get my attention on anyone else but him. I said, "Do you know of any photographers in particular who were angry at her? Were there any threats?"

"Not that I know of," he said with obvious reluctance.

I thought of that note the marquess had discovered: STOP INTER-FERING OR WE WILL MAKE YOU STOP. This new information certainly provided a context in which that message made sense, but it seemed utterly outlandish.

I said, "I have heard that your own relationship with her was somewhat fraught."

"Fraught? Oh, nonsense. We disagreed occasionally, that's all."

I knew he was lying—the way his eyes cut away from mine, the way he shifted his weight—but an accusation would merely end the interview in hostility. I asked instead, "Do you know of anyone else she argued with?"

"Only the Cemchelarna Foundling School Board, and I'm sure you already know about that."

"Yes," I said. "Thank you for your help."

He failed to hide how glad he was to see me leave.

X

As unlikely as Osmer Bazhevar's theory seemed, it was, painfully, the best explanation I had yet found for the note. The person who wrote that note was angry at the marquise, and in the photographers of Amalo, I had finally found someone who had reason to be angry.

Now I needed to talk to a photographer.

I knew where the photographers' studios were, on Dawn Street in the Zheimela along with the brothels. But I could not imagine that they would talk to a prelate, and my calling forbade lies and ruses. I went to find the only person I could think of who might be able to help me.

At least Pel-Thenhior was easy to find. It was not a night the Opera performed, so I found him in his mother's teahouse, the Torivontaram.

"Two nights in a row?" he said as he waved me to the second chair at his small table.

I knew I was blushing again, but said, "Do you know any photographers?"

"*Photographers?* Should I be insulted?"

"No, I'm sorry," I said, my blush becoming painful. "I should have explained first. I am witnessing for the Marquise Ulzhavel, who was murdered, and the person I spoke to this afternoon thinks the photographers—or, I suppose, *a* photographer—murdered her because she was trying to get them banned from Amalo."

"You realize that theory is insane," said Pel-Thenhior.

"I know," I said, "but it's the only theory I have."

"So you want to what? Ask a random photographer if he killed the Marquise Ulzhavel?"

Put like that, it did sound insane. "No," I said. "But I don't know anything about photographers or photography. I don't know if they even knew what she was doing. Thus, I need to talk to a photographer."

"And I'm the first person you thought of," said Pel-Thenhior. "That's certainly not a compliment."

I couldn't tell if he was amused or offended. "I'm sorry," I said again. "I just don't know anyone else to ask."

"Has a photographer never petitioned you?"

"Not yet."

"Well, it's hardly the worst thing anyone's ever said about me. Come sit down and have dinner with me, and after that we can go find a photographer."

"*After?* Won't it be too late?"

"Photographers, like other undesirables, keep very late hours," said Pel-Thenhior.

※

Over dinner, Pel-Thenhior told me about the ongoing production of *The Siege of Tekharee*, which I had seen performed earlier that fall. "Poor Davaro," he said. "She's really been thrown in the lion pit with this as her first production with the company. It's a hard opera your first time through it."

"But not after that?"

"Anything's easier the second time."

That was true enough.

"She's very good, though," Pel-Thenhior added, as if I had expressed doubts. "Just as good as Arveneän and much easier to work with. Well, she'll *be* as good as Arveneän when she's got some experience. I admit she's not there yet."

"How old is she?"

"Nineteen," said Pel-Thenhior. "She's been singing in neighborhood operas since she was thirteen. This is the first time she's ever been paid enough to live on. She is a very happy young lady."

"I can imagine," I said. A thought occurred to me. "Do you accept foundlings?"

"Foundlings? You are full of surprises tonight. The question has never arisen, but I see no reason why we wouldn't. I know there are foundlings in Wardrobe. Ulsheän hires them to hem things and rip out seams and whatnot, and lets them work their way up from there. Why?"

"No real reason," I said, but found myself telling him about Isreän.

"That is very sad," said Pel-Thenhior. "It's a pity you can't find her employer. He ought at the very least to pay for the funeral."

"Even if we found him, he would never admit fault. That sort of man never does."

"Unconscionable," Pel-Thenhior muttered. He might have said more, but at that moment his mother came out of the back and said in Barizhin, "Iäna, your zhornu needs to speak with you."

Pel-Thenhior made a face, but said, "I beg your pardon—and please don't go anywhere! I'll be back as soon as I can." He got up and followed his mother.

I waited. I finished dinner and drank tea and felt more and more awkward. But the longer I waited, the more ridiculous it seemed to give up and leave, especially since Pel-Thenhior had explicitly asked me to wait. Other customers came and went, and I began to wonder nervously when the Torivontaram closed, or if it was one of those establishments that stayed open all night.

But the servers didn't seem worried. They brought me more hot water and generally behaved as if this happened all the time. Maybe it did.

It was nearly two hours before Pel-Thenhior returned, and when he did, he was accompanied by a goblin woman with the same golden-yellow eyes as his.

"I am so sorry!" Pel-Thenhior said. "I could not get away any faster. This is my zhornu, Adreän Pel-Venna." The word he used—"zhornu"—could mean cousin either literally or figuratively.

"Othala," said Min Pel-Venna in a strong Barizheise accent. "I have a question."

"Of course," I said.

"It is about a stillbirth." She hesitated.

"Go on."

Reassured, she said, "It is my sister-in-law's child. Since the birth she has been very ill, for no reason that our cleric can discover, and finally today I asked her about her dreams, and the idiotic woman tells me she's been dreaming about her dead child every night."

"Oh no," I said.

"That is what we wonder," said Min Pel-Venna. "I know that it is a very rare occurrence, but—"

"No, you're quite right," I said. "Dreams are one of the surest signs of a revetheralin."

"Can you do anything about it?"

"Yes," I said. "Is now a good time?"

"You think it cannot wait until morning?"

"If she's been nursing a revetheralin for a month, then, no, it cannot wait."

"All right," said Min Pel-Venna. "Come with me, then."

I looked at Pel-Thenhior.

"Iäna can come if he likes," said Min Pel-Venna.

"Art sure, Adreän? Won't Armedis mind?"

"Armedis is too worried about Cholan to notice," Min Pel-Venna said. "Come on."

I shrugged into my overcoat and followed her, Pel-Thenhior behind me. We didn't have very far to go, just around the block and up two flights of stairs to a small, shabby apartment with a thin and worried-looking goblin man in the front room.

"Who is this?" he said in Barizhin, giving me a suspicious look.

"The Witness for the Dead," Min Pel-Venna said in Ethuver-azhin. "He may be able to help Cholan."

"She isn't dead!" he said, softly but with great vehemence.

"Of course not," Min Pel-Venna said briskly. "But she might be nursing a revetheralin. Othala Celehar will be able to tell."

He turned to me, an awful expression compounded of hope and horror on his face. "Can you? Truly?"

"Yes," I said. "Where is your wife?"

"In there," he said, nodding toward the back room. "Asleep. She sleeps a great deal since the baby was born."

"Of course," I said. That could be a natural response to what had happened . . . or it could be the exhaustion caused by a revetheralin. "If I may? It will take only a moment to know."

"Yes," he said. "Please."

I opened the door and knew before I stepped inside.

I stepped inside anyway, because I didn't want to have to try to explain how I knew, but I could feel the death in the room.

A revetheralin was not like a ghoul; a ghoul was nothing but dead flesh and hunger, while a revetheralin was a kind of haunting, but one that only happened to women whose babies were stillborn. Scholars argued over whether it was truly the spirit of the dead infant or some kind of opportunistic malice, but two things were true: it appeared in the woman's dreams as her dead child, and it could kill.

It had almost killed this woman already.

She was heavily asleep, an elven woman, little more than a girl, with harsh lines of grief and exhaustion marking her face. The tracks the revetheralin left were not visible, but I could see where it had mauled her, all the same.

I stepped back out into the front room and said, "Yes."

Mer Pel-Venna shut his eyes for a moment, then said, quite lev-elly, "What must we do?"

"You must leave this apartment. It knows how to find her here."

"All right," he said, although that was no small thing to ask.

"But most of it *she* has to do."

"I cannot ask her to stop grieving our child."

"No, of course not. But it's not the grief that draws it. It's the despair."

"Despair?" he said.

"The fact that there's a revetheralin shows her despair. And that is what she has to stop."

"But why should Cholan despair?" he said, more to Min Pel-Venna than to me. "We are both young and healthy. Yes, this first attempt ended in tragedy, but there's no reason to think our second child will not live."

"I don't know," Min Pel-Venna said. "That's a question for Cholan."

"You can ask her now," I said. "You need to wake her up. The longer she's asleep, the more likely it is to come back."

"She has to sleep," he said.

"Yes, but *not here.*"

"All right," he said and went into the back room.

"You're certain," Min Pel-Venna said softly.

"Yes," I said. "It's not actually a thing one can be uncertain about."

"Is there anything you can do for Cholan? Some way to keep it from finding her again?"

"There are prayers," I said, "but really, she needs to have *less* to do with Ulis. A pilgrimage to the Sanctuary would be a good start."

Mer Pel-Venna returned with his arm around Merrem Pel-Venna. She looked even more fragile awake, also frightened.

"Good evening, Merrem Pel-Venna," I said. "I am Thara Celehar, a Witness for the Dead."

"G-good evening," she said. "Is it true, then?"

"I'm afraid so."

Her face twisted; she turned to hide it in her husband's shoulder. Muffled, she said, "It was my only comfort."

"It was not your child," I said, deciding to leave scholarly arguments out of it.

"I knew it couldn't be," she said. "But it just seemed . . ."

"Cholan," Mer Pel-Venna said gently, "we can have another child."

"I know," she said. "I do know. But—"

"Later," he said. "Othala Celehar says you can't sleep here anymore, so right now we need to figure out where you're going for the night."

"With me, of course," said Min Pel-Venna. "Don't be silly, Armedis. Cholan, let's pack a bag for you." She shepherded Merrem Pel-Venna into the back room.

Mer Pel-Venna said, "Thank you, othala. I thought she was going to die before we could figure out what was wrong."

"I follow my calling," I said.

For the first time, Mer Pel-Venna seemed to notice Pel-Thenhior standing behind me. "Oh," he said with obvious dislike. "Iäna."

"Don't mind me, Armedis," Pel-Thenhior said. "I'm just here as Othala Celehar's guide. Is there anything more you need to do here, Celehar?"

"No," I said. "I have given them the best advice I have. Good night, Mer Pel-Venna."

He now looked merely bewildered. "Good night, othala. Thank you."

Pel-Thenhior shut the door behind us with a decisive click.

As we came out onto the sidewalk, Pel-Thenhior said, "Do you still want to find a photographer?"

"Yes."

He eyed me with some doubt. "It means going to the Zheimela, and this is not a very pleasant time of night at which to do that."

"No, it is not," I said. I considered the matter again, but came to the same conclusion. "I have no other track to follow. Yes, let us go to the Zheimela."

"All right," he said, pulling his braids free of the coat collar and settling them with a toss of his head. "This is probably a foolish thing to be doing, but let us do it anyway." He started walking at a brisk clip, south toward the Dachenostro and the Coribano line that would take us as far as the ferry docks. Of the tram lines, only the Zulnicho crossed the Mich'maika.

"You don't have to do this," I said, half trotting to keep up with him. "I have no wish to put you to so much trouble."

"I don't mind a little trouble," Pel-Thenhior said. "Oh, sorry! I'm walking too fast." He slowed down enough that I could match stride with him.

We were silent for only a few moments before he began talking about his new opera. *The Grief of Stones* was based on a Barizheise novel about a lighthouse keeper and his family and the tragedies that befall them after the wreck of the *Grief of Stones* on their rocks. Part of the novel is the court case, as the survivors of the wreck swear the lighthouse was not lit, while the lighthouse keeper and his family swear it was; part of the novel is the string of bad luck that starts the morning after the wreck, when the lighthouse keeper's wife dies. Then one daughter runs off with a pirate; the other one dies in childbirth. His son's wife goes mad, talking about the ghosts of drowned sailors and the horrible creatures of the deep. The judiciar rules against them, and they are bankrupted paying restitution. Finally, the lighthouse keeper is confronted, on the crow's nest platform at the top of the lighthouse, by the ghost of the captain of the *Grief of Stones*; he admits that he did not light the lighthouse on the night of the wreck because he had been paid by the *Grief of Stones*'s competitors to be sure she did not make it to port. Only he and his son knew. The ghostly captain tells him there's a curse on his family, that all of these terrible things have happened because of his unscrupulous greed. The lighthouse keeper, unable to bear the guilt, flings himself from the top of the lighthouse; the captain's ghost disappears. The son, who heard everything, climbs up and says the only thing left to do is to swear an oath of penury and tend the lighthouse for the rest of his days.

Pel-Thenhior was writing out of order. He had the first scene and the last scene, and was going through and writing what he called the "good bits." Then he would go back and fill in the rest. "If I've done it right, there won't be much to fill in because the whole opera will be good bits. Just some transitions and getting people on and off stage."

I had been trying to keep track of the characters Pel-Thenhior was jettisoning, combining, outright inventing. "It sounds like an opera with more parts for men than women."

"Yes," said Pel-Thenhior. "It's the opposite of *Zhelsu* in that as in many other respects. It will please the traditionalists. And then the *next* opera, I can do something shocking again. If you're shocking every time, people get bored and stop paying attention, and I'll take any reaction to my operas except boredom."

"Even a riot?"

"They *cared*," said Pel-Thenhior. "So, yes, even a riot."

)(

The photographer's studio was in Dawn Court, off Dawn Street, where the Guild brothels in the Zheimela were clustered. We went up the court to the dome and four columns of the pump house, and there Pel-Thenhior stopped. "The city's two most successful photographers are here," he said. "Nathomar to the north and Zhikarmened to the south. Where do you want to start?"

"Does it matter?"

"Nathomar is more likely to talk, but Zhikarmened is the better photographer."

I decided to skip over the implication that he'd seen enough of both their work to judge. "I need the one who talks," I said, and Pel-Thenhior nodded. He led the way to the north side of the court and a glass door lettered in gilt NATHOMAR PHOTOGRAPHY. A bell jangled when Pel-Thenhior pushed the door open.

The front room of Nathomar Photography was paneled in brown velvet and had two chairs upholstered to match. There was no one waiting, but the door had barely closed behind us before a young elven man in his shirt-sleeves came out of the back room. His eyebrows went up, but he said, "Good evening, othala, Pel-Thenhior. What are you doing here this time of night?"

"I'm just here with my friend," said Pel-Thenhior, and Mer Nathomar turned his inquiring expression to me.

I could not lie about my calling. "My name is Thara Celehar, and I am—"

"The Witness for the Dead," Mer Nathomar finished for me, his smile shifting from professional to genuine. "I read about you in the papers all the time. I was very glad that you survived the ghoul in Tanvero. It must have been terrifying."

Usually, when people said things like that, I said, *I follow my calling,* and changed the subject. But I needed Mer Nathomar's goodwill. Thus, I said, "I hope never to have to do that again."

Mer Nathomar made a warding gesture and said, "But how can I help you? Are you here because of a petition?"

"Yes," I said and hoped Mer Nathomar would stop anticipating my words. "I am witnessing for the Marquise Ulzhavel and have discovered I need to speak to a photographer."

Mer Nathomar's bright blue eyes seemed guilelessly surprised. "The Marquise Ulzhavel, othala? I thought her death was natural."

"No," I said. "She was poisoned."

"*Poisoned?*" He made a warding sign again. "But why?"

"That is the question I am endeavoring to answer," I said.

The puzzlement on Mer Nathomar's face and in the set of his ears looked real. "I'm happy to help in any way I can, but I don't quite see how your witnessing has brought you here."

"She was trying to get photographers banned from the city," I said.

Mer Nathomar laughed. "Someone's always trying that and has been since Varenechibel banned photography from the Untheileneise Court. If we killed all our detractors, we wouldn't be able to move for the bodies."

"Were you aware of the Marquise Ulzhavel's campaign?"

"Oh, yes," said Mer Nathomar. "I keep abreast of city politics."

"But you didn't consider the marquise a threat?"

"Not yet," said Mer Nathomar. "She hadn't made it past alienating all her friends."

"I beg your pardon?"

"The *amateur* photographers. A number of them are noblewomen, so the first serious hurdle for anyone who wants to ban photography is the influence of the amateurs, which is considerable."

I had had no idea there was such a thing as an amateur photographer.

"What if you *had* found her troublesome? What would you have done?"

"Well, I certainly wouldn't have killed her. That's for opera, not for real life." Pel-Thenhior stirred beside me, as if about to object, but said nothing. "Photography may be disreputable, but we have some powerful patrons, starting with the Procurers' Guild."

"Then you wouldn't have sent her an unsigned note warning her to 'stop interfering'?"

"How melodramatic," said Mer Nathomar. "I assure you, I sent no such note."

"Might Mer Zhikarmened?"

Mer Nathomar laughed. "I can just imagine him doing it. No, othala, I don't think he would, although you can certainly ask him. In general, we try to avoid attracting attention, and sending unsigned notes is a very good way to get people much too interested in your activities. After all, the note's no good if your recipient can't figure out what you're talking about, and if they *can* figure it out, they can probably figure out who you are, too."

"You sound like you've given the matter some thought," said Pel-Thenhior.

"I've received my fair share of unsigned notes," said Mer Nathomar.

"So you think the note might not have come from a photographer at all," I said.

Mer Nathomar shrugged. "It's certainly a question I would ask."

"Pel-Thenhior says you and Mer Zhikarmened are the two most successful photographers in Amalo. Do you think a less successful photographer might feel differently about the marquise's opposition?"

Mer Nathomar thought about his answer. "I think threatening a marquise, even anonymously, is something no *professional* photographer would be stupid enough to do. And how would they have known how to get the note to her? How did she receive it? Through the post?"

"No one knows," I said. "Her husband found it among her things after her death."

"Well, *that's* bothersome," said Mer Nathomar.

"There was no envelope with it," I said, "which might suggest she did *not* receive it through the post."

"Or that she discarded the envelope," said Pel-Thenhior.

"Or that, yes."

"Because if she *didn't* receive it through the post," pursued Mer Nathomar, "then I don't think a professional photographer could have gotten it to her. An amateur might have, though."

"No," I said, "if it didn't come through the post, it must have . . . No, it must have come through the post; otherwise, she couldn't have received it except by someone handing it to her, which rather defeats the purpose of not signing the note in the first place."

"True," said Pel-Thenhior. "Sorry, Nathomar, you're not cleared yet."

"I don't suspect Mer Nathomar of anything," I said.

"Thank you," said Mer Nathomar. "Are you quite sure the note is about photography?"

"No," I said, "it's only the most likely subject. It has been very difficult to find *any* reason someone would want to murder the marquise."

"There are always reasons," Pel-Thenhior said darkly.

"That is very true," said Mer Nathomar. "Have you talked to the servants, othala? *They* will know."

I hadn't talked to the servants because it had seemed so clear that the danger came from outside the Ulzhavadeise compound. But if that was not true . . . And then I thought of a question I had stupidly failed to ask Ulzhavar about the workings of hezhelta.

"I know who I need to speak to," I said. "Thank you for your patience, Mer Nathomar. You have been very helpful."

"I am glad to hear it," said Mer Nathomar. "It was a most interesting conversation."

We exchanged bows, and Pel-Thenhior and I departed. "Was that true, or just politeness?" Pel-Thenhior asked as we came out of Dawn Court.

"No, it was quite true," I said. "There is a question I must ask the Master of the Mortuary, and depending on his answer, I may know who the murderer is."

"That's quite a question," said Pel-Thenhior.

"I should have asked it before. Now it has to wait until tomorrow afternoon."

"We could go and wake him," Pel-Thenhior offered; as far as I could tell, he was sincere.

"No," I said, "it's not necessary. If the murderer is who I think it is, they aren't going to hurt anyone else. And if I'm wrong, there's no hurry, because I have not the least idea of where to look next."

"You're not going to tell me who you think the murderer is, are you?"

"A false accusation is a terrible thing."

"Will you at least tell me later, when you know?" Pel-Thenhior said plaintively.

"Yes," I said, a little startled.

"It will keep eating at me, otherwise," he said.

We boarded the ferry and crossed to the north bank of the Mich'maika, leaving the Zheimela behind.

Ж

I was relieved in the morning to find Tomasaran waiting for me in the Prince Zhaicava Building, not wandering lost somewhere in Cemchelarna.

She said, "You look tired."

"I sleep badly," I said, not wanting to discuss the reasons I had not slept the night before.

"That is unfortunate," she said sympathetically. "One of my sisters—my Rozhemadeise sisters—has suffered that way since she was a small child. My mother tried every remedy that anyone told her, but Tanzheio still goes sleepless many nights."

"I, too, have tried a great many things," I said, feeling a sudden surge of sympathy for Tomasaran's sister, "all of them more or less useless."

"That is what Tanzheio says."

"In any event, there's nothing really to be done about it. Certainly, no need to worry."

She looked doubtful.

"I've been this way for years"—which was not something I had meant to tell her—"I'm accustomed to it."

"How uncomfortable."

I shrugged, though I knew my ears were lowering. "It is not pleasant, no. But it could be worse." Much worse. The nightmares I had had after Evru's execution had been worse. I would take sleeplessness any night rather than endure one of them again.

"I will not fuss over you," Tomasaran promised. Then her mouth went wry and she added, "I have been told often enough that I haven't a maternal bone in my body."

Here was something else I had not thought to be curious about. "Do you have children?"

"One son." Her ears were low, and she looked down at her hands. "The Tomasada disowned me, but they did not disown him, and I could hardly take him away from his proper family."

What did one say to that? "I'm sorry," I said awkwardly. "That must be a painful situation."

"It is less painful here than it would be in Eshvano. Here at least I have something of value to contribute—or I will, when you think I am ready to begin witnessing. There I had nothing of any value to anyone, and nothing to do."

I thought of the months I had spent at the Untheileneise Court, believing that I had forfeited my calling, with nothing to do but stare at the walls and try to avoid my cousin. "I understand," I said. "And I don't know . . . I'm not sure how I would know when you're ready. Which is not to say that I object to teaching you! Just that I am in the dark, too, about how we go about it."

She nodded. "No one really knows what to do with me. Is it so uncommon, to find a calling as an adult?"

"Mostly," I said, "the people who find callings as adults are the people who are called to be hermits. And mostly, the people who find that they can speak to the dead are people who are already learning to be prelates of Ulis, because those are the people who most often touch dead bodies. Usually, it comes on fairly slowly. I can't tell you when I started hearing the dead, because by the time I realized it, I'd been doing it for months. And I truthfully have never heard of someone finding their calling with a single touch."

"I am unique," said Tomasaran bleakly. "Huzzah."

"Do you *feel* called to Ulis? Or is it just that you hear the dead?" I regretted asking the question instantly. It was a horrible thing to ask anyone.

"I don't know," Tomasaran said. "I have been faithful to the gods all my life, but I have never felt *particularly* drawn to Ulis. I am trying, now, to be more open to him, but I don't really know what to do."

"Record your dreams. Meditate on them. You know the prayer of compassion for the dead, and there are other prayers to Ulis that you can learn."

"I . . ." She looked taken aback. "Meditate?"

"Is that not part of the practices you learned as a child?" I said, taken aback myself.

"No," she said. "I was taught that meditation was goblin nonsense." We stared at each other.

I had grown used, in the agnostic south and especially at the Untheileneise Court, to the idea that many people did not worship in the way I had been taught—or, indeed, at all—but I had found Amalo to be a much more observant city, and with the large numbers of goblins and part goblins in its population, goblin practices were widely accepted. Of course, Tomasaran had not grown up in Amalo.

She said, "I'm sorry, othala. I didn't mean that the way it sounded."

I could have picked a fight, but she wasn't to blame for the way she had been raised. I said, "Meditation can be a useful tool, especially if you are trying to do something like determining a calling."

"What if I don't?" she said, with such urgent anxiety that I knew she had been wrestling with the question for some time.

"I don't think Ulis would have given you the ability to hear the dead if he didn't want your service. But perhaps it is harder to feel as an adult."

"Perhaps," she said, as if she found it unlikely. "Will you teach me the prayers you spoke of?"

"Certainly," I said, and I spent that morning, uninterrupted by petitioners, in teaching Tomasaran the prayers I had learned as a novice. I did not teach her any of the deeper practices, for she had no basis on which to understand them, but the simple prayers to Ulis in his various aspects, plus the prayer of compassion for the dead that she already knew, would give her a starting point.

After lunch, we returned to the Sanctuary of Csaivo, where we found Ulzhavar in the mortuary, teaching a crowd of novices basic anatomy and autopsy practices. He saw us and said, "Hello, othalei!"

"I have a very quick question," I said.

"Then I will be glad to answer it quickly."

"How fast does hezhelta work when ingested?"

"That *is* a quick question, for the answer is, very quickly indeed. Sometimes less than a minute."

"Less than a *minute*?"

"Yes. That is the only good thing to say about it: unlike calonvar, it does not prolong its victims' agony."

"Thank you," I said. "I could have saved myself a good deal of trouble if I'd thought to ask you that at the autopsy."

"Much of any kind of investigation is asking the right questions," Ulzhavar said to his students, and Tomasaran and I slipped quietly away.

It was a short walk to the Ulzhavadeise compound, and I debated whether I should speak to the marquess or to Min Tativin first. The question turned out to be moot, for when I rang the bell, the marquess was in the front hall, looking at a portrait.

"This is our wife," he said to us, "as she was when we were married."

The portrait was a formal one, showing a young elven woman in all her jeweled finery. She was pretty enough, but what struck me was the directness of her gaze. The portrait painter had captured something of her personality in the way her painted eyes looked at her audience, direct and brisk and amiable. I regretted her death sharply now, in a way I had not before.

"When was the last time you saw her?" I said.

"At breakfast that morning, before she went to her meetings. We spoke only of trivial things."

"The last time we saw our husband, we fought," Tomasaran said. "It is a bitter memory."

"Yes," said the marquess. "Have you found our wife's murderer?"

"We need to ask Osmin Tativin a question," I said, "and then we will be able to tell you."

"All right," said the marquess, although he was eyeing me sharply. "You will find her in the solarium. She is helping us to sort our wife's papers. The marquise kept *everything*."

Perhaps that was reason enough to explain why she had kept the note.

"Thank you," I said. "This won't take long."

I remembered the way to the solarium. Osmin Tativin was seated at the secretary-desk, surrounded by stacks of paper. I tapped on the door and she twisted around. Her eyes widened when she saw me.

I said, "Did you write the note?"

"What?"

"We know you killed her," I said. "But did you write the note?"

"We do not know what you are talking about!" She stood up as she said it.

"Yes, you do, Osmin Tativin. The poison that killed the marquise works in less than a minute. You told us you saw her die. Either you killed her or you know who did."

"We do not know what you are talking about," she said again, but weakly.

"You murdered her, Osmin Tativin. Why?"

"It might have been the maid! She brought the tea!"

"We did not know there was tea. Is that how you got her to ingest it? Did you offer her a cup of tea?"

She shook her head, not in answer but in distress, and a voice said from behind me, "Did you do this thing, Esmeän?" The marquess had entered the room as silently as a cat.

"I had to!" she sobbed, her formality crumbling with her resolve. "She was going to dismiss me!"

"*Dismiss* you?" said the marquess. "But she often told us that she didn't know what she would do without you."

"Why was she going to dismiss you, Osmin Tativin?" I said.

"Someone gave her these," said Osmin Tativin, taking a small stack of papers out of one of the secretary-desk's pigeonholes.

A single glance was enough to explain the marquise's reaction.

"It was right after our father died," said Osmin Tativin, then abrogated formality in a rush: "I was destitute, desperate! But the marquise said she would have to think about her response, and it had been three days! And I *knew*."

"But what have you gained by killing her?" said Tomasaran. "You are still without a position and she can no longer give you a character."

"She hadn't told anyone yet, but I . . . we knew she would. This way, nobody had to know, and we could get another position."

"And for this you killed our wife?" the marquess said.

"We are sorry!" said Osmin Tativin. "We didn't want to do it, but we could see no other way." She put her face in her hands and wept.

The marquess turned to me, as stone-faced as ever. "What must we do?"

"First, we must get the Vigilant Brotherhood to take her into custody. Then, as the Witness for Tomilo Ulzhavel, we must find a judiciar who will take our deposition. This is a simple case. We doubt the judiciar will demand more witnesses. We witnessed her confession. There is little else to be said."

"Then justice will be quick," the marquess said. "We will send a boy to the watchhouse."

"We will await them," I said. There was no reason to make him spend any more time in the same room as his wife's murderer.

"Thank you, othala," said the marquess. "Your devotion to your duty is greatly appreciated."

"We follow our calling," I said. There was nothing else I could say.

X

After the Brotherhood had come and gone, taking the unresist-ing Osmin Tativin with them, I said to Tomasaran, "There is still one mystery remaining."

"There is?"

"Who gave the marquise the photographs?"

"Does it matter?"

I stared at her.

"It doesn't change anything. Osmin Tativin murdered her, not this other person."

"But this other person is part of the marquise's death. She was murdered *because* they gave her the photographs."

"Are you saying they're guilty of the murder?"

"No. Not guilty." I struggled for a moment with how to explain it to her, since she had so little of the necessary grounding in the tra-ditions of the Witnesses for the Dead, traditions that every prelate of Ulis knew without thinking. "The person who gave the marquise the photographs is connected to her through her death, and if I am to Witness for Tomilo Ulzhavel, I need to trace that connection."

"What if you can't?"

"The Witnessing remains incomplete. And I keep trying."

"It just seems like wasted effort."

"That depends on your definition of 'wasted,'" I said. "It is the only thing left that I can do to honor the marquise."

"Oh," said Tomasaran. "But what will you do?"

I crossed the room to the secretary-desk and picked up the pho-tographs, doing my best not to look at them. "I know someone who might be able to tell me more about these. And that seems as if it might be a fruitful starting place."

"You know a photographer?" Tomasaran looked as though she couldn't decide whether to be scandalized or impressed.

"You meet a great many people as a Witness for the Dead." That was far more sententious than I had intended to sound, but I couldn't help it being the truth—and it left the subject of my rela-tionship with Pel-Thenhior alone.

We left the Ulzhavadeise compound with plenty of time left in the afternoon to go and schedule our depositions—perhaps even give them, depending upon how busy the Judiciary was.

"How long does it take?" Tomasaran asked me as we rode the tram back up the hill.

"The deposition or the trial?"

"Well, both."

"The deposition need not take more than a couple of hours. The judiciar's judgment can take anywhere from a day to a month, depending on the judiciar."

The Judiciary was housed in the Amal'theileian, which was a grand conglomeration of palace styles through the centuries. The rulers of Amalo had apparently never torn anything down, preferring to build around and above and below, connecting the various wings with colonnades and open staircases and the occasional artful courtyard.

Tomasaran initially balked at going inside, insisting that she wasn't "important enough."

"Of course you are," I said. "You are a witness to a confession of murder, and I need your deposition. Come on."

It was true that the Amal'theileian was intimidating—although it was nothing compared to the Untheileneise Court—but, "Part of being a Witness," I said, "is not being intimidated out of doing your duty. Think of it as practice."

"All right," she said, but I heard the uncertainty in her voice.

I led Tomasaran at a brisk pace through the bustle and confusion of the Amal'theileian's marble halls to the Office of the Judiciary. The Witnesses' waiting room was about half full—judicial Witnesses waiting their turn.

"Othala Celehar!" said one, and I recognized Witness Parmorin, who had witnessed for the *Excellence of Umvino*.

"Good afternoon," I said, and remembered to introduce Tomasaran. "Are you waiting for a deposition or an assignment?"

"Assignment," she said with a sigh. "Always the hardest. At least if you're waiting to depone, you have the deposition to occupy yourself with. But what brings you here?"

"We are witnessing for a murdered woman," I said, indicating Tomasaran along with myself.

Parmorin made a ritual warding gesture. "Then you must want to put your name in the queue. I don't think there are very many deponents here, so you might even get in today."

"That would be best," I said, with a sigh of my own, and went up to the desk.

I didn't know the clerk on duty. "Good afternoon. We are Thara Celehar, a Witness for the Dead. Our colleague, Othalo Velhiro Tomasaran, and we need to make depositions about a murder."

"Of course, othala," the clerk said, writing our names down in his ledger. "Mer Holvathar should be able to hear you this afternoon."

"What happens now?" Tomasaran asked as we took two chairs together in the corner of the room where I could see the door.

"Now?" I said. "Now, we wait."

$$\text{\Large X}$$

Mer Holvathar was a short, stout elven man in vigorous middle age. His manner was brusque, but he was a good listener. He was patient with Tomasaran's nervousness, asking questions when she needed direction. She again proved to be capable of giving clear testimony of what she had heard and seen; she needed only practice to be able to give, unprompted, a deposition that would meet a judiciar's standard.

I gave my own deposition carefully, being sure to explain each step of the process by which I had realized Osmin Tativin's guilt. It was important to show that I had more than just her confession, since people could and often did recant confessions of wrongdoing.

"Thank you, othala," said Mer Holvathar. "That is all very clear. You will be notified of the judiciar's decision."

"Thank you," I said, and Tomasaran and I made our departure.

After I parted from Tomasaran for the day, I found that I wasn't ready to go home. I decided to visit Anora, for I had a great deal

I wanted to talk to *someone* about, and I knew Anora could be trusted.

He was in the middle of a funeral when I reached Ulvanensee. I settled myself on one of the benches in Ulvanensee's brick portico and waited peacefully—at least, that was, until I recognized one of the two mourners as Subpraeceptor Azhanharad. Then I waited intently. When the funeral was done, I was easily able to intercept Azhanharad's habitual frown as he strode for the exit.

"Subpraeceptor," I said.

"Othala," said Azhanharad with wary neutrality. "What brings you here?"

"A need to talk to Othala Chanavar. Yourself?"

"We buried that little suicide from the other day. Isreän."

"No one claimed the body?"

"No one even *inquired* about the body," said Azhanharad. "We buried her according to Ploraneise rites and pray that that was correct."

"It almost certainly was," I said. "We have never heard of one of the other sects running a foundling home."

"Not in the Airmen's Quarter at any rate," said Azhanharad. Then, briskly, "We have other business we must attend to this afternoon. Good day, othala."

"Good day, Subpraeceptor."

Anora found me a few minutes later and said, "Well, that was very sad."

"Isreän? I spoke to her for Azhanharad a few nights ago."

"We waited as long as we could, hoping someone would claim the body, but no one did."

"What didst thou name the child?"

"The subpraeceptor chose the name. He came with the gravestone already complete. The child's name is Aivaru."

"That is a very pretty name," I said.

"The subpraeceptor is as capable of poetry as any man. Didst need to speak to me?"

"I hoped thou wouldst come to dinner with me."

"Of course!" Anora said. "Let me change my clothes and give my prelates some instructions for the night, and we can be off."

He strode off down the northwest passage, and I leaned on the half wall and stared out at Ulvanensee, grim and dusty and the resting place of who knew how many thousands of bodies. Even the Catacombists' Guild didn't know the full extent of the catacombs beneath Amalo; Anora had told me that the maps of what lay deep under Ulvanensee had been lost centuries ago.

Anora returned in a dark brown frock coat with gray embroidery and said, "Wilt object to the Chrysanthemum?"

"Not at all," I said.

He paused mid-stride to peer down at me. "It will be quite all right if thou wishest to go somewhere else."

"Why should I wish that?"

"Thou'rt always so *agreeable,* Thara. I worry that thou'rt merely going along with what I want because thou dost not want the bother of disagreeing."

"If I had some better suggestion, I assure thee I would offer it."

"Wouldst thou?"

"I promise," I said. "I like the Chrysanthemum. Come on."

He started walking again. "All right. But I worry sometimes."

"I know thou dost. I wish thou wouldst not."

"It worries me that thou dost still grieve."

It was my turn to stop abruptly. "Grieve?"

Anora gave me a severe look. "Art going to deny it?"

"I don't . . ." But I *couldn't* deny it, not when grief still sat like a heart made of lead in my chest.

"Thou needst not tell me of it, for I have no intention of prying. But I have watched thee these past six months, and it seems only barely to have lightened."

I did not know if Anora knew I was marnis. I knew I did not want to tell him. "It is kind of thee indeed to worry," I said, "and things . . . things are not as bad as they were."

"That reassures me remarkably little."

"It is the best I can do."

"If thou didst *want* to talk of it . . ." Anora said hesitantly.

"I thank thee, but I do not," I said. "Let's just go to dinner."

"All right," Anora said, and started walking again, although I was aware of him watching me.

I said, "I wanted to tell thee about the Marquise Ulzhavel."

"Didst find her murderer?"

"I did," I said, and we talked of the Marquise Ulzhavel—and of Osmin Tativin—for the rest of the evening.

After I left Anora, I walked to the canal docks and boarded an eastbound ferry. It was crowded and uncomfortable with people, all talking loudly. I found a seat beside two goblin men having an intense conversation—in rapid and colloquial Barizhin, so I did not have to try not to listen—and did my best to be patient, although I felt restless and discomfited. Whatever Anora knew or didn't know, whatever gossip about me said—and I did not delude myself that there was not gossip—I hadn't thought my grief for Evru was so obvious, that it could be read on my face, my clothes, the set of my ears. The thought was unnerving and made me eye my fellow passengers warily, although they were much too involved with their own business to pay any attention to me.

I found my way from the dock to Dawn Court. There seemed to be some sort of celebration going on in Mer Zhikarmened's establishment; I ducked gratefully into Mer Nathomar's.

The waiting room was empty, but again it was only a matter of moments before Mer Nathomar appeared.

"Othala Celehar!" he said. "I did not think to see you again. And certainly not so soon."

"I did not think to be here again so soon, either," I said. "But events progressed unexpectedly this afternoon, and I have something I would like your opinion on."

"*My* opinion? You must mean photographs, then."

"Yes." I took them out of my inner coat pocket and handed them to him. "Anything you can tell me about them."

Mer Nathomar looked, and his ears flattened. "Let's not do this out here. Come on."

I followed him into the back, which turned out to be a much larger space than the waiting room suggested, but full of a jumble of furniture and odd things like birdcages and fake plants and a giant plaster dragon's head. There was a clear area against one wall, with a gaslight chandelier, two gaslight torchieres, and a boxy object made of wood and glass, mounted on a stand, that had to be a camera.

Mer Nathomar said, "How did you even get these photographs?"

I explained about Osmin Tativin. Mer Nathomar, looking at the photographs with increased interest, went through them one by one. He said, his blue eyes very steadily meeting my gaze, "You understand that I myself have never taken pictures such as these."

"Yes," I said. I certainly understood that he would not tell me if he had.

"All right. Any photographer would be able to tell you *some* things about them. They look like they were taken in a professional studio. The model seems most unwilling, which could mean several things, but your information tells us that she really *is* unwilling, and that narrows the field quite a bit. Most photographers would refuse an unwilling subject, but there are a few who prey on women like Osmin Tativin, who have been forced to the expedient of posing for pornographic pictures. Their audience for such pictures is narrow but very . . ." He paused, searching for the word he wanted. "*Committed*, let us say."

"Meaning there aren't very many photographers who would have taken these pictures."

"Correct. Moreover, there are certain recognizable habits that all photographers get into. The props they use or the poses they favor. And *this* one"—he sorted through the pictures to find the one he wanted—"shows the habits of a particular photographer."

I looked at the picture. Mer Nathomar said, "That pose, with her in front of the mirror and looking over her shoulder at the camera, is peculiar to Mer Anvina Renthalar, who is exactly the sort of person you'd expect him to be."

"Is he the sort of person who would give photographs like this to the woman's employer?"

Mer Nathomar grimaced. "It's certainly not something he'd *hesitate* to do, but he wouldn't do it without a reason. Money is a compelling one."

"But nobody seems to have asked the marquise for money. The note—if the note was sent by the same person as the photographs—just wanted her to stop 'interfering.'"

"And that's peculiar, because Renthalar would think that was pointless. Are you *sure* the note belongs with the pictures?"

"No, but it seems the most probable of several unlikely scenarios. The note and the pictures together make more sense than either does separately."

"What did the note say?"

"'Stop interfering or we will make you stop.'"

"That really couldn't be more vague, could it?"

"No," I said with some feeling.

"And *that,* at least, is not Renthalar's style. He would be specific about what he wanted and probably specific about what he was threatening to do."

"So Renthalar *took* the pictures, but somebody else wrote the note and gave the photographs to the marquise."

"That would be my guess," said Mer Nathomar. "But I must admit that I have as little to do with Renthalar as possible. I may be misjudging him."

"At least I know where the pictures came from."

"Yes. I'm quite sure about that. I've seen that pose too many times not to recognize it."

"Where is Mer Renthalar's studio?"

"I can't tell you that!" He sounded almost shocked.

"Why not?"

"Othala . . . Look, I don't mind your questions because I don't have anything to hide. I really *don't* deal in that sort of thing. Most of Mer Renthalar's business, to the contrary, is dependent on everything staying hidden. He won't answer your questions, and he may decide that you are a threat, in which case they'll be pulling you out of the Mich'maika in a couple of days."

"Then how can I proceed?"

He regarded me for a long time, frowning thoughtfully, then said, "Maybe I know someone you should meet." He gave me a side-long glance. "She is a Guild prostitute."

"I've talked to Guild prostitutes before," I said.

"All right, then," said Mer Nathomar. "Come on."

"Now?" I said.

"She'll be awake now," said Mer Nathomar. "She won't be in the morning." He shepherded me back through the front room and out into the court, locking the door behind us.

"I am putting you to a great deal of trouble," I said.

He waved that away. "Business is slow tonight. And I'm pleased to be able to help Amalo's only Witness for the Dead."

"I have a . . . an apprentice, I guess you'd say, so I'm not really the only one."

Mer Nathomar laughed. "Even so."

I followed him out of Dawn Court, down the street, through a bewildering assortment of alleys, and out into another court, this one lit by paper lanterns hanging from the great tree in the center.

"How lovely," I said.

"You wouldn't expect that of the Guild, would you?" Mer Na-thomar said. "It was the girls' idea and now the Guild masters take credit for it." He went up to a door in one of the buildings surround-ing the court, where a massive goblin man was leaning against the wall, looking bored.

"Good evening, Tanata," said Mer Nathomar.

"Good evening, Mer Nathomar," said the goblin man. He eyed me suspiciously. "Is the prelate with you?"

"Yes," said Mer Nathomar. "He'll cause no trouble."

"All right," said Tanata, and opened the door. "Welcome to the Cinnabar Cat."

Inside, it was not cinnabar. Everything was in cool, tasteful blues and greens, including the gowns worn by the prostitutes. It was a clever choice, for those colors brought out the elven women's eyes and provided a striking contrast with the goblin women's coloring.

An older elven woman, wearing an ornately embroidered turquoise half-jacket over a very simple but beautifully tailored dress in a deeper turquoise, came up to us. Her hair was dressed with lacquered combs and a strand of turquoise glass beads. She wore her Guild insignia as a locket at her throat.

"Mer Nathomar!" she said, sounding professionally pleased but also puzzled. "Were we expecting you?"

"No," said Mer Nathomar. "I need to speak to Erthalo. Is she free?"

One of the watching women—an elven girl wearing a shockingly low-cut deep blue dress and an elaborate silver choker necklace— stepped forward before the Guild master had decided on what she was going to say.

"I'm free now, if it's quick," the elven girl said.

"It is," said Mer Nathomar.

"Oh, all right," said the aggrieved Guild master. "You can use the Pearl Room if you're *quick*. If you *aren't* quick, Mer Nathomar, I will charge you for her time."

"Fair enough," said Mer Nathomar, and we followed the elven girl—Erthalo—down a hallway and into a room decorated entirely in white.

"Some of our patrons have imperial fantasies," said Erthalo.

I was fairly sure that was illegal, but I was here as Tomilo Ulzhavel's Witness, and other questions of legality were outside my remit.

Mer Nathomar closed the door and said, "I need you to show him."

Her hand went to her necklace. "Why?"

"To persuade him he doesn't want to go asking Anvina Renthalar any questions."

"Oh. Goddesses, no, othala, you don't want to do that." She undid the clasp of her necklace and took it off.

The scar stretched halfway around her neck. I could only be amazed that she was still alive.

She said, "I threatened to go to a Witness about Anvina's blackmail schemes. That night, this happened. I am lucky that he did a bad job."

"And you didn't go to a Witness?"

"Do I look insane? No, I did not. But I don't model for Anvina anymore, either."

"I thought his models were all . . ."

"What he calls 'special cases'?" Her mouth twisted. "He *prefers* the girls that come to him as a last resort, but if it's a bespoke photograph where a patron wants a particular thing to be happening, he gets better results with the girls who are pretending."

"Can you tell me," I said and hesitated, then tried again. "I am witnessing for a woman who was murdered in consequence of being given some of Mer Renthalar's photographs, and I'm trying to find out how they got to the person who gave them to her."

"*Murdered?*" said Erthalo in horror. "Over *photographs*?"

"It is complicated," I said, "and I cannot explain if we are to keep this meeting quick. I'm trying to find out how the photographs got to the . . . to the murdered woman."

Erthalo made a warding gesture. "Anvina probably couldn't help you with that, even if he was willing to try. He's got big volumes of photographs in his studio, and his patrons can go through and pick out whichever ones they want. He'll make reproductions and he doesn't keep records."

"So it's not his patrons he blackmails?"

"No, of course not," she said. "He blackmails the women who come to him because they have no other means of raising money."

"But if they have no money, what good does it do him to blackmail them?"

"Mer Renthalar is a patient man," Erthalo said with a shiver. "He can afford to wait until the poor woman is married and respectable and thinks she can forget about him."

There was a sharp tap at the door, and Erthalo fastened her choker around her neck. "I'm sorry I couldn't be more help, othala."

"Thank you," I said. "I appreciate your honesty."

She hesitated at the door. "Mer Renthalar is a bad person, othala. Don't go near him." And then she was gone.

"Let us be off before Sosavin decides to charge us for the room," said Mer Nathomar.

I followed him out. We were back in his studio before either of us spoke again.

"She gives sound advice," said Mer Nathomar.

"Yes," I said. "I have no desire to cross Mer Renthalar."

"But you do not have the information you want."

"No, although it certainly seems that, whoever sent the photographs to the marquise, they would not have had any difficulty obtaining them."

"No," said Mer Nathomar. "It is part of Mer Renthalar's business. He probably wouldn't be able to tell you anything about the person who bought those pictures."

"Probably not," I said. I knew what he wanted, and I said, "I will not go near him."

"Thank you, othala. I will sleep better."

The bell on his front door jangled, and he pointed me out the back door while he went toward the front.

All the way home, I thought of Erthalo and her brutal scar and watched my fellow travelers uneasily.

X

Tomasaran was not waiting for me in the morning, but she arrived a few minutes after I did. "Good morning, othala," she said, taking the petitioner's chair.

"Good morning," I said. "We need a third chair."

"I suppose so," said Tomasaran. "How does one go about getting a third chair?"

"I have no idea," I said.

"The cartographers will know," she said. "I will go ask them."

She was gone longer than I expected, but returned carrying a plain wooden chair like the two the office had had when I had been given it. "There," she said, setting it down at an angle to my desk. "The cartographers had an extra. Min Talenin said otherwise you have to requisition furniture from the stewards' office and that can take a week or two." She sat down.

"Do they need the chair back?"

"No," said Tomasaran. "Min Talenin said it was just collecting dust."

We sat silently for several moments before I was able to come up with a topic of conversation. "Are you finding Merrem Nadaran's boardinghouse comfortable?"

"Oh, yes," said Tomasaran. "Far more comfortable than I would be in the Tomasada compound."

"Then you do not regret following your calling?"

"No," she said, "although I worry about how much I do not know. I thought about it last night, and I think you are right that I need to know about benefices and what prelates of Ulis do if I am truly going to be a Witness for the Dead. I had no idea it was so complicated until Othala Veltanezh started talking about the registers."

"The prelacy of Ulis is not a mystery," I said, "but very little is shared with laypeople."

"Only funerals," said Tomasaran.

"Perhaps we can ask Othala Chanavar if you could spend a day or two with him. Nothing will teach you the business of being a prelate faster than watching the operations of a cemetery like Ulvanensee."

"I would like that," said Tomasaran. "Maybe—"

There was a timid tap at the door.

Tomasaran and I both stood up.

The petitioner was a middle-aged bourgeoise elven woman, respectably dressed, whose face held a complicated mixture of nervousness, embarrassment, and determination. I was surprised she was alone, but it made me aware before she began that her petition was of surpassing importance to her—but something that she could not tell her husband or any of her male relatives.

"Are you Othala Celehar?"

"We are, and this is our colleague, Othalo Tomasaran."

She nodded to Tomasaran and turned back to me. "Othala, we are Ceiliän Bralisharan, and we have come to you about our friend Neshiro Mulinaran."

"Yes?" I said.

"We have been friends with Merrem Mulinaran for many years, and she was always a woman who told stories. Lies, our husband called them, but we did not and do not believe that she intended them to be taken seriously. But . . ." She stopped and wrestled with it for a moment, then started on what seemed to be a fresh track. "Merrem Mulinaran died three days ago. She had no children and no family in Amalo, and we are distant cousins, for our mothers were both Dechaladeise. She appointed us her executrix."

She stopped; this time it did not appear that she was going to be able to start again. I said, "If you have come to us, you must have a question you need to ask her."

"Yes!" she said. "Who is the dead body in her attic?"

After a moment, I said cautiously, "That seems like a very reasonable question."

Having gotten the question out, she was able to tell her story in a coherent fashion. As Merrem Mulinaran's executrix, she had to make an inventory so that things could be matched with bequests, or marked for sale, and so that outstanding bills could be paid. She had started by going through the whole house, top to bottom, except that at the top, in the attic, she had found a bulky package wrapped in bedsheets. She unwrapped it—blushing now as she admitted to curiosity—and found a body.

"He was not *recently* dead," she told us. "Indeed, he seemed to have been there for many years. He was quite . . . dry."

"And you have no idea of who he might be?"

She hesitated.

"You have an idea," I said encouragingly.

"It was Neshiro—Merrem Mulinaran's way to tell stories, as we have said. And she told many different stories about the death of her husband. Sometimes, she said she'd killed him."

"But not always?"

"No. More often, she said he died of iärditha shortly after they came to Amalo. But sometimes she said other things."

"You believe she murdered her husband?"

"We do not know!" She gripped her hands tightly together, as if afraid of what they might do. "That is why we have come to you, othala. Because the only person who knows is Neshiro."

"All right," I said. "It is a rightful petition. Let us go ask Merrem Mulinaran about her unexpected lodger."

"Oh, we need not go anywhere," said Merrem Bralisharan. "We brought her with us." And she produced from her bag a squat black box.

Merrem Mulinaran had been cremated, according to the stipulations of her will, but Merrem Bralisharan had not yet scattered her ashes. "We found Mer Mulinar—if that is who he is—while her body was at the crematory. We knew we had to . . ."

Disregard her friend's wishes until the mystery was solved. An awkward fix to be in. "Yes," I said. "We will know very quickly if Merrem Mulinaran has the answer you need."

She handed me the box. In it were Merrem Mulinaran's ashes and a striking peacock brooch.

"It was her only real piece of jewelry," said Merrem Bralisharan.

I said the prayer of compassion for the dead and touched the brooch with one finger; I immediately found myself surrounded by the still vivid presence of Merrem Neshiro Mulinaran. For once, my difficulty was not that the dead were almost beyond answering questions; rather, the problem was that Merrem Mulinaran was *too* present. It was hard to concentrate long enough to put the question together.

But when I did, she answered at once.

I held the box out so that Tomasaran could touch the brooch, which she did, although she jerked her hand away after a few seconds. "You are correct, Merrem Bralisharan," I said. "Merrem Mulinaran murdered her husband."

"Oh *no*," said Merrem Bralisharan.

"They had just moved to Amalo, where they had no family and no one knew them. There was no one to ask after Mer Mulinar when he disappeared, and it was years before she was close enough to anyone to invite them into the house. There was no difficulty in just . . . storing the body like any awkward piece of furniture."

"But why?" said Merrem Bralisharan, who looked on the verge of tears.

"We do not know," I said. "Merrem Mulinaran's memory was only of her own cleverness."

"How like her," Merrem Bralisharan said dismally.

Mer Mulinar, of course, had not left a will, or if he had, his widow had destroyed it. Merrem Bralisharan and I decided the best thing to do was cremate him and scatter his ashes in the Zhomaikora. "A body this old is very unlikely to rise as a ghoul," I said, "but on the other hand, it does not hurt to be certain."

"It was foolhardy of her to keep him for so long," Merrem Bralisharan said.

"It was."

"We do not understand how she could do it."

I considered the memory of Merrem Mulinaran in my head. "She does not seem to have felt that she did anything wrong."

"Neshiro was very much a person who believed that if she did a thing, it could not possibly be wrong. But we did not imagine it could extend so far."

We were silent for a moment, and I said, "We cannot tell you why she wanted him dead."

"She never spoke of him fondly. And they were childless. Perhaps Mer Mulinar was contemplating divorce . . ."

"Far better to be a widow."

"Yes," said Merrem Bralisharan, although she looked horrified at her own theory.

"Her estate must make restitution."

"How? Mer Mulinar has no heirs."

"A donation to the Ulistheileian," I said. "For Ulis is the god she wronged."

"When the bequests and the bills are done, we will donate the rest."

"What did her will stipulate?"

Merrem Bralisharan shook her head. "She left the remainder of her estate to us, but we do not want it. Truthfully, othala, there will not be a large amount. Merrem Mulinaran seems to have been very bad at paying her debts."

"It is the spirit of the gift that matters," I said, "not the gift itself."

"The spirit of the gift is whole-hearted," said Merrem Bralisharan. "*Very* whole-hearted." And she shuddered.

When she was gone, Tomasaran said, "Do you have many petitions like that?"

"That petition is unique in my experience," I said. "I have never heard of another case of a murderer storing their victim like an old sofa."

"She was very clever."

"She was. Also utterly unprincipled. We are lucky that she was not also ambitious, or she might have left a trail of bodies like rose petals wherever she went."

Tomasaran made a noise that was not a laugh. "Your analogy is striking, othala."

"And a trifle untoward, yes," I said. "You will find I am not the only prelate of Ulis with that problem."

"I was not offended. Just startled."

"It has been a startling morning," I said.

※

Merrem Bralisharan was our only petitioner that morning. Tomasaran rather hesitantly produced a pack of cards from her frock coat pocket, and we played argis until noon—a child's game, but by that same token, a harmless one. If someone caught us, it was much easier to excuse than pakh'palar.

At noon, when our obligation to this literal office was done, Tomasaran asked, "Do you have need of me this afternoon, othala?"

"I . . . might," I said, reconsidering in the middle of telling her she was free to go. "It depends."

"Depends on?"

"How you feel about something that is not strictly prelate's business."

"What do you mean?"

I explained about Osmin Temin's school and showed her the note I'd been given.

She examined it. "And you're sure this isn't just some child's ill-conceived joke?"

"If it is, then every girl I saw was part of the joke, and they should all consider a career in opera, for they are extremely talented actors. It's not a joke."

"What do you intend to do?" she said, with commendable caution.

"Talk to the school's neighbors, first of all," I said. "It's not so different from witnessing for someone who has died in the middle of a quarrel—which happens more often than one might like to think. In order to witness for them, you have to find out the truth of the quarrel, but you can't find that out from the dead person."

"They'll only tell you their side of it," Tomasaran said.

"Exactly. Thus, you ask the neighbors. You ask the coworkers. You ask the families. You try to build up the truth from all these different pieces. That's what I want to do with Osmin Temin's school, and I would be glad of your help if you want to come. But only if you want to! This is only very tangentially related to being a Witness."

"It sounds like good practice, though," Tomasaran said. "Yes, I will be glad to come."

On the Abandoned Bridge, we passed a storyteller recounting the slaying of the dragon Erzamagria, which sounded a little different knowing that the slayer was an agent of the Clenverada Mining Company and that there was no maiden to be rescued, only a fortune in gold ore.

When we reached Goshawk Street, we separated, Tomasaran taking the east side of the street while I took the west.

I'd told her to try businesses before houses. Homeowners were often alarmed at having a prelate of Ulis on their doorstep, as if we brought death rather than following it. Clerks and shopkeepers tended to be calmer—and frequently had better information, given that they spent their days with the shop windows, paned or the much more expensive plate glass, looking out on the street.

I found out very quickly that no one liked Osmin Temin. The shopkeepers said she was unfriendly, haughty, as if her rank precluded her from having to be polite. They admitted, some of them grudgingly, that she always paid her bills promptly and in full. More than one person observed that Osmin Temin seemed to have come into some money recently.

"Not that you'd know it from looking at the girls, poor little mites," said a matronly part-goblin bakery owner. "Out in all weathers without proper coats, and you can't tell me, othala, that they're getting enough to eat. Skinny as sticks, the lot of them."

Other shopkeepers noted that the girls were all extremely well-behaved. "She says she teaches 'em manners, and I guess she does at that," said the elven owner of a pastry shop a block from the school. "They wait their turn, speak up nicely, it's always 'please, sir,' and 'thank you, sir,' and there's none of that atrocious giggling. Not from Osmin Temin's girls."

No one reported anything particularly suspicious, and several people would clearly have liked to. When I met up with Tomasaran again, she had gotten much the same answers: Osmin Temin was disagreeable but a good customer; the girls were threadbare but polite; Osmin Temin herself had been dressing better over the past few months. "And no one said anything about a student asking for help," Tomasaran finished. "Which surprised me a little. If they're willing to ask a complete stranger for help, why wouldn't they ask somebody they know?"

"It's a good question," I said, "and I have the answer to it. Everyone dislikes Osmin Temin, but they speak very fondly of her deputy, Min Orbelin. I'm sure the first thing any of them would do would be to talk to her."

"Do you think they'll tell her about us?"

"Probably, but there's nothing for it."

"I don't know what I would have told them if they'd asked why I was asking so many questions, but nobody did."

"Your clothes and hair mark you as a prelate," I said. "People in Amalo tend not to ask about a prelate's business." It wasn't that way everywhere; in Lohaiso, the people were endlessly nosy.

"Oh," said Tomasaran, to whom this aspect of her calling had clearly not occurred. She shook her head sharply, then asked, "What do we do now?"

"I know what I'm going to do, but I think you'd better not."

"Why?" she said, almost indignantly.

"Because I don't want you to have to explain yourself to Dach'othala Vernezar. Or possibly to the Amal'othala."

"The Amal'othala! What is it you plan to do?"

"Talk to the local prelates. The possibility exists that one of them will report me for being too inquisitive."

"Is that a crime?"

"It's unbecoming to a prelate of Ulis. The Amal'othala will probably say I have transgressed my calling."

"That sounds very serious."

"He can't actually do anything to me but set a penance. The Archprelate appointed me. Only he has the authority to remove me from office. But your situation is quite different, and I don't think you should come."

"Are you sure?" she said, sounding both crestfallen and relieved.

"Yes," I said. "I don't want to get you in trouble. Go home, and I'll see you tomorrow."

"All right," she said. She left me at the alley between Goshawk and Pigeon Streets, and I regrouped myself. It was time to find the local ulimeire.

※

Othalo Prenevin was very young, a mousy elven woman whose coat of office was even shabbier than mine. She recognized me—as many prelates did—and came bolting to her feet. "Othala Celehar! How . . . how can we help you?"

"What do you know about Osmin Temin's school?"

"The school on Goshawk? They have never needed our services."

That was a weaseling answer. As a beneficed prelate, she had to know the ins and outs of her neighborhood. "No gossip?" I said bluntly.

"Gossip!" She tried to look horrified, but did a poor job of it. "I nev— That is, we do not gossip."

"Then you are the first Ulineise prelate in the history of the world who does not."

Her face was scarlet. "I mean . . . we talk to people, of course."

"Of course."

"We have heard nothing *bad* about Osmin Temin's school," she said, wringing her hands. Her ears were flat.

"But you have heard something?"

"Only . . . only that Osmin Temin is spending money very freely for someone in charge of a foundling school."

I had heard the same thing. "Have you heard where the money is coming from?"

"Only speculation. Osmin Temin won't say."

"Someone asked?"

"Someone tried," Othalo Prenevin said, "but Osmin Temin just walked away from them." She hesitated, then added, "Osmin Temin is very rude."

I had heard that, too.

"And none of the teachers knows?"

She shook her head. "They don't gossip." A thought seemed to strike her. "You might ask Othas'ala Delemar. He talks to Osmin Temin sometimes."

It was transparently a ploy to get rid of me, but I doubted she knew anything more anyway. I asked for directions to the othasmeire and set out afresh.

This part of Cemchelarna seemed to be all row houses, narrow but respectable. The othasmeire clearly dated back to the days when Cemchelarna was fashionable. It was imposing, even soot-tainted and with its copper dome gone to verdigris. The mosaic floor was missing tiles, and the sanctuary seemed cavernous with the great darkness of the dome rising above the marble pillars.

I stopped at the last edge of light and called, "Hello?"

After several moments of silence, a voice called back, "Hello? Is someone there?"

"I was hoping to speak to Othas'ala Delemar."

"Well, that's easy enough. I am Othas'ala Delemar. How can I help you, othala?"

He'd finally gotten close enough that I could see him: an elven man, as old as the Marquess Ulzhavel or older, wearing shabby vestments and a strand of crystal beads in his long prelate's plait— which was unorthodox, but not forbidden. He was a little stooped, but still vigorous, and his pale blue eyes were sharp.

I said, "I am trying to find out more about Osmin Temin's school."

"That's an odd hobby for a Ulineise prelate. What is your name?"

"Thara Celehar."

"You're Prince Orchenis's pet Witness for the Dead, the one the Curneisei hate. What are you doing out in Cemchelarna? And why in the world are you interested in the foundling school?"

"I am a Witness for the Dead. I was appointed by the Archprelate, not by Prince Orchenis." The other part was true enough.

"That's as may be," said Othas'ala Delemar. "It's not a secret that you're here because the prince needed a way to get around Dach'othala Vernezar. They've been at odds for years."

I knew Prince Orchenis had asked the Archprelate to appoint me to Amalo to maneuver around Vernezar—it was one reason Vernezar disliked me—but I hadn't realized that the move was so transparent to people who were neither Vernezar's staff nor Prince Orchenis's court. No one before Othas'ala Delemar had been brazen enough to tell me. *Everyone* had warned me about the Curneisei when I first came to Amalo, so much so that avoiding the area south of the Amal-Athamareise Airship Works had become reflexive.

"No matter," said Othas'ala Delemar. "You said you were asking about Osmin Temin's school. What did you need to know?"

"Does she treat the girls well?"

"Well?" said Othas'ala Delemar, eyeing me with a mix of puzzlement and suspicion. "What do you mean by *well*? She makes them work, if that's what you're asking. It is not a school for shirkers."

That sounded ominous, but perhaps I had become predisposed

to find everything I was told about the school ominous. Or perhaps it was my growing dislike for Othas'ala Delemar.

"I've heard the girls don't have adequate clothing for bad weather," I said.

"Oh, nonsense," said Othas'ala Delemar impatiently. "They just whine because they don't get fashionable clothes." His face cleared. "If it's a girl you're looking to place there, I can assure you that she will be well trained and easily able to find work when she leaves."

I realized in horror that he thought I had an illegitimate daughter I was trying to disburden myself of. I felt my face go scarlet and my ears go down, and I said, "I assure you, it is nothing of the sort."

He looked amused and said, "It's no business of mine. Your girl will be well taken care of at Osmin Temin's. Good day." And he vanished back into the darkness of the othasmeire.

I reminded myself of the impossibility of proving a negative and did not shout after him. The more I denied it, the more he would believe it to be true.

)(

Dissatisfied and uncertain, I made my way back from Cemchelarna to the Veren'malo. There, instead of doing the sensible thing and going home, I walked to the Vermilion Opera and went in.

It was early evening; technically, the part-goblin boy at the ticket window shouldn't have let me past, but he recognized me and waved. I waved back and went through the first set of double doors to the foyer with stairs to the balconies and narrow passageways to the boxes on the ground floor. I circled to the left and entered Pel-Thenhior's box. He was not there, but I was content to wait. He would arrive eventually.

The curtain was up, so I sat down and watched the people preparing for the evening's performance.

As I watched, a screen rose, revealing the set for *Zhelsu*. For all that the costumes were drab (by opera's standards), the set for *Zhelsu* was towering and elaborate with gearwheels and copper pipes. The centerpiece was a giant wheel that actually turned, and its remorseless revolutions were an image Pel-Thenhior had put to good use. Right now there was a goblin stagehand three-quarters of the way to the top doing maintenance; I kept having to make myself look away from his precarious position. Another goblin stagehand was sweeping the floor of the stage, and a third was carefully cleaning the footlights.

Pel-Thenhior was standing in the middle of the stage with a harried-looking elven man, discussing something in low voices. A little group of chorus members were standing by the footlights on the far side of the stage, practicing a tricky harmony. There was a general air of busyness and purpose that I found soothing after a long afternoon of talking to people without results.

After some time, a part-goblin man came out and said, loud enough to carry, "They'll be opening the house in fifteen minutes." On this cue, the stagehands and the chorus members disappeared; the elven man said, "Thank you, Iäna," and strode off stage. Pel-Thenhior spoke to the part-goblin man for a few moments; then they went together into the wings. Ponderously, the curtain began to close. Almost immediately, Pel-Thenhior's door into the box opened.

"Othala Celehar!" he said cheerfully as he sat down in the other chair with his notebook and pen. "Welcome! Have you come for the opera or some other reason?"

That was a good question. I said, "I would certainly like to see the *whole* opera, but I would also like your opinion on something."

"I think you've got that backwards. Aren't I supposed to be the one asking advice of a prelate?"

"Please don't," I said and made him laugh.

"You are welcome to my opinion, for whatever use it is to you. We have a minimum of half an hour before the curtain rises again. Tell me."

"It won't take *that* long," I said, and told him about Osmin Temin's school.

He listened with focused attention, and when I reached my inconclusive conclusion, said, "Surely this is not your problem to fix. Can you not take the note to the board of governors?"

"I don't think there *is* one," I said. "Osmin Temin seems to be in control of the money."

"Which is suspicious all by itself. There are good reasons not to have the person in charge of revenues also be in charge of expenditures. And from what you've said, it is not at all clear where the money is coming from."

"No, it isn't. But not from tuition."

People were beginning to enter the auditorium, beautifully dressed elves, mostly in couples, although I saw several single men. There were goblins and part goblins among them, though not many; I saw one magnificent goblin dowager in plum taffeta who was being escorted by two men, almost certainly her sons.

"So," said Pel-Thenhior. "You have two mysteries. Whatever it is the girls want to be stopped, and the source of the money Osmin Temin spends."

"It seems possible," I said, "that they are the same mystery."

"Possible," Pel-Thenhior agreed, "but I'm puzzled by what could have the girls so scared."

"Yes. And so secretive. There are many people in their neighborhood whom they could have asked for help."

"Starting with the othas'ala."

"Yes, although I admit that Othas'ala Delemar would not be my first choice of confidant."

"You make me curious," said Pel-Thenhior.

Someone tapped on the door leading backstage.

"I'll be right back," said Pel-Thenhior. He left his notebook and pen on his chair, and I heard him saying, "What seems to be the problem, gentlemen?" as the door closed behind him.

Pel-Thenhior was gone long enough that the audience settled as much as they were going to, and the curtain went up.

*Zhelsu* starts with the adult chorus onstage singing about work in a dreary, monotonous, and horribly infectious tune. Pel-Thenhior had said once, with every sign of satisfaction, that he expected to be cursed in the streets.

Pel-Thenhior came back just as the overseer came on stage to yell at the chorus for singing, and then to perform his own smug aria. Pel-Thenhior nodded to me as he picked up his notebook and pen and sat down, and then he uncapped his pen and started taking frenetic notes.

I watched the first act of *Zhelsu* with considerable interest, since I had seen only bits and pieces of it, never the whole thing. Min Vakrezharad was magnificent from the moment she stepped on stage, her voice pure and unwavering. Min Nesthin, the replacement for Min Shelsin, was excellent as Zhelsu's closest friend, and Mer Mesunar as the overseer was almost *too* convincing; the greedy way he watched Zhelsu made my skin crawl.

The first act ended with the overseer's proposition to Zhelsu and her horrified retreat from the stage. The curtain came down; Pel-Thenhior straightened from his hunch over the notebook and said, "They're doing quite well, really."

"You're a perfectionist," I said.

"Of course," said Pel-Thenhior. "If you aren't always striving to become better, you stagnate. The only thing Arveneän and I ever agreed on."

"Doesn't it become frustrating?"

He laughed. "It is *always* frustrating. Ask Othoro about her second-act aria. But it is better than becoming bored with one's own performance."

"Does that happen often?"

"Oh, yes. Many great singers stop trying after a while, because their performance is good enough that no one's going to complain about it, and they feel as if that's all that's necessary. They don't feel the need to *strive* for— But I beg your pardon. I get carried away on that subject. You were saying that the othas'ala was perhaps not someone the girls would confide in."

"Perhaps I do him an injustice."

"I doubt it. And in any event, if they're passing notes to you, they have clearly not been successful at finding help closer to home."

"But what can I *do*? I don't have evidence of anything I could take to a Witness. I have no legal right to interrogate Osmin Temin, and no way to make her answer my questions."

"Perhaps," said Pel-Thenhior, "you need to find out what Osmin Temin isn't telling you."

"A very sensible suggestion. But *how*?"

"Go look," said Pel-Thenhior. "In her office. We could do it tonight."

"Are you suggesting I should break into the school?" I said, aghast.

"Unless you can think of a better way," Pel-Thenhior said, and that was when the curtain rose for act two.

Act two of *Zhelsu* is the reaction to the overseer's proposition. One by one, the people close to Zhelsu—her mother, her closest friend, her lover—fail to help her, and when the overseer traps her, she has no one to turn to, no recourse except to jump into the manufactory's machinery and end her life. The scene was even more harrowing in its full context—I heard some faint screams from the audience when Min Vakrezharad flung herself over the catwalk railing—and only seconds later the opera ended with Min Rasabin's piercing shriek.

This audience was generous with their applause. Pel-Thenhior disappeared backstage again, though again he left his notebook, like a promise that he was coming back. I watched the audience leave, bright and glittering and probably untouched by Zhelsu's story except the scandal of an opera about manufactory workers and the goblin woman singing the lead.

Pel-Thenhior, when he came back, said as if continuing a conversation, "Mer Dravenezh was in the Parzhadada box tonight. I am relieved."

"Relieved?"

"He missed so many performances I was afraid he'd been fired. But I saw him tonight, alone as always."

"Do you think he comes for his own enjoyment or at the marquess's behest?"

"I don't know. It's one of the many things I've never dared to ask

Parzhadel, just as I never ask him what Mer Dravenezh *says* about the performances. He's very attentive, I know that much."

"It's more than you can say for most of the audience."

He laughed. "They're paying better attention than you think they are. They noticed *Zhelsu* quickly enough that first night, although that may have just been Othoro."

"Do any of the other opera companies have goblin principals?"

"Not hardly," Pel-Thenhior said. "The most they'll do is to have goblins in the lower half of their choruses. Before my voice changed, I was determined to be the one to change that." His mouth quirked. "I suppose I *am* changing that, really, although it will take more than one opera. But if you want to make a living as an opera singer in this city, you have to perform elven opera. There's no way around it."

"Do people perform other kinds of opera?"

"People perform the Barizheise operas all the time in neighborhood operas. But those are . . ." He shrugged in a comprehensive dismissal of amateur opera. "So I will keep giving Othoro major roles, and the next opera I write—not *The Grief of Stones,* the one after that—will be so shocking it makes *Zhelsu* look tame. Which is when other companies will start trying to steal it."

"*Steal* it?"

"Oh, yes," he said, darkly amused. "There is no honor among the operaneisei. The Amal'opera wouldn't stoop to such things, but the Parav'opera and the Silmar'opera, and the Chelim'opera and all the rest of them . . . They probably—no, certainly—won't cast any goblins and they'll reconstruct the score and libretto from memory, and they'll put on *terrible* productions—which will be some comfort. As will the knowledge that they're all copying an opera written for a goblin lead."

"Have you ever put on any Barizheise operas?" I asked, and his humor brightened.

"Goddesses of mercy, no! Barizheise opera is either a series of bloodbaths or interminably boring recitations of the characters' lineages, or both at once. And even if I wanted to, Parzhadel would never let me. He's far too canny a businessman for that."

"But he doesn't object to *Zhelsu*?"

"Scandal makes money," Pel-Thenhior said dryly. "We're earning back the damage from the riot very quickly, and *Zhelsu* still has most of its run to go. *And* everyone in Amalo knows it's the opera that caused a riot." He smiled suddenly. "And some people even profess to enjoy it. You shouldn't let me go boring on and on about opera, you know. I can and have talked about this sort of thing all night long." He tucked notebook and pen into one of his inner pockets. "You were going to persuade me to help you break into the foundling school."

"I was?"

"Well, it doesn't make any sense the other way around."

I said, "But I'm by no means convinced that breaking into the school is the right thing to do."

"Do you have another idea?"

"No."

"Of course not. Otherwise, why would you come explain the whole thing to me?"

"I wasn't trying to make you help me."

"I know that. I'm volunteering because you certainly shouldn't be doing such a harebrained thing alone. Besides, my curiosity has been aroused."

"Can I talk you out of it?"

"Of course, but I really think it's your best option. We can go right now and get it over with."

"Right *now*?"

"It's past midnight, so everyone will be in bed, and not close enough to dawn that anyone will be getting up. It's the perfect time."

"You sound like you've done this before."

"Nothing like *this*, but I will admit to my share of escapades in my youth."

"Then I suppose I must defer to your experience."

"You never snuck out after curfew?"

"No."

He raised his eyebrows at me, but I had no intention of elaborating.

"Well," he said, "I don't mean to force you into it, but it's the only useful idea I have."

"Which makes it the only useful idea either of us has. It's just . . . What do we say if we're caught?"

He laughed. "If we're caught, I don't think what we say is going to matter. The best course, as a friend of mine used to say, is *don't get caught*."

"How wise of your friend," I said dryly.

"Well, it *is* good advice," said Pel-Thenhior.

"I suppose so. But the easiest way not to get caught is not to do foolish things after midnight."

"You don't think we should do it."

"No," I said, "although I do greatly appreciate the offer. But I think I am going to follow my own advice and go home. Good night, Pel-Thenhior."

"Good night, othala. Let me know if you change your mind."

I thought there was very little chance of that.

𝑋

There were no petitioners the next morning. In the afternoon, I walked with Tomasaran down to Ulvanensee, where Anora was delighted to have another prelate for a few days.

"You will learn how to dig graves," he warned her. "It is impossible to keep a sexton in this cemetery. Those that do not object to the workload quickly realize that Ulvanensee is haunted, and that's the end of that."

"Haunted?" said Tomasaran; to her credit, she sounded more intrigued than alarmed.

"Oh, no proper ghosts," said Anora. "But things move themselves—there's no denying it—and there are graves where the dirt is always disturbed no matter how many times you rake it smooth."

"All right," said Tomasaran.

"Good, good," said Anora.

I said, "Just come back to Prince Zhaicava when you feel as though you've learned enough."

"Of course, othala," she said, smiling.

X

I had been considering my next step in the matter of the pictures. Mer Nathomar's opinion that I should not talk to Mer Renthalar seemed worth paying attention to. It was unlikely that Mer Renthalar *could* help me, even if he would want to, which also seemed unlikely, and I felt that I did not want his attention turned toward me if I could avoid it. I could keep him as a last resort.

I had decided to try starting at the other end: how the pictures got into the marquise's hands. It had happened at a city council meeting, which meant that one of the Amal'theileian's stewards almost certainly witnessed at least part of what occurred.

I had never had occasion to speak to one of the stewards before, and I had no idea which one of them I wanted. My best and simplest option was to ask the first one I saw and follow the path wherever it led.

The Amal'theileian stewards were liveried servants—a reminder to the city government of the power of the principate, and also some insurance against bribery. It was not that liveried servants could not be bribed, but most of them took their oaths of fealty very seriously, and they were more likely to be offended than tempted.

The first steward I spoke to, a tall elven man, impressive in his livery of white and gold on black, was able to tell me the stewards who were assigned to the city council's chamber. When I asked how to find them, he said, "The city council's chamber and offices are their domain. They'll be there."

Although I had never had reason to attend a session of the city council, I knew where their chamber was, far enough north in the south wing that one heard the trams only as a distant rumble. The mayor's office sometimes had lines of petitioners stretching out into the main hall.

Everything in the south wing was new, having been built by Prince Orchenis's father, so the hallways and rooms still mostly followed the lines laid out by the architect. The council chamber was easy to find, although I had to climb the stairs to the public entrance, which was at the top of the gallery. As I had hoped, there was a steward there, engaged in the self-evidently endless task of cleaning the gallery seats.

This steward, another tall elven man, listened attentively to my question and said, "I don't remember anything of the sort, othala, but you should ask Dovinar. He'll be at his duty post, which is the mayor's office and the door to the floor of the chamber." I thanked him and went back down the stairs and then followed the signs to the mayor's office, where a tall, gaunt-faced elven man was mopping the marble floor. He stopped when he saw me and stood with both hands on the mop handle in a way that suggested he was prepared to use it against me if he had to.

"I am looking for Dovinar," I said.

"You have found him, othala."

I explained again about the marquise and the photographs.

Dovinar thought carefully and said, "I remember the Marquise Ulzhavel. She was a lovely old lady, and we were all saddened by her death. And I *do* remember the last time she attended a council meeting, because she was scheduled to speak to the council and didn't. That was the meeting three months ago."

"Why did she not speak?"

"She gave no reason. She simply said she could not speak and left. I had not connected it with the package."

"What package?"

"A flat package, not quite as big as a book. I was requested to give it to her by a lady, and there did not seem to be any harm to it."

"Can you remember anything about the lady?"

Dovinar thought dutifully for several moments. "She was not as old as the marquise, and she was very well dressed in dark brown velvet with embroidery of red and gold flowers. Her hair was dressed with tortoiseshell combs and red lacquer tashin sticks. She was . . ."

"Yes?"

"She was polite, but only barely, and she did not stay to see her package delivered. She gave it to me and immediately left."

"And you gave the package to the marquise?"

"The lady said it was something the marquise had forgotten or something she needed—I can't remember exactly what she said."

"Did you see the marquise open it?"

"No. I couldn't stay. My duty post is out here and it was a busy night."

"How long was it, do you think, before the marquise left? Five minutes? Half an hour?"

"It wasn't as much as half an hour," said Dovinar, "because that was when she was scheduled to speak. But closer than that, I can't tell you. Does it matter?"

"I don't know," I said. "It might. Where was the marquise when you gave it to her?"

"There is an anteroom where speakers wait for their turn before the council." He pointed at a door a little farther along the hall.

"Was she alone in the antechamber?"

"There were two or three other people in there. It would be easy to find out who they were—their names will be in the proceedings of that meeting."

"Yes, of course," I said. It would be a pointless exercise. I didn't need to know more about the package; I needed to know more about the lady who brought it.

But Dovinar could remember nothing more about her, although he thought he would recognize her if he saw her again.

I thanked him and went home, where I spent the rest of the afternoon cleaning. All I had succeeded in learning was that Anvina Renthalar had not given the photographs to the marquise himself, and in fact might have no interest in the matter at all. Someone else was involved, whether she was instigator or merely courier.

And how to find her I had no idea.

X

When I reached the Prince Zhaicava Building the next morning, I was surprised to find Witness Parmorin waiting for me.

"Min Parmorin! Is there something we can do for you?"

"Perhaps," said Parmorin. "We do not know. First we must tell you that we have been selected to witness for Esmeän Tativin."

"Oh," I said.

"She has told us the whole story. Do you still have the pictures?"

"We do. We are still trying to find out who sent them to the marquise."

"An interesting question," Parmorin said. "May we see them?"

"Of course," I said. I had put them in a desk drawer, carefully wrapped so that even in the improbable event of someone going through my desk, they wouldn't see them by accident. I took them out, unwrapped them, and handed them to Parmorin.

She kept her face still as she looked at them, but her ears twitched. "Those are horrid," she said, handing them back.

"Yes," I said.

Parmorin said, "Thank you, othala. We did not want to look at them, but felt we must."

"You are thorough in your witnessing," I said.

"Yes," said Parmorin. "Even when it does no good."

Parmorin had been gone only a few minutes when an elven subpraeceptor I did not know knocked on the door.

"Good morning," I said warily.

He bowed. "Othala Celehar?"

"Yes."

"I am Subpraeceptor Mobrasar of the Cemchelarna watchhouse. My colleague Subpraeceptor Azhanharad says that you have assisted him with found bodies several times."

"Yes," I said, and tried not to let my relief show. For a moment when he said Cemchelarna, I had been afraid that Othalo Prenevin or Othas'ala Delemar had reported me as a nuisance.

"We, ah, have found a body, and could use some help."

"Of course," I said.

We took the Coribano line, and Subpraeceptor Mobrasar told me what he could about the body, which wasn't very much. She had been found in the dark hours of this morning under the Abandoned Bridge, in one of the few places where an object could fall from the bridge to the pavement covering the Cemchelarna River.

"Looks like suicide," said Subpraeceptor Mobrasar, "but there's no note on the body, so we can't say for sure. And we don't know who she is."

"Do you get a lot of suicides?"

"Our fair share," he said with a grimace and a twitch of his ears. "Not as many as the Mich'maika, but there's a few every year."

"Do they often leave notes?"

"As a rule. People who jump off the Abandoned Bridge know they're going to be found, and they generally seem to want their affairs to be tidily managed. People who jump in the Mich'maika or the Zhomaikora don't seem to care as much."

We got off the tram at the Eshaimi ostro, which was in the same building as the watchhouse, although we had to go around the outside to reach the watchhouse door. The watchhouse had no crypt and no cold room; they had put her on the long table in their meeting room, using sheets from their tiny infirmary. They had laid her out as decently and respectfully as they could. I walked up the room and stood by her head. She was part goblin, her black hair frizzing out of two rope-thick braids. I was reaching to touch her forehead when I took a good look at her face and froze.

"Othala?" said Subpraeceptor Mobrasar.

"I *recognize* her," I said. "She's from Osmin Temin's foundling school." It was the part-goblin girl who had given me the note.

"Oh," said Subpraeceptor Mobrasar, sounding as shocked as I felt. "Do you know her name, othala?"

"No," I said, "but we can find out if she still does." I said the prayer of compassion for the dead and touched her brow.

Darkness and fear, my heart banging against my breastbone, the terrible sense of dangling over empty space, fingers cramping on brick, and then sharp bites of pain as someone stabbed at my fingers again and again, until finally I couldn't hold on any longer, and I fell.

And jerked away from the corpse, my knees nearly buckling.

"Othala? Are you all right?"

"Yes," I said. "Yes, I'm fine. But it wasn't suicide."

"Oh no," said Subpraeceptor Mobrasar, possibly involuntarily.

"Someone shoved her over the parapet of the Abandoned Bridge."

"Who?"

"She never saw their faces. Her name was Tedoro."

"No family name?"

"She was a foundling. She had none."

"Then I suppose the school is the only place to notify of her death."

"She had no other home," I agreed. "Will you petition me?"

"What, on her behalf?" Subpraeceptor Mobrasar said, shocked. "We can't do that. Only her family can properly petition a Witness."

"But she *has* no family," I protested.

"That's as may be," said the subpraeceptor. "We are aware that Subpraeceptor Azhanharad likes to assume a paternal role in these cases, but we consider that offensive to the dead and deeply inappropriate."

I bit back argument. His ears showed there was no point, and I would only alienate him further. "You will let us know if you change your mind."

"We will," he agreed, but we both knew he wouldn't.

He bowed to me, and I bowed back, then went up the hill and returned to my office for the rest of the morning.

But it was almost as if the dead girl—Tedoro—was following me. I was ambushed by flashes of her death, the dark, the wind, the nauseating swirl of lights. Had she screamed? I didn't remember her screaming, but that didn't mean anything. And while the Abandoned Bridge was practically a street carnival by day, it was not safe in the night. If she had screamed, no one would have investigated.

My hands hurt; I kept looking at them, expecting them to be bleeding, but they were unharmed. And the waves of vertigo made me long to be able to lie down.

They were familiar symptoms. I'd gone too far in, as my teacher

Othala Pelovar would have said. Speaking to the dead successfully was a delicate balance. You had to reach out far enough to find the remnants of the spirit that lingered around the body, but not so far that the memory of death invaded you, as Tedoro's death had done to me. It would wear off over time. Meanwhile, I could only be irritated at myself for making a mistake I'd stopped making before I was sixteen.

I could not face food, so at noon I went directly to the Vermilion Opera. I didn't know when Pel-Thenhior would get there, but I needed to talk to him when he did.

X

Unfortunately, I was not the only person who needed to talk to Iäna Pel-Thenhior that afternoon. When I cautiously entered the auditorium, Min Rasabin was already seated on a folding chair on stage, and Mer Dorenar and Mer Beronezh were standing off to one side, not quite in the wings.

"Hello, Othala Celehar," Min Rasabin said when I'd come far enough down the aisle that she could identify me.

"Hello, Min Rasabin," I said, trying not to be obvious about how glad I was to sit down.

Mer Dorenar looked around from his conversation with Mer Beronezh and bowed. "Othala Celehar."

"Good afternoon, Mer Dorenar," I said.

"You must be here for Iäna," said Mer Beronezh, sounding worried.

"Yes. I just have a question to ask him. It will only take a moment."

"Oh, no, that's fine. Just as long as you're not here to tell us someone else has been murdered."

*No one that you know,* I almost said, but managed to stop myself with a simple "No."

"It must be very trying always to be the bringer of bad news," said Mer Dorenar.

The sympathy was entirely unexpected, and I floundered for a moment, trying to find the right response. "It is the nature of my calling," I said finally, since that at least had the virtue of being true.

I had been notifying people of their loved ones' deaths since I was eight, and one of the many things I liked about my current position was how little of that I had to do.

Mer Dorenar nodded. "My sister was called to be a cleric of Csaivo. There are parts of it she does not like, but she says she would not trade it for anything."

I hadn't felt that way in Aveio—had in fact been praying nightly for a way out long before I became involved with Evru—but Aveio had been an exception and a nightmare in more ways than one. "Yes," I said, although I could not quite muster a smile.

"So there's no difference between serving Csaivo and serving Ulis?—I'm sorry! I didn't mean that the way it sounds! Obviously there are quite large differences. I meant the calling."

Poorly phrased though it was, I understood his question. "No, there's no scale with, I don't know, Salezheio at the bottom and Anmura at the top. A calling is a calling."

"I meant no offense."

"No, of course not. None taken."

Min Rasabin turned the conversation, whether deliberately or not, by asking Mer Beronezh a technical question, and they were all quickly involved in the topic. I sat and listened to them, and the light-headed feeling of vertigo finally began to go away.

By the time Pel-Thenhior appeared, there were ten people on stage: four principals, five members of the adult chorus, and Merrem Matano, the matron of the children's chorus. Only three of them— Min Rasabin, Mer Beronezh, and Merrem Matano—were specifically waiting for Pel-Thenhior; the rest had simply shown up for work.

Pel-Thenhior greeted people cheerfully as he came down the stage, saying, "Just a minute," to Min Rasabin and Mer Beronezh; he paused as Merrem Matano came up to him, but at the same time caught sight of me.

"Othala Celehar! Why are you here at this hour of the day?"

"I need to speak to you for one moment. I promise it will not take longer."

Pel-Thenhior looked from me to Merrem Matano. She said, "I can wait one moment."

"Thank you, Davelo," Pel-Thenhior said, then came the rest of the way down and vaulted off the stage to talk to me. "Are you all right? You look awful."

"I'm fine," I said. "The undertaking we talked about last night? I want to go tonight."

His eyebrows went up. "Are you serious?"

"As serious as death."

"All right," Pel-Thenhior said immediately. "Meet me at the Torivontaram tonight and we'll go."

"Thank you."

"Are you sure that's all you need? You really don't look well."

I stood up and hoped he couldn't see the effort. "I'm going home to rest. I'll see you tonight."

"Fine," he said, although he sounded doubtful and his ears dipped for a moment. "I'll see you tonight."

As I started up the aisle, I heard Merrem Matano say, "That was your 'one moment,' Mer Pel-Thenhior."

)(

What did one wear to break into a foundling school? Certainly not my coat of office, which would have been inappropriate on a number of levels and was also too expensive to risk. I examined my three frock coats—rusty black, dark green, and dark blue—and finally decided that the blue coat was probably my best choice.

Late that night, I took the tram back up to the Veren'malo and wound through its alleys to the Torivontaram. Pel-Thenhior was seated alone at a back table and waved me over vigorously. He asked at once, "What is wrong? Yesterday you were emphatic that you would not do it; today you insist that it must be done at once."

"There's a dead girl," I said, and told him about Tedoro.

He listened intently and said when I was done, "And you're quite sure it's the girl who slipped you the note."

"Quite sure," I said.

"And you think she was murdered because of whatever it is that Osmin Temin is doing?"

"The girls were right to be scared."

"It would seem so. Well, I have no objection to doing the thing tonight. You'll just have to walk with me to my apartment. It's on the way and I'm not doing any of it in this coat." The coat was watered gray silk; I wouldn't have risked it, either.

"All right," I said.

"Don't let it eat at you," he said. "You couldn't have predicted this."

"Yes, but I could have gone last night when you suggested it. She might still be alive if I had."

"*Might,*" said Pel-Thenhior. "It might be. But it also might be that nothing you could have done would have saved her. She might already have been dead by the time *Zhelsu* was over. We have no way of knowing."

"No, I know," I said. My ears were low and I could not gather the energy to lift them. "I just . . . I should have moved more quickly."

"And if you'd had the faintest idea that someone would find this matter—whatever it is—worth killing over, you would have. But you didn't know. You couldn't have."

A young goblin woman in a dark green dress came out of the kitchen and immediately approached the table. "Zhornu," she said. I was glad of the excuse to end the conversation, for Pel-Thenhior and I had begun to circle like two dogs chained to one stake.

"Zhornu," Pel-Thenhior said, though not warmly.

"I need thee to speak to her," she said, obviously on the assumption that he would know what she was talking about.

And her assumption was correct, for he said at once, "No."

"*No?* Just like that?"

"Getting in the way in one of Mama's arguments is like getting in the way of a slamming door," said Pel-Thenhior. "Thou canst speak to her thyself."

"But she won't *listen* to me!"

"What makes thee think she will listen to me? She never has before."

"But—"

Merrem Pel-Thenhior appeared in the doorway to the kitchen and said in Barizhin, "I can hear you two all the way in the back. Come into the kitchen and let us discuss this matter"—and then a word I did not know but that was probably either "quietly" or "reasonably."

Pel-Thenhior said, "I'm sorry about this, Celehar. I'll be back as soon as I can."

"It's fine," I said, and Pel-Thenhior followed his cousin into the kitchen.

One of the servers, a skinny goblin boy with a Pelanran's golden eyes, came over and said, "Can I bring you anything, othala?"

I reckoned up the money I had on me and said, "A four-cup pot of black orchor, please. I foresee that I'm going to need it."

✕

When Pel-Thenhior returned, I had drunk two of the pot's four cups and was wondering about a third.

"Is that orchor?" Pel-Thenhior said.

"It is."

"You are a genius," he said and poured himself a cup. He sat down. "I apologize. Although at least this time I haven't brought back a problem for you as well."

"How is Merrem Pel-Venna?"

"Better," said Pel-Thenhior. "It hasn't found her, and she and her husband are consulting with a Csaiveise who specializes in midwifery. They are determined that the next child will be born healthy."

"That will keep it away more surely than anything else," I said.

"Will it? I'll tell . . ." He hesitated fractionally, then continued, "a friend to tell Armedis. He's not speaking to me."

I wondered what word he'd censored himself on, but asked, "Why not?"

"Old stupid reasons," said Pel-Thenhior. He drank the rest of his orchor, then said abruptly, "Have you changed your mind?"

I wished I could. "No."

"All right. Off to Cemchelarna."

I was glad to be moving, even if it was toward something I did not want to do.

Pel-Thenhior was a brisk walker. Although he remembered after half a block to moderate his pace, I still had to work to keep up. After several minutes of silence, he said, "I told Parzhadel the truth. About Tura."

"Are you sure that was wise?"

"No, of course I'm not sure. But he is my patron. The Opera's business is his business. Also, he's as close-mouthed as a snapping turtle."

"It is your decision," I said. "I only worry for Mer Olora's unnamed lover. It would be a great pity if all his efforts to protect this person came to naught."

Pel-Thenhior gave me a quizzical, sidelong look. "Those efforts included murder."

"And suicide. I didn't say he made good choices, for he did not. But the sincerity and urgency of his efforts cannot be doubted."

"No, I suppose not. Do you not think, as Arveneän's Witness, that the truth should come out?"

"We agreed that it should not. And Subpraeceptor Azhanharad agreed, as well."

"No, I know. I just . . ."

"She didn't die because she was going to tell the truth. She died because she was trying to profit from the secret. And being her Witness does not make me her champion."

"It doesn't?"

He might have been teasing. I said, "I advocate for the truth of how she died. And if Mer Olora were still alive, I would be advocating that he be tried so that justice could be done. But he visited justice upon himself."

"I think your position is contradictory."

"It is not a situation I have been in before. But I am *not* going to claim that Arveneän Shelsin was an innocent or that the goal she was striving for when she died was a good one. In truth, I would rather thwart her."

"And thus you wish to prevent the scandal from breaking, since scandal is certainly what Arveneän would have done if she did not get the money."

"Yes," I said. "You understand."

"Yes," said Pel-Thenhior. "I think I even agree."

We took the tram to Belvorsina III, and then walked to Pel-Thenhior's building. He had a whole flat rather than just a room, and I had to remind myself that envy was a corrupting passion.

I waited in his main room. His desk was elaborate with the geo-metrical carvings popular a hundred years ago, and on it were stacks and stacks of paper, some of it ruled for musical notation, some of it filled with writing in a strong Barizheise hand. I was slightly shocked at the number of photographs he had pinned to his walls; they were all of women beautifully dressed and beautifully coiffed, solemn faced or smiling tiny secret smiles. One of them was posing with the giant plaster dragon's head I had seen in Mer Nathomar's studio.

Pel-Thenhior was gone barely five minutes before he returned in a plain burgundy coat and with his braids tied in a horsetail down his back. He was carrying a dark-lantern. "There," he said. "I am at least somewhat less inappropriately dressed for this venture."

"You don't have to do this."

"And leave you to go alone? No, I thank you. Besides, I am, in a quite reprehensible fashion, looking forward to it." He grinned at me, almost daring me to argue with him.

"All right," I said. "I have no real wish to dissuade you."

"Very good," he said. "Let's be off."

He led the way from his apartment to Lacemaker Street; from there, I led to Goshawk Street and Osmin Temin's school. We ex-plored the alleyways until we found the back of the school: a grubby little courtyard and an awkwardly jutting ell with a door that proved to be unlocked.

"Well, *that* was easy," Pel-Thenhior muttered.

On the other side of the door was a mud room, with a bench along one wall and a row of galoshes under it. The door to the rest of the school was locked.

"I suppose they've no need to worry about someone stealing a bunch of old galoshes," Pel-Thenhior said ruefully. "What do we do now?"

"Let me . . ." I stood on tiptoe and felt along the door lintel. My fingers almost immediately encountered a key. "Here."

"Was that a lucky guess, or do people just have no idea what a Ulineise novitiate entails?"

"Lucky guess," I said, although the other was true as well. I unlocked the door while Pel-Thenhior turned the dark-lantern to give the minimum possible light; then I very carefully pushed the door open.

The door opened into a kitchen, which we crept through as cautiously as mice around a sleeping cat. From there we found ourselves in a hallway that seemed to run the length of the house and was so narrow we could not walk side by side.

Pel-Thenhior picked a door and very gently tried the knob. It was locked. He tried two more, also locked. Then he tried the door directly opposite the kitchen, and it opened on stairs going down. He looked at me, and I shook my head and pointed up.

He closed that door and tried the one next to it, which revealed the stairs going up we wanted. We ascended the stairs, narrow and steeply pitched, and at the top found ourselves in a hallway I recognized. I was able to find the head of the main staircase, and from there I knew roughly where Osmin Temin's office was, although I could not lead us straight to her door.

Pel-Thenhior tried one door and found it locked, but the next one opened, and when we peered in, it was Osmin Temin's office. Even if I hadn't recognized it, I would have known by the size of the desk.

We went inside, and Pel-Thenhior carefully closed the door behind us before he opened the dark-lantern a degree or two more. He set it on the desk and said in a whisper so soft it barely reached me, "I'll take this side." We both started opening drawers.

The first drawer on my side held a pen-wiper and an ink-blotter and nothing else.

Pel-Thenhior snorted in sudden amusement.

"What?" I said.

"Your Osmin Temin is a treasure hunter," he said. "She's got a little library here of pamphlets about the Hill of Werewolves."

"Oh dear," I said. "I wouldn't have thought it of her. She seemed quite relentlessly pragmatic."

"But money hungry," said Pel-Thenhior.

"True," I said. "In any case, I don't think those help us."

"It's unlikely to be why the poor girl was murdered," Pel-Thenhior agreed, and we returned to our search.

The second drawer was locked.

"That's promising," said Pel-Thenhior.

"Yes, but it does us no good."

"The lock's probably a very simple one."

"That does us no good either, unless you . . ."

Pel-Thenhior grinned at my expression. "Let me borrow a couple of hairpins."

I took two hairpins out of my braid and handed them to him, moving to the side so that he could get at the drawer.

"Mind you," he said, crouching down, "I didn't say I was any *good* at this. But I lose my desk key all the time."

"You could stop locking it," I said.

"I'd rather, if someone wants to go through my papers, that they have to work for it." We were silent for several minutes; I was about to suggest that we give the whole thing up as a bad idea, when he said, "Aha!" and slid the drawer open.

All that was in it was a stack of maybe twenty cards, bigger than playing cards, but still small enough to be tucked in a pocket. The upward-facing side of the top card was blank.

"Well," said Pel-Thenhior, and raised his eyebrows at me.

"Yes," I said and turned over the top card.

And dropped it in shock.

"What?" said Pel-Thenhior, but he had already picked it up. "Oh. Oh dear." We stared at each other, and Pel-Thenhior finally said what we were both thinking: "What is *pornography* doing in a foundling school?"

"I have no idea," I said. I took the photograph back again and held it carefully in the lantern's light. An unhappy hunch struck me; I picked up the rest of the cards and fanned through them before pulling one out. "That's Tedoro."

"We need Nathomar. I wish we could take these to him."

"We can't," I said. I put the cards back in order and set them back as I had found them, then closed the drawer. "I hope you can lock it again."

"Yes, it's just the reverse of unlocking it. And then I'll give your hairpins back."

"All right."

It didn't take him as long to lock the drawer, and he handed me back my hairpins, which I put in a trouser pocket rather than trying to repair my braid without the use of a mirror.

"I still think Nathomar's the person we need," said Pel-Thenhior.

"I agree," I said. "Let's go."

"You don't want to . . ." Pel-Thenhior gestured at the desk, which had drawers we hadn't even touched.

"No," I said. "I think we've found the thing we came here to find."

"Probably," said Pel-Thenhior, although he looked dissatisfied.

"I don't think we should linger," I said. "Who knows when the kitchen staff start their day?"

"Point," said Pel-Thenhior and picked up the dark-lantern, closing it almost to nothing again. We retraced our steps out of the school, both of us heaving a sigh of relief when we were back in the courtyard.

Pel-Thenhior opened his lantern to provide more light, and we started for the Zheimela and Dawn Court and Mer Nathomar's photographic studio.

After a few blocks, I said, "But why give a note to me? Why not go properly to a Witness?"

"I don't know," said Pel-Thenhior. "Although her murder does suggest a reason."

"Terror," I said bleakly. "Then she probably *did* die because she passed the note to me."

"Or because she did something else equally foolhardy. Not *everything* is your responsibility."

"I know," I said and turned the subject. "What in the world can Osmin Temin be involved in?"

"If it was *one* girl's picture, I would assume that an enterprising young lady had found a source of pocket money and Osmin Temin had found out and either confiscated the picture or had it ready for a confrontation over disgracing the school and so on and so forth."

"That doesn't make sense with giving me a note asking for help in stopping 'them' and it doesn't explain the new source of money *Osmin Temin* seems to have found."

"No," Pel-Thenhior said slowly. "But I'm willing to venture that that *is* the source of Osmin Temin's money. She's making her students pose for a photographer and keeping what they earn for herself. Plus, of course, the blackmail material."

"Even after they graduate, these poor girls aren't going to make enough in wages to tempt a blackmailer."

"You can blackmail people for things other than money, and I feel that Osmin Temin is a person who would be very alive to the possibilities. I suspect she was blackmailing Tedoro."

"Into doing *what*?"

"Perhaps Osmin Temin wanted to *stop* her from doing something."

"Like going to a judicial Witness? In which case, why the half measure of giving me a note?"

"You said you thought maybe she wanted to avoid getting the Judiciary involved."

"Maybe," I said. "But it doesn't make sense. If Osmin Temin was blackmailing her with the photograph, why would she do *anything* that might result in someone seeing it?"

"I doubt she expected us to go through Osmin Temin's desk," Pel-Thenhior said dryly.

"Fair. But let's consider the other side. For Osmin Temin to be using those pictures for blackmail, she can't have any qualms about showing them to people, and that makes no sense at all. It would ruin the reputation of her school in a heartbeat if word got out that one of her students was a photographer's model."

"You don't play pakh'palar, do you?"

"Not often, why?"

"Don't," said Pel-Thenhior. "But do consider the possibility that Osmin Temin might, hypothetically, have been bluffing."

"Bluffing?"

"Threatening to show a pornographic picture to someone and actually being willing to go through with it are very different things," said Pel-Thenhior. "She could have been counting on Tedoro not realizing that."

"Oh, this is nonsense," I said. "We don't have enough information for any of this 'hypothetically.'"

"Then you need more information," Pel-Thenhior said promptly.

"Yes, but I don't know how to get it."

"For tonight, the best we can do is consult Nathomar, though it is only in fairness to him to say that he may not be able to help."

We had gone straight south on Goshawk Street, knowing that we would be unable *not* to find the canal. Residential became industrial became warehouses and the smell of the canal became steadily stronger. We came out on the bank only a few yards away from a ferry stop.

We sat down to wait, and Pel-Thenhior said, "I'll have to remember that sneaking around other people's houses is exhausting."

"Thank you for coming with me," I said.

"You're welcome, although I need no thanks. I just hope . . ." He hunched a shoulder. "No, never mind. Let us talk of something else."

"I could ask you about the photographs on your walls."

"And I could tell you that they are photographs of my friends."

"Are they all prostitutes?"

"You don't mince words, do you?"

"I'm sorry," I said. "I didn't mean that the way it sounded. I just meant that I knew prostitutes had their photographs taken, to adorn the walls of the brothels."

"That's true. But there are other women of the demimonde, who will never be respectable and therefore can enjoy the luxury of having themselves photographed. I have a friend who is a dealer in a gambling house, for example. Opera singers are the same."

I remembered Arveneän Shelsin and all her patrons.

"Thus," continued Pel-Thenhior, "I have many friends who have given me their photographs, and I like having them where I can look at them. I'm not running a brothel in my spare time or whatever you were imagining."

"Nothing like that. I was merely curious."

"Understandably," Pel-Thenhior admitted.

I saw the ferry's light approaching. Between midnight and dawn, the ferries, like the trams, ran once an hour, so we were lucky in our timing.

The ferry was mostly empty—it would be full on the return trip west. We took seats together and Pel-Thenhior said, "I think we should change the subject."

"Yes," I said. "Tell me about the new opera."

"Oh, it's coming along. My biggest problem is in trying to give the women distinct characters—they have none in the original—because I want them to have some kind of *presence* on stage. Or at least for the audience to be able to tell which is which."

"That seems like a reasonable thing to do."

"Well, I'm not helping my cause by rearranging the characters to suit myself. At the moment, the women are all just 'father's wife,' 'son's wife,' 'sister.'"

"Is the father's wife not the son's mother?"

"Now *there*'s a thought," said Pel-Thenhior. "A *second* wife. That could put her at the same age as the other two and explain why the faithful lighthouse keeper is betraying the trust reposed in him. A young wife with expensive tastes is a terrible thing."

"I suppose so," I said, and he laughed.

"In opera it is. And it also makes the relationship between the women more interesting if the mother-in-law is the same age as the daughter-in-law and the spinster sister."

"Yes," I said, more feelingly than I meant to.

"Personal experience?"

"My father's second wife was younger than my eldest sister. It became quite uncomfortable at times."

"That sounds unpleasant," said Pel-Thenhior, "but it is just the thing for opera. I now have a triangular relationship between the three women, especially if the daughter-in-law and the sister band together against the outsider." He pulled his notebook out and began jotting notes. "I beg your pardon, but if I don't write this down, I will have forgotten important parts of it by morning."

"Of course," I said, and Pel-Thenhior wrote notes to himself until the ferry reached its Zheimela dock.

Ж

This time, the brown velvet waiting room was not empty. Two part-goblin women and an elven man were waiting; the man and one of the women in the chairs, the second woman kneeling with her skirts spread around her like a dropped flower. The man had a Procurers' Guild ring prominent on his hand, which made it not hard to guess that the two women were prostitutes.

"Good evening," Pel-Thenhior said cheerfully.

The man nodded. The two women smiled.

Pel-Thenhior and I stood by the gas sconce and waited. No one said anything.

The waiting seemed endless, especially as I was beginning to feel the lack of sleep in my bones, but eventually Mer Nathomar emerged from his back room, escorting a lovely part-goblin woman. "There you are," he said. "Give me a week and you can come get the prints."

"That's fair," said the pimp as he and the first two women stood up. They left, the three women chattering brightly, and Mer Nathomar turned to us. "Well," he said, "good evening, friends! Othala Celehar, this is getting to be a habit. What can I do for you?"

"We have something we would like your opinion on," I said. "But maybe not out here?"

Mer Nathomar's eyebrows shot up. *"Again?"*

"Again?" said Pel-Thenhior.

"Othala Celehar was here last night with a question."

"Unrelated to this," I said.

"In any event," said Mer Nathomar, "come back into my studio."

The studio was still a chaos like the back room of a secondhand shop. Mer Nathomar said, "I can find chairs if you want to sit."

"I don't think this will take long," said Pel-Thenhior. "What we need your opinion on is some pornography we found in an unexpected place."

Mer Nathomar's ears went down at the word "pornography." "I am not a pornographer."

"I didn't say you were," said Pel-Thenhior.

"We're not really interested in pornographers," I said. "There's been a murder."

"Another one?" he said.

"Nothing to do with the marquise," I said.

"That hardly makes it better," said Mer Nathomar. "But all right. What does a murder have to do with pornography, of all things?"

"That's what we're trying to find out," Pel-Thenhior said. "What's the penalty for making pornography?"

"You know as well as I do," Mer Nathomar said. "Six months hard labor in the quarries, which—between the accidents and the iärditha—is *this close* to being an outright death sentence."

"Would you murder to avoid it?"

"Me personally?"

"No, hypothetically. If pornography were a thing a person was doing, might they commit murder to avoid that sentence?"

"And keep a profitable scheme going," I said.

"A person might," Mer Nathomar said carefully.

"Do you know of anyone who *would*?"

"Hypothetically?" said Mer Nathomar.

"Hypothetically," agreed Pel-Thenhior.

"Yes, several," said Mer Nathomar.

"Oh good," said Pel-Thenhior.

A thought struck me, and I asked, "Do the models suffer the same penalty as the photographer?"

"I don't think anyone's ever brought a Witness against a model," said Mer Nathomar. "But, yes, I suppose they would."

"It explains why they don't want to go to a judicial Witness," I said to Pel-Thenhior's puzzled look.

"But they're children," Pel-Thenhior said.

"They may not know that that protects them," I said.

Pel-Thenhior said to Mer Nathomar, "We are hypothesizing that the headmistress of a foundling school is in a scheme to use her students as models. And clearly not paying them."

"Wait," said Mer Nathomar. "You mean that someone is taking pornographic pictures of *children*?"

"Girls between thirteen and sixteen," I said.

"Legally still children," Mer Nathomar said. "Never mind what I said before. If I was in a scheme to make pornography of children, I would *definitely* murder to protect my secret."

Pel-Thenhior said, "Is there a market for that sort of picture?"

"Abhorrent as it is, yes. There always is."

"So there's nothing inherently implausible in the idea."

"No, not at all."

"Do we have anything we can take to a Witness?" I asked.

Mer Nathomar's ears showed puzzlement. "Forgive me, othala, but you *are* a Witness. Aren't you?"

"I'm a Witness for the Dead. Not a judicial Witness."

"But there's that dead girl," said Pel-Thenhior.

"I have to be petitioned," I said. "I can't just witness for whomever I please. And the Cemchelarna Brotherhood did not want my help."

"Why in the world not?" Pel-Thenhior asked.

"It isn't, strictly speaking, in their remit, and Subpraeceptor Mobrasar is apparently a stickler for the rules." I hoped I didn't sound as bitter as I still felt.

"But if she has no family," said Pel-Thenhior, "who is going to petition for her? What if no one does?"

"Then no one will witness for her," I said, "and whoever murdered her will not be punished."

A thought struck Pel-Thenhior. "I petitioned you for Arveneän. Can I petition you for Tedoro?"

"It's more *customary* for the family to petition the Witness for the Dead, but there's no rule that says it *has* to be."

"Was that a yes?"

"Yes. You can petition me for Tedoro."

"Excellent. Shall I come to your office, or can we do it right here?"

"There's nothing sacred about my office. A photographer's studio is as good a place as any other."

"Then I petition you to witness for Tedoro, who has no family and no one to speak for her."

"I accept your petition." And I was inwardly, reprehensibly, pleased at how disconcerted Subpraeceptor Mobrasar was going to be when I showed up in the afternoon.

"What does that mean in practical terms?" asked Mer Nathomar.

"It means I can go ask questions at that school, and the Brotherhood has to let me. Even Witnesses for the Dead get immunity from interference, although it does not mean our questions will be answered."

Pel-Thenhior suddenly looked worried, his ears dipping. "Isn't that awfully dangerous? They've already killed one person."

"I won't go alone," I said, "and killing a Witness always creates more trouble than it solves. Always."

"We will hope they are wise enough to know that," said Pel-Thenhior.

✕

I slept a few hours, and in the morning, I went to the Red Dog's Dream for oslov and their Airmen's Blend. Then I took the tram up to the Veren'malo and the Prince Zhaicava Building, and my office, the post, and the papers. I had no petitioners and spent the morning writing up my notes. Then I went to Ulvanensee to persuade Tomasaran to come with me out to Cemchelarna.

I found her with two of Anora's prelates—Vidrezhen, an elven woman, and Erlenar, a half-goblin man—engaged in whitewashing the prelacy, which there was no denying it badly needed. They were also all breathless with laughter.

Tomasaran's eyes widened when she saw me. "Othala Celehar!" she said, still too out of breath for it to be much more than a gasp, and Vidrezhen and Erlenar were suddenly absorbed in spreading the whitewash evenly across the yellowing plaster.

"Tomasaran," I said, feeling very tired, "there is nothing in the oath you swore that forbids you from laughing."

"No, othala," she said, still looking abashed.

"And even if there were, what am I going to do? Tell Anora?"

The absurdity of it—for Anora would only laugh at me if I tried any such thing—reached her, and she smiled. "All right."

"Good." And I was pleased to see the whitewashing get a little less rigorous, too. "I came to ask if you would accompany me on an errand to Cemchelarna."

"Cemchelarna? More about the school?"

"Yes, although our first stop is the Cemchelarna watchhouse."

"The watchhouse? But—?"

"You'll want to clean up," I said.

She looked down at herself. "Oh no."

"I assume those aren't your only pair of trousers."

"No. That is—these are an old pair of Othalo Vidrezhen's. My own are . . . I'll just go clean up." She fled hastily down an already whitewashed hallway.

I looked at Vidrezhen and Erlenar, neither of whom was looking at me. "Am I really so terrifying? I don't mean to be."

Vidrezhen said, "Othalo Tomasaran thinks very highly of you. And you can be a little . . ." She hesitated, either trying to find the right word or trying to judge my reaction. "Formidable."

"Formidable?" I said. I was short, slight of build, and perennially shabby, and the sessiva had left me with a graveled and ugly voice. What was there in that that was formidable?

"It isn't a bad thing!" Vidrezhen said. "Anora is always telling us we need more gravity if we ever want to stop being junior prelates."

"Yes, well," I said, "it's true that that is a requirement of our calling. I suppose I might . . ." Pel-Thenhior had told me I didn't laugh enough. Was this the same observation from a different angle? "In any event, I am not intentionally intimidating you, and if it seemed that I was, I apologize."

"You have no need to apologize, othala," said Erlenar, clearly as uncomfortable as Vidrezhen, but valiantly doing his part. "You have done us no wrong, and we took no offense."

"Thank you," I said and decided we would all be happier if I waited for Tomasaran outside.

When she emerged, some fifteen minutes later, properly dressed as a Witness for the Dead and her hands and face clean of whitewash, she said, "What has happened, othala?"

"Please, call me Celehar," I said on an impulse of loneliness.

"All right. Celehar." She seemed startled, but not displeased. "But what happened? Why are we going to the watchhouse?"

"A girl has died," I said. "The girl who gave me the note. Her name was Tedoro."

"Oh no," said Tomasaran. "How *awful.*"

"It's worse," I said. "She was murdered."

"Murdered? Are you sure?"

"That's why we're going to the watchhouse," I said. "So that you can see for yourself."

"All right," Tomasaran managed after a pause that was probably longer than she would have liked it to be.

We took the tram to the Eshaimi ostro and circled it to the watchhouse.

Subpraeceptor Mobrasar was surprised to see us. "Othala Celehar? Did you forget something?"

"In a manner of speaking," I said. "We have been petitioned to witness for Tedoro. Have you buried her yet?"

"But . . . but she has no family! We confirmed it with the school! How . . . ?"

"We found a friend," I said. "Has she been buried? If she has, she will have to be exhumed."

"No," he said, still seeming amazed. "She is to be buried at noon tomorrow."

My opinion of Osmin Temin, already low, sank further.

"And where is her body?"

"At the municipal ulimeire. Othala Umenar is preparing the body."

"Thank you," I said. Umenar was my least favorite of Anora's friends, the sort of man who caused trouble just to prove he could. "When you spoke to the school, did you learn anything else about her?"

"She would have turned sixteen in two weeks," said Subpraeceptor Mobrasar.

"Then she was getting ready to leave the school?"

"Yes, and she had found employment. It is very sad."

"Yes," I said, although "sad" was not the word I would have used to describe the murder of a fifteen-year-old girl. "Thank you, Subpraeceptor. Where is the municipal ulimeire?"

He gave me directions. It wasn't very far, and Tomasaran and I walked briskly, for the day was chilly.

The municipal cemetery was called Ulvoranee, and it was probably five hundred years old, built—like the othasmeire on Goshawk Street—at the time that Cemchelarna was a fashionable residential district for courtiers and bureaucrats. The main building was stone with marble facing, and the courtyard had at one time had a fountain in the center, although that had been turned off centuries ago. We found Umenar, a middle-aged elven man with a sour face, preparing Tedoro's body according to Ploraneise custom. He was not pleased to see us.

"Well, Celehar," he said. "What brings you here? Don't tell me you're after this one—who'd you find to petition for her?"

"A friend," I said, again not specifying whether it was her friend or mine.

"Since you're here," he said ungraciously and stepped away from the body. Then he saw Tomasaran behind me, and his sour look deepened. "Who is this?"

"Othala Umenar, this is Othalo Tomasaran." I could be polite, even if Umenar wouldn't bother. "I'm teaching her how to be a Witness for the Dead."

Umenar's eyebrows went up, but whatever he was thinking, he did not say.

I said to Tomasaran, "Try her."

She hesitated, then nodded and started saying the prayer of compassion for the dead. I joined her, that being the best support I could offer.

Tomasaran stepped forward and touched Tedoro's linen-swathed shoulder. For a moment, she was frozen, then she staggered back.

"Take a deep breath," I said. "Murders are hard to deal with."

She nodded. "That was . . ."

"Yes," I said.

"Is that all you need?" said Umenar. "Because I've got other things to do today."

"What have you done with her clothes?" I said.

"Her *clothes*? They're in the bin of things to go in the incinerator." He pointed to a bin against the wall.

"Let's look at them," I said to Tomasaran. "There might be something useful."

Tedoro's clothes made a pathetically small heap at the bottom of the bin. We took them out piece by piece, checking for pockets and finding several, but there was nothing in them except a couple of half-zashanei and a pilgrimage token that I did not recognize, a tightly braided loop of ribbon with a disc of polished and faceted clear quartz hanging from it.

It wasn't Amaleise, but she could have acquired it in any second-hand shop in the city. I tucked it into an inner waistcoat pocket. "I'll see if I can find anybody who recognizes it."

"Is it important?"

"It might be," I said. "It might not."

Umenar cleared his throat impatiently, and I nodded to Toma-saran. Real discussion could wait until we were out of Umenar's domain.

"Thank you, othala," I said, and we left.

We had walked several blocks before Tomasaran said, "Is it always like that?"

"Like what?"

"Witnessing for a murder. Is it always so . . . ?"

"Vivid?"

"Horrible."

"In my limited experience, yes."

"You are not of great comfort," she said wryly.

"I'm sorry. I can't be."

"No. I suppose it's really little different from if one witnessed a murder personally, only . . . closer."

"Much closer," I said. "You will find that all violent deaths are unpleasant to witness for."

"Does it get any easier?"

"You will grow more accustomed to it. I do not know that 'easier' is the word I would use. On the other hand, you will not see many murders."

"How many have you witnessed for?"

I reckoned the tally as we walked. Two in Lohaiso, one in Aveio (though for the horror of the memory, it was in a category by itself), the victims of the crash of the *Wisdom of Choharo*—though I had only witnessed, properly speaking, for the emperor and his three sons—and then Arveneän Shelsin and the Marquise Ulzhavel and now Tedoro. "Nine? Ten? I think I've counted correctly."

"That seems like a great many," said Tomasaran.

"Yes," I said, for there was no point in denying it. "But it is not most of what you will do. Other deaths are not as . . . as charged as a violent murder. I wish she'd known the person who killed her."

"She never saw them," Tomasaran said, half as a question.

"No. It was too dark and it happened too fast. All we know is that someone wanted her dead badly enough to make sure she fell."

"It is *horrible*," said Tomasaran.

"Yes," I said, because there was nothing else to say.

We had walked to Goshawk Street and now stopped in front of Osmin Temin's school. I wanted to say something encouraging but failed to think of anything that would not be patronizing. I climbed the steps, Tomasaran close behind me, and rang the bell.

Presently, the door was opened by an elven girl who had been crying, her white skin blotched and her eyes swollen. She was visibly startled to find two Witnesses for the Dead on the doorstep, and I said, without forcing her to find words, "We've come about Tedoro."

She burst into tears, and it was some moments before she was able to say, "Please come in, othala, othalo. We will tell Osmin Temin you are here."

Tomasaran and I stood close together, almost back-to-back. From somewhere upstairs we heard a door slam; both of us jumped a little.

Presently, Osmin Temin descended the staircase, as graceful and self-assured as any courtier—although I noticed that this time, rather than having me brought to her, she was coming to me. It might mean nothing, or it might mean a great deal.

"Othala Celehar!" she said, as if this were both a social visit and a pleasant surprise. "What can we do for you?"

"We've come about Tedoro," I said, and I saw a flicker of anger on her face, a sharp twitch of her ears, before she composed herself to be sorrowful.

"Of course," she said. "The Brotherhood brought us the dreadful news yesterday. But—forgive us—we do not quite understand why you are here."

"We have been petitioned to witness for Tedoro," I said.

"*Petitioned?*" she said in manifest disbelief. "By *whom*?"

"Does it matter?" Tomasaran said. "The girl was murdered."

"And of course we want justice for her," Osmin Temin said hastily. "But we just don't understand who could have petitioned for her. This school was the closest thing to a family she had."

"And yet you did not petition for her," Tomasaran said, not quite an accusation.

Osmin Temin looked affronted and said, "We were not sure the matter was worth Othala Celehar's time."

"A murder?" I said.

"*Was* it murder, then? We understand she fell."

"She had help," Tomasaran said darkly.

"That is terrible, and of course you want to investigate. You are welcome to talk to the girls, and we will answer any questions we can."

The sudden concession was suspicious. I said, "How long had Tedoro been a student here?"

"Almost three years. We don't take them younger than thirteen."

"Was she a good student?"

"Fair," said Osmin Temin with the barest shiver of a shrug.

"Did she have any particular friends? Anyone who might know where she was going the night she died?"

"We suppose so, but what does that have to do with anything? She fell off the Abandoned Bridge—it was obviously footpads."

It wasn't footpads, but I wanted a chance to talk to the students before I drove Osmin Temin into a corner.

I said, "Perhaps you are right, but we would still like to talk to the other girls and the teachers."

"The *teachers*?" She wanted to refuse, but after a scowling pause, she said, "All right. You can sit in this classroom—it's unused this time of day—and we'll have one of the girls come to you."

"Thank you," I said. I was in truth not sorry to have a chance to sit down.

Tomasaran followed me, but did not sit, instead pacing along the slate board at the front of the room. "You must know she's lying!" she burst out as soon as Osmin Temin was out of earshot. "That wasn't footpads."

"No," I agreed. "They don't murder, as a general rule, and they certainly wouldn't murder her *before* they tried to rob her."

"And what's to say this girl—any of the girls—will be truthful?

Aren't they more likely to tell us what Osmin Temin wants us to hear?"

"Perhaps," I said. "But their conversation will be instructive nonetheless. Come sit down. You'll frighten them, pacing like that."

"Oh, all right," said Tomasaran, and she sat down next to me at one of the long tables that apparently served the school as desks.

The first timid knock turned out to be the elven girl who had answered the front door. Her name was Asavo, and she was fourteen. Her answer to all of our questions was "I don't know," and I couldn't tell if it was because that was what Osmin Temin had told her to say, because she was too upset to think, or because she genuinely didn't know. After Asavo came Orimeän; after Orimeän came Melnaro. I began to get snippets: one girl who told us Tedoro was Osmin Temin's errand-runner, another girl—several girls—who had overheard Min Orbelin encouraging Tedoro to stay at the school as a teacher when she graduated. One girl, finally, a goblin named Kelmaru who would admit to being Tedoro's friend, said, "She would never have stayed."

"No?" I said.

"She hated it here," Kelmaru said.

"Why?" said Tomasaran, but Kelmaru looked away and said, "I don't know."

It wasn't time to push yet. I didn't want word getting back to Osmin Temin that I knew about the pornography before I was ready to confront her. I let Kelmaru go, and the next person who came in was not a student, but Min Orbelin, Osmin Temin's second-in-command.

She was elven, plain-faced, her hair dressed in a single braided bun. Her eyes were rather obscured behind her spectacles, and I could not read the expression on her face. She was steadfastly noncommittal in her answers, like Osmin Temin trying to paint Tedoro as an ordinary, unmemorable student.

Here I found I wanted to push a little. "We are told that you asked her to stay as a teacher."

"Who told you that?" she said sharply.

"Several people," I said. "Is it true?"

She had no natural gift as a liar; she floundered for several seconds before she said, "We are short-handed and could always use another teacher."

"But why Tedoro?" I said. "Why not one of your outstanding students?"

Her laugh was harsh. "We're a foundling school, othala. We don't *have* outstanding students. Is there anything else? We do have a classroom to get back to, and it's nearly sundown."

"We should leave off for the day, then," I said, for I had no desire to be wandering around strange parts of Cemchelarna in the dark. Not with Tedoro as a particularly pointed object lesson. "We'll come back tomorrow and talk to the girls we haven't seen yet and the other teachers."

"You seriously intend to talk to everyone in the school?"

"Of course," I said. "How can we hope to find the truth if we don't?"

She did not answer me.

✕

The next morning, a petitioner was waiting for me, a part-goblin man in his late middle age, his thick black hair streaked with iron gray, and the wrinkles around his eyes deepening from lines into folds. "Arnekesh doesn't think you can help," he said without preamble, "but I say it doesn't hurt to try."

"Um," I said. "Thank you?"

"He finally agreed to try when I said I wouldn't agree to scattering the ashes unless we did. So he's not very happy about this."

"I may *not* be able to help," I said. "I often can't. But why don't you tell me about it, and I'll help if I can."

"Thank you, othala. I'm afraid you'll find the matter rather trivial, though."

"That's not mine to judge," I said, and did not add that I would be grateful for something trivial.

He nodded and said, "It's the scone recipe."

"I beg your pardon. The *scone* recipe?"

"It does sound trivial, doesn't it? But our bakery is famous in Tenemora for its scones, and Vulathmened was the only person who knew the recipe."

"The recipe makes that much difference?" I said. "You can't just find another recipe for scones?"

"Vulathmened's scones . . . He made them every morning and we asked him how he made them and our customers asked him how he made them, and he'd smile and promise to tell Arnekesh or me, but he never did. Half our steady business is those scones, and people have been *polite* about the recipe Arnekesh is using, but it's not the same and we all know it."

"And if people stop coming to you for your scones . . ."

"We rely on that business. So it is a trivial matter, but it's important to *us*."

"It is a valid petition," I said. "I'll help if I can."

His face creased around his smile.

Tomasaran appeared just as I was locking the office door. "We have a petitioner," I said. "Do you want to come?"

"Of course," said Tomasaran. "Where are we going?"

※

The ashes were in the bakery—it did not seem to have occurred to anyone that it was an odd place to keep them—and we traveled to Tenemora, to the stop after the insane asylum and two blocks east. The bakery was not prepossessing, although it smelled delightfully of cinnamon rolls, and Mer Honibar's partner, Mer Arnekesh, another part goblin, was waiting for us at the back door with a scowl.

"We shouldn't be bothering you with this, othala," Mer Arnekesh said immediately.

"I have no other petitioners this morning," I said, "and my mandate says nothing about sitting in judgment on the questions my petition-ers wish to ask the dead. I am happy to ask Mer Vulathmened about the scones on your behalf."

"How was the take this morning?" Mer Honibar said pointedly.

Mer Arnekesh wavered a moment, then said, "Oh, all right," and led the way into the kitchen, where the smell of cinnamon rolls sur-rounded us.

Mer Vulathmened's ashes were in a cylindrical pottery con-tainer, the sort used by the Ishvaleisei in their funeral rites and called a revethbrul. The lid was bound on with a heavy, dark green ribbon. I untied it carefully while I said the prayer of compassion for the dead, putting lid and ribbon in a clear spot on the long stone counter, and delicately touched the ashes with one finger.

Mer Vulathmened had died quite peacefully in his sleep, so I did not have the memory of his death to contend with, only the diffi-culty of asking a relatively complicated question. It took a long time for Mer Vulathmened to answer, but when he did, the answer was simpler than I'd expected, although possibly not as helpful as Mer Honibar had hoped. *Nutmeg.*

"Nutmeg," I said, and Mer Arnekesh burst out, "Does he think we haven't *tried* nutmeg?"

"It's all the answer I can get for you," I said, "and it was very clear. Othalo Tomasaran?" I offered her the revethbrul; she touched the ashes gingerly, and after a lengthy pause said, "Yes. Nutmeg."

"But I *tried* nutmeg," said Mer Arnekesh. "A week ago. And it wasn't right."

"Maybe that's not what he meant," I said.

"You're the one who said 'nutmeg,'" Mer Arnekesh snapped.

"No, I mean . . . Where do you keep your nutmeg?"

"Here," said Mer Honibar, and pulled down a box from a high shelf. He handed it to me in exchange for the revethbrul of Mer Vulathmened's ashes.

When I opened the box, I found a jumble of nutmegs, clearly hiding nothing. But the box itself was surprisingly shallow, much shallower than it looked like from the outside.

"Is this, by chance, Mer Vulathmened's box?" I asked.

"Well, I *think* so," said Mer Honibar, "although it's been so long I can't say for sure. Why?"

I turned the box in my hands, then turned it upside down, making a pile of nutmegs on the counter.

"What," Mer Arnekesh began, but I shook the box sharply, and the interior fell out, followed by a yellowed piece of paper and a ten-zashan coin. Mer Honibar pounced on the paper.

"This is it!" he cried, unfolding it with almost more haste than care. "Look, Arnekesh!" They bent their heads together over the paper and were silent for a moment, reading anxiously.

"This *is* it!" said Mer Arnekesh. "Othala, I beg your pardon."

"There is no need," I said. "It is my calling."

X

At noon, Tomasaran and I attended Tedoro's funeral. All of the girls from the school were there, with Osmin Temin and Min Orbelin and the two other teachers acting as shepherds. Everyone wore shabby dark clothing; full mourning was costly and only Osmin Temin was wearing black on black on black. I noticed that her clothes looked very new. Afterwards, we returned to the foundling school and our seemingly endless, seemingly fruitless questioning of the students. (One teacher, Min Tesavin, referred all questions back to Osmin Temin; the other, Merrem Caltavezharan, seemed too frightened to speak.) I had lost count of the students by the time we came to Sukelo, a goblin, probably fifteen or just turned sixteen, her black hair in thick plaits and her eyes round and reddish orange and angry.

At first, scowling and mistrustful, she would not talk to us, which I could have told her was foolish, since it only increased the impression that she had something to tell. Finally, for this was clearly the right place to push, I said, "It may help you to know that we already know about the photographs."

I would have been well served for my reckless extrapolation if she had said, *What photographs?* But she went the color of ashes. "You *know*? But how . . . ?"

"I've seen them," I said. "She makes you pose for them, doesn't she?"

"If you don't pose when it's your turn, you don't eat," Sukelo said. "I *tried*, othala. I swear I tried. But you get so hungry it makes you stupid."

"I'm not blaming you," I said.

Tomasaran asked, "Why didn't you go to a Witness?"

Sukelo shook her head tiredly, as if this was a question she had been asked—or had asked herself—many times. "We're all implicated. Besides, Osmin Temin never lets us out on our own long enough to get to the Amal'theileian. Min Orbelin is always there. They send—sent—Tedoro on errands, but they knew they didn't have to worry about her."

"Why not?" said Tomasaran.

"She's the one who bullies the first-timers into it. Osmin Temin didn't even make her pose anymore. And she was so close to getting out . . ."

"Tedoro gave me a note asking for help," I said.

"*Tedoro* did?" She thought furiously for a moment. "Is it true that she was murdered?"

"Yes," I said.

"Whoever killed her, Osmin Temin is to blame."

"Oh?" I said.

"Why else would Tedoro be on the Abandoned Bridge after dark? She wasn't *stupid*."

"You mean Osmin Temin sent her there?"

"Yes."

"I am afraid of the possibility that her actions got her killed," I said. "Would Osmin Temin do that?"

"She's threatened to often enough," said Sukelo.

"*Could* she?" said Tomasaran.

"Oh, yes," Sukelo said immediately. "Mer Renthalar would do it without blinking."

"Mer Renthalar?" I said, startled.

"The photographer. Him or his brother. They're awful. And even if he wouldn't do it himself, I'm sure he knows people who would."

"Can we go to a judiciar?" said Tomasaran.

"As Witnesses *vel ama*," I said, "we're only interested in Tedoro's death. We'll have to go to a judicial Witness about the rest of it."

"That seems unnecessarily complicated," Tomasaran said. "Can't we just . . . ?"

"No," I said. "It's outside our remit. And really the person who should go is Sukelo. You and I can only offer hearsay testimony."

"I can't go," Sukelo said. "I don't want to go to prison, either."

"How old are you?"

"Fifteen, as best anyone can guess."

"If you're under sixteen, the Judiciary considers you still a child. You wouldn't be prosecuted."

She stared at me for a very long time, then said slowly, "Osmin Temin was lying."

"Osmin Temin seems to do that a lot," Tomasaran said.

"But still," said Sukelo. "They'll never listen to me, will they? A goblin foundling?"

"That doesn't matter to the Witnesses," I said.

She gave me a very dubious look. "And if they do . . . It will ruin the school. Where will we all *go*?"

"Surely one of your teachers can keep the school running," said Tomasaran.

"No, you don't understand," Sukelo said. "They're all part of it."

"*All* of them?" Tomasaran said, shocked.

"Osmin Temin made sure," Sukelo said. "So that none of *them* could go to a Witness."

"Oh dear," said Tomasaran.

"Yes," said Sukelo.

"Osmin Temin has been very cunning," I said. "But, Sukelo, think. If Osmin Temin had Tedoro murdered, what's to prevent her from having one of the rest of you murdered?"

"If she suspects you of helping us . . ." Tomasaran said.

Sukelo put her face in her hands. "I've been in here too long. She'll never believe I didn't talk, will she?"

"You have to go to a Witness," I said. "It's the only way you can protect yourself."

"You've trapped me," she said.

"You were already trapped," I said. "We're showing you a way out."

She looked at me resentfully. "What happens to *me*, then, if I go to a Witness? I can't come back here. I have no money, no family."

"We will ask the Witness," said Tomasaran. "This can't be the first time they will have encountered that kind of problem."

"At worst," I said, "the Brotherhood will let you sleep in a jail cell for a few nights, until we can find something for you."

"You promise you'll find something?" said Sukelo.

"One way or another," I said. "Yes, I promise."

She did not move. "That takes care of me, I suppose, but what about the other girls?"

"How many students are there, all told?" asked Tomasaran.

"Thirty-eight. I mean, thirty-seven. Too many to rely on the charity of the neighborhood."

I was about to suggest seeking the advice of the othas'ala, but then remembered my impression of him.

But then again, perhaps I had misjudged him. "Othas'ala Delemar?" I said.

Sukelo laughed. "Him? He'd sell us straight to the Guild."

"Any of the other neighborhood priests?" said Tomasaran.

"Othalo Prenevin?" I said. "That ulimeire is probably big enough to shelter thirty-seven girls."

"She *might*," said Sukelo, although she sounded doubtful. "She's an awful gossip, though."

"At this point," I said, "gossip is the least of your worries."

※

Finally, we got Sukelo moving, however reluctantly, but we were almost immediately halted again by an elven girl waiting in the hallway. I recognized her from the previous day, but couldn't re-member her name. She was in a state of high agitation. "Sukelo!" she said, almost shrieked. "What's going on?"

"Nileän," Sukelo said. "The Witnesses know. About the pictures."

"Oh no," Nileän said. "They can't!"

"It's true," Sukelo said. She and Nileän were standing hand-clasped in the middle of the hall like any pair of star-crossed lovers. "And they want me to go to a judicial Witness."

"Oh *no*," Nileän said again, so clearly terrified that for a moment I wanted to say, *Never mind. We will forget it.* But Tedoro had been murdered, and I could not forget.

Instead, I said, "The Witness will understand that you were co-erced."

"Do you think so?" Osmin Temin said from behind me. "Or are you just telling them lies to get them to do what you want?" She was standing in the hall with four older elven girls, all of whom looked grimly terrified.

"Our calling forbids us to lie," I said.

Osmin Temin laughed. "Really, Othala Celehar. Do you expect *anyone* to believe that?"

For a moment, I was too appalled at her cynicism to speak.

She pressed her advantage. "In any event, we regret to inform you that *no one* will be going to testify for a judicial Witness, and in fact you are going to have to be very cooperative if you want to leave the school at all. The doors are all locked, and our girls are armed, which you are not."

I realized that one reason the girls looked so terrified was that each of them was holding a knife.

"You can't be serious!" Tomasaran said.

"Oh, we are, we assure you," said Osmin Temin. "We're all going to go down to the basement now, and then Othala Celehar is going to do us a favor."

"A *favor*?" I said. "If you think this is any way to ask for a favor, you must be mad."

She laughed, and I wondered if in truth she wasn't a little bit insane.

"Oh, we think you'll oblige us. We can have your friend killed just as easily as Tedoro."

It was far more threat than confession—I thought she probably didn't know what counted as a confession to a Witness. Either that or she didn't care, which was a very bad sign.

I said, "Suppose everyone puts the knives away and we discuss the matter?"

"No," said Osmin Temin. "We have the advantage and we intend to keep it. Now come along. It's really not an unpleasant basement and should make a relatively comfortable place for Othalo Tomasaran to wait."

Her four girls started toward us, looking determined even though I would have wagered none of them had the least idea of how to use a knife on another living creature. I might have been able to get the knife away from one of them, but that still left three.

Tomasaran was looking at me. "All right," I said to her. "I don't want anyone to be hurt."

"All right," Tomasaran said reluctantly, and we let ourselves be herded, with Sukelo and Nileän, down into the basement to a room that looked as if it had been used as a classroom, with an easel at the front of the room and rows of tables and chairs.

"Please," Osmin Temin said mock-graciously, "have a seat."

Tomasaran and I sat together at one table, and Sukelo and Nileän sat at the next. They were still holding hands. Osmin Temin's four girls stayed at the back of the room, and Osmin Temin herself went to the front and stood next to the easel. She looked at us like a teacher at an unpromising class and said, "You know, of course, that there is treasure hidden under the Hill of Werewolves."

We stared at her. It was so utterly not what I had expected her to say and seemed so utterly irrelevant to the situation, that it was some moments before I managed to say, cautiously, "We have of course heard the *stories* about treasure under the Hill of Werewolves."

"It's real," said Osmin Temin, "and we know how to find it."

Another stunned silence. I thought of the pamphlets Pel-Thenhior had found. They had a pragmatic purpose after all.

Tomasaran said, "And you're telling us because . . . ?"

Osmin Temin heaved a sharp, exasperated sigh. She said, "We need Othala Celehar's help."

"*My* help?" I said, abrogating politeness and in that moment not caring. "How can I possibly be of help to you?"

"The problem," said Osmin Temin, "is that there is a guardian. A revethavar."

"Those only exist in stories!" Tomasaran protested.

"Why do you think there are ghosts on the Hill of Werewolves?" said Osmin Temin. "The revethavar causes them."

*That* was certainly not an answer I had considered when Prince Orchenis asked me the same question.

"How do you know it's a revethavar?" Tomasaran said.

"Our late father," Osmin Temin said, as if it pained her. "He devoted his life to studying the history of the Hill of Werewolves. He found ancient documents in the archives of the Amal'theileian that talked about the slaughter of the Wolves of Anmura and the destruction caused by the revethavar. He collected accounts of people who disappeared around the Hill of Werewolves, and many of them were treasure hunters. It was his belief that they had encountered the revethavar. He knew the location of an entrance to the revethavar's tomb, and he would go to the Hill of Werewolves and stare at it, but he never went in. He took us with him when we were a child. We have gone in, but never very far."

"Why not?" Tomasaran said.

"We have no desire to encounter a revethavar," said Osmin Temin. "But it has occurred to us that a true Witness for the Dead would be able to speak to it."

"What good does that do?" I said.

"It might do a great deal of good. You might be able to calm it. You might be able to destroy it."

"You have an exaggerated opinion of our abilities," I said.

"How do you know?" Osmin Temin said, and I greatly disliked the light in her eyes. "Have you ever encountered a revethavar?"

"Of course we have not," I said.

"Then you don't know," she said, almost triumphantly.

"It is not necessary for us to encounter one to know that this idea is insane," I said. "Your whole story is insane."

Her face darkened. "We weren't asking for your opinion, othala. We were explaining what we are going to do."

"We?" I said, for she had distinctly used the plural: what *we* are going to do.

"You don't think we're going to let you go alone, do you?" Her smile was unpleasant. "We're just waiting for a friend to arrive, and then you and we will go together."

"You aren't serious," I said desperately.

"We are entirely serious," she said. "We find that for some reason we need to leave Amalo in a great hurry, and our current funds are hardly sufficient."

"So you're going to try to *rob a tomb*?" Tomasaran said.

"No," said Osmin Temin. "With Othala Celehar, we are going to *succeed* in robbing a tomb. We have been thinking about this for a long time, but we never thought we would be able to persuade a Witness for the Dead to accompany us—until you were kind enough to give us the leverage we need. You may think we are insane, Othala Celehar, but you will come with us, or we will have our friend kill Othalo Tomasaran." Her smile was full of knives. "Just as we had him kill Tedoro."

Nileän burst into tears. I felt much the same.

## X

Osmin Temin's "friend" turned out to be a tall elven man with a blandly unmemorable face. She did not introduce him. They left the room for several minutes, and when they returned, Osmin Temin said, "All right, Othala Celehar. Let us be off."

"Osmin Temin, you must know that this is madness," I said.

"Madness or not, it is the only option you have left us," she said. "Now *come*, or we will have our friend start breaking Nileän's fingers."

Nileän gave a faint shriek and began sobbing again.

"Leave her alone!" Sukelo said angrily. "It's not *her* fault."

"That is up to Othala Celehar," Osmin Temin said smugly. She knew she had me cornered.

"All right," I said.

Tomasaran said, "Celehar, don't!"

"I have to," I said. "I don't want anyone to be hurt."

"That should include yourself," Tomasaran said, glaring like a cat at Osmin Temin.

I shrugged helplessly and followed Osmin Temin out of the room. She had two of her knife-wielding girls come with us, which was regrettably well calculated. Osmin Temin by herself I might get lucky enough to overpower, but three against one was, I knew, more than I could handle. And it would only take one of them to run back to the school and tell Osmin Temin's friend to go ahead.

We did not speak on the journey to the Hill of Werewolves. Osmin Temin was serene in the knowledge that I could not escape her without effectively murdering Tomasaran, and the two girls regarded me with a mixture of terror and determination that said plainly, without need of words, that they believed they would kill me if necessary, and that belief was one I did not want to put to the test.

We reached the Hill of Werewolves still with a margin of daylight. Osmin Temin led us unhesitatingly through the gardens around to the northeast side of the hill, where the gardens ended in a steep drop-off. Heedless of her expensive mourning clothes, Osmin Temin descended the slope in a series of long, skidding steps.

The two girls and I looked at each other. None of us wanted to follow her.

"Merciful goddess," Osmin Temin said in exasperation. "Come *on,* Celehar! We don't have much daylight left!"

I wanted to point out that that was her fault, not mine, but I held my tongue and descended the slope—ungracefully, but without breaking anything. The girls followed.

At the bottom of the slope, Osmin Temin led us farther into the wasteland, farther and farther, until we came to a dry creek bed. She climbed down into it, and now we followed her up the creek bed toward the looming darkness of the Hill of Werewolves. We ended up bent double, almost crawling, as the thelavis vines, some as thick as my wrist, had twined together to make a roof. Shortly after that I realized I was walking on bricks, not stones, and this wasn't a creek bed, but an abandoned waterway.

After a wretched eternity, we came to a massive iron grille, which was clearly there for the express purpose of keeping people like us out. But something had shifted in the centuries the grille had been there and at the lower right corner there was a gap between the grille and the stone, large enough for a determined person to get through.

Osmin Temin slid through with the ease of much practice. I hesitated, and she said, "There's no point in balking here. Don't worry about the dark—I've had a lantern stashed here since I was their age," with a nod at the two girls. She picked up a burlap-wrapped object and revealed it to be an owl-light, which she proceeded to kindle.

She was correct; there was no point in balking here. With a small, hopeless prayer for my coat of office—it seemed almost certainly doomed, but I could not bear the thought appearing in my shirt-sleeves in front of Osmin Temin—I edged through the gap between grille and stone.

It was cold inside the Hill of Werewolves—not merely chilly, but bone-cold. That didn't seem like it could be anything but a dire warning, and I tried one last time: "Osmin Temin, this is a fool's quest. Please. Nothing good can come of this."

"Shut up and don't be a coward," she said and started into the dark.

I looked at the two girls standing on the daylight side of the grille. "Go with Osmin Temin," one of them said, and they were still clutching their knives. The gap between the grille and the stone was narrow enough that they would have ample time to catch me before I was even free enough of the grille to run.

I could see no alternative. I turned and followed Osmin Temin.

Ж

After a short walk, we came to a place where there was a bridge over the waterway. We climbed up, holding the lantern for each other in turn; then Osmin Temin again took the lead, as if she knew exactly where she was going.

It was apparent immediately that this place beneath the Hill of Werewolves was sacred to Ulis. The owl-light showed floor mosaics in which I could pick out jaguars and jackals, and every time Osmin Temin flashed it around, there were carvings of the moon—or of wolves, the aspect of Anmura that was most favorable to tasks undertaken after dark.

It seemed to be getting colder.

"How do you know where to go?" I asked Osmin Temin.

"Our father had maps," she said. "One of them had belonged to the Wolves of Anmura and the others were made by people who went exploring. Not *all* of them disappeared."

"Then what makes you think there's still treasure here?"

She laughed. "We *know* there's still treasure here. No one has ever bested the revethavar, and it guards the vault where the Wolves of Anmura hid their treasures when they realized they were going to be attacked."

"Did you not say that this is the revethavar's tomb?"

"It is," she said. "The praeceptor committed suicide by ritual to become a revethavar. The first thing he did was seal the crypt with himself inside."

"Then how do you expect to get in?"

"Ah," said Osmin Temin. "The revethavar only sealed the entrance that led to the outside. The entrance that led to this"—she waved her hand expressively—"he left open, since none of these halls lead outside, but only back to the crypt itself. He didn't plan for the gap in the grille."

"But why didn't he block the entrance when people started exploring?"

"We do not know," said Osmin Temin, "but we would guess—"

The owl-light's beam suddenly revealed a boot.

We both startled, and Osmin Temin directed the light toward

that lump of shadows, which turned out to be a skeleton still entangled in the remains of its clothes.

"And there's a solution to a mystery," Osmin Temin said, "if only we knew who it was."

"And how he died," I said. I was murmuring the prayer of compassion for the dead as I approached the corpse. I touched its forehead, intending only to make formal recognition of the death, and I jerked back as if the corpse had bitten me. I almost felt as if it had.

"What?" said Osmin Temin.

"The spirit is still ..." I swallowed hard. "Normally, the spirit leaves the body within two or three weeks of death. But this spirit has been frozen here for two hundred and fifty years. He was strangled to death by empty air."

"The revethavar," said Osmin Temin. "Well, we know his reach extends this far. Can you sense him?"

"Only the cold," I said. "If you'll wait a moment, this spirit needs to be released."

"Do it on the way out," said Osmin Temin and went briskly onward.

I did not dare to hesitate in following her.

We walked past other bodies, glimpsed tangentially as the owl-light illuminated bits and scraps of cloth and bone. Osmin Temin would not stop for me to find out if their spirits, too, were trapped, or even to offer a prayer. "How many people do you think have died down here?"

I had asked as if she were a friend or a colleague; she did not respond in kind, only saying, "Oh, a score probably," in an indifferent voice. "Some of them most likely got lost, or had their light give out, and starved to death. If the revethavar didn't get them first."

I shivered, imagining that slow starvation in the dark.

We turned right, and the mosaics gave way to polished marble; the owl-light now caught carvings of the sun and a bas-relief of running wolves, and beneath that the phases of the moon.

"We're close," said Osmin Temin. "Be—"

But whatever she wanted me to be—ready or careful or something else—I never learned, for at that moment the owl-light cast the shadow of a standing person, and we both realized the revethavar had been waiting for us.

I could see it only by the shadow. I could never quite focus on the thing casting the shadow, just as I could never quite hear its voice, only moaning like the wind or like two great stones grinding together. I knew what it said; the words were there in my mind, burning cold and full of cruel amusement: *Well. Treasure seekers. I've been expecting you.* And the understanding, whether from the revethavar or from my own horrified logic, that the reason it had left that entrance unblocked was precisely in order that people would come. It wanted prey.

I was on my knees without any memory of my legs bending. *And what's this? One of you can hear me? How novel. I may not kill you right away after all. But this other one . . .*

I felt its attention shift away from me and could do no more than gasp thankfully for air.

Osmin Temin was saying something, but between the noise of the revethavar and the roaring of my heartbeat in my ears, I could not hear her. I saw, however, when the shadows wrapped around her throat and her eyes went wide. I lurched to my feet and tried to help her, but there was nothing around her throat to be pried away, only the revethavar's laughter.

In desperation, trying to distract it, I reached out as I did with ghouls and, without any expectation of success, tried to find its name.

I found howling anarchy, like being in the middle of a storm where everything felt at once sharp and unbearably heavy and also ruinously old. The revethavar had been a living man two millennia ago, or possibly slightly more, and it remembered every day of those two thousand years.

It had gone insane centuries ago, if *insanity* was even the right word for something so monstrous.

I searched desperately for its name, but had not found it—if it was even there to be found—before the revethavar noticed me and swatted me aside like a bothersome fly.

The blow knocked me physically into the wall, and I had done Osmin Temin no good, for the revethavar's grip on her had not slackened. I watched, too dazed to move, as her face darkened and her eyes bulged. She strangled to death on empty air, and I could not help her.

Then the revethavar turned its attention back to me. It did not attack me physically; it was intrigued by the fact that I could hear it and began experimenting, as a cruel child might with a trapped cat, to discover how best it might hurt me, utterly indifferent to—or even pleased by—the damage it did. I struggled to stay conscious under the revethavar's assault, struggled still to find its name, as the only hope I had was that it could be defeated in the same way as a ghoul. Otherwise, it would destroy me and then kill the husk of a body that remained.

I could not tell if it did not realize what I was doing, or if it merely considered me no threat, but it did nothing directly to stop me. It tore at me like a handful of knives, and I sought deeper and deeper, hearing my own breath coming in harsh gasps, as if in physical exertion. My vision was going black around the edges when I caught the faintest flicker of memory, the last shred of the man the revethavar had been.

"Hasthemis!" I tried to shout but it came out as a bare whisper. "Hasthemis Brulnemar! I know your name and bid you rest."

The revethavar howled in earnest and attacked me with its raking knives, but its name, so deeply buried for so long, was like the keystone of a vast arch.

"Hasthemis Brulnemar," I whispered again. "I know your name. I know your death." Ritual suicide, with two prelates of Ulis chanting a ceremony that they should never have learned. The bite of the knife along one arm and then the other. Standing and watching the blood pool. "Hasthemis Brulnemar, you have been wrongly kept from your slumber. You must rest. Hasthemis, let the darkness take you."

*No,* the revethavar said, now desperate. *Do not destroy me.*

But it was too late. Even if I had wanted to, I could not have stopped the cascade of ruin as two millennia of decay finally caught up to Hasthemis Brulnemar.

"I know your name, Hasthemis Brulnemar," I said, my voice a little stronger. "Let the darkness take you."

It shrieked: protest and despair. I felt the air harden against my throat for a moment, but the last substance of the revethavar broke and fell away, and I was alone with Osmin Temin's corpse.

It was a long time before I could move, but then I crawled across to her, whispering the prayer of compassion for the dead. I put a hand out to touch her, although I didn't know why. It was too soon; it would be overwhelming.

I touched her and there was nothing.

It was as if I had reached for something and discovered my hand was missing.

I made a painful noise and scrambled away from the body. I found myself kneeling, my arms wrapped around myself, my breath coming in great painful shudders. I couldn't think; there was nothing in my head except great flapping wings of panic. I had never had that happen with a fresh corpse; even with long-dead bodies there was *something*, a sense of absence, of an empty chamber, but this was as if I'd reached out and touched a stone, something that had never held life and never would.

Shudders turned into racking spasms until I retched, although there was nothing in my stomach except bitter green bile. When my body finally calmed again, I realized the *other* problems facing me. Osmin Temin was dead, and I could not ask her corpse for the path out of the revethavar's tomb. There was the owl-light—which had fallen from Osmin Temin's hand but had landed right side up, as it was weighted to do—but I did not know how much fuel it had left.

That meant that if I wanted to get out of the tomb, I had better do something about it *now*. I got to my feet, which was a struggle in itself, skirted wide around Osmin Temin's corpse, and picked up the owl-light. It was reassuringly heavy, and the knot of fear in my stomach eased slightly.

But I still had to find my way out.

I knew the first step: go back to where the marble floor became mosaics and turn left. I discovered that I was completely disoriented, so that I had to cast up and down the corridor to find the mosaics. I tried the wrong way first and came to a doorway flanked by snarling wolf statues that I knew I had never seen before. I turned around quickly—I did not want to know what other horrors the tomb might hold and I had no interest in the treasure Osmin Temin had died for—passed her body again and soon came to the mosaics and the left turn I was certain of.

From there, I realized with mingled amusement, horror, and relief, I remembered the way to the last body we had passed. When I came to it, I said the prayer of compassion for the dead; my voice was always graveled and harsh, the result of surviving the sessiva when it scythed through Lohaiso, but now it was only the husk of a whisper. I could not bring myself to touch the body—something I had observed in other people but never before in myself. I swallowed hard and slowly found my way from body to body like the rose petals in the wonder-tale, until I came to that first body, the one that had strangled to death on nothing like Osmin Temin. I forced myself to touch it, and it was like touching any ordinary object.

From there, I found the bridge and the waterway . . . and remembered the two girls waiting at the grille.

What was I going to tell them?

Would they even believe the truth?

I sat for a long moment on the bridge before sliding down into the waterway, trying vainly to think of a lie I might tell. But even assuming I could tell a lie plausibly, which was doubtful, no lie would conceal the fact that Osmin Temin was not with me. And I could not think of any reason that she would allow me to return without her, except incapacity. Or death.

But sitting there until the owl-light ran out of fuel was not a better option.

I followed the waterway through the dark beneath the Hill of Werewolves and had to blink tears out of my eyes when I finally saw cold moonlight ahead of me.

I came to the grille, and both girls bolted to their feet. One said,

"Where is Osmin Temin?" but the other said, "Othala, are you all right?"

I looked at her blankly, and now both of them were staring at me in alarm.

"There's . . . blood," said one, gesturing at my face.

"Blood?" I said, as if I'd never heard of it before. I touched my cheek and my fingers came away sticky.

"What *happened*?" they said in ragged unison.

I told them the truth about the revethavar and Osmin Temin's death. To my surprise, they believed me.

They told me their names—Balaro and Ziniän—and Balaro said, "Othala, you need a cleric."

"I need a member of the Vigilant Brotherhood," I said. "Othalo Tomasaran and Sukelo and Nileän are still in grave danger."

"Let's get out of here first," Ziniän said practically. "Then we can worry about finding a watchhouse."

"That's reasonable," I said, though at that moment reasonable was the last thing I wanted to have to be.

I edged between the grille and the stone. Balaro and Ziniän helped me up on the other side, and we progressed slowly as far as the drop-off we had skidded down in daylight. Looking at it from the bottom, I wondered if I could make it up. The girls looked at me as if they were wondering the same thing. I had to try, for I was afraid of what might happen if Osmin Temin's "friend" was left without instruction overnight.

"All right," I said. "We have to."

Between the three of us we clawed and scrambled, dragged and pushed, and made it to the top of the slope, all of us bruised and scratched, with raw palms and torn clothing.

"The gate will be locked," I said.

"We can climb over," Balaro said stoutly, and indeed between the three of us, we could, although we were neither graceful nor swift.

"Where do we go now?" asked Balaro.

There was something heartening in the realization that they did not intend to desert me. "I have to get to the Chapterhouse," I said, for it had taken no particularly cogent thinking to see that Subpraeceptor Azhanharad was the only member of the Vigilant Brotherhood whom I had any hope of persuading to listen to my wild story.

"The Chapterhouse?" said Ziniän. "In the Airmen's Quarter? That's half the city from here."

I said, "I know."

Balaro said, "Othala, you can't get on a tram looking like that. They'll throw you off. Let us find a cleric first."

I was desperately torn. On the one hand, I wanted to get to Azhanharad as quickly as possible. On the other, Balaro was right about the tram. The conductor was highly unlikely to be sympathetic to a ragged and bloody prelate. I did not need a mirror to tell me I looked like a madman.

"But how are we to find one?" I said and was alarmed at how feeble I sounded.

"There must be one nearby," Ziniän said optimistically.

"We lose nothing by looking," Balaro said. "We might find a watchhouse, which would be almost as good, even if Othala Celehar does not want to explain the situation to them."

"Yes," said Ziniän. "Come, othala. Standing here all night truly gains us nothing."

They were right, and I was embarrassed at needing two fifteen-year-old girls to tell me what to do.

It was late, and the area around the Hill of Werewolves was working-class and respectable. Everyone was asleep except the three of us, and we waded slowly through the darkness from one streetlight to the next, looking for either the red lantern of a watchhouse or the green lantern of a cleric.

We found a green lantern first.

I sat down on the stoop without quite meaning to, and Balaro rang the bell vigorously. The cleric must have been awake, for it seemed no time at all before she was letting us in, an elderly elven woman with her hair hanging in thick white braids against her shoulders.

Ziniän had to help me up, and the cleric's scrutiny was sharp as she said, "Gracious! What has happened to you?"

"It is a long story," I said, "and I need urgently to speak to a man in the Vigilant Brotherhood's Chapterhouse."

"We said we had to find a cleric first," Balaro said.

"Yes," said the cleric. "I think that was for the best." She led us into her consulting room, which was clean and orderly and yet contained two comfortable chairs along with the stone-topped table, and a brown tabby cat who opened one eye to inspect the intrusion. "I am Revano Galinin. Tell me how I can help."

I did not know where to start.

"Hmm," said Othalo Galinin. "Let us start with the obvious. What is your name?"

"I am Thara Celehar, a Wi—" I broke off.

"You are the Witness *vel ama* for the dead," Othalo Galinin said calmly. "I have read about you in the newspapers."

"Not anymore," I said. "My calling has been taken from me." Said aloud it sounded both nonsensical and terrible.

"That seems very drastic," said Othalo Galinin. "Just a moment." She left the room, only to return with a basin, a towel, and a steaming jug of water. "Now. What happened?"

"It will sound like the ravings of a lunatic."

"Even though the moon is full, I do not think you are mad. Tell me your story, Othala Celehar."

I obeyed her, although I could not recount it in an orderly or logical fashion, and I could not tell if she believed me. By the time I finished, she had cleaned and bandaged my hands, washed the blood off my face and failed to find a wound that could have produced it, and persuaded me, having ordered Balaro and Ziniän out of the room, to take my trousers off so that she could attend to my knees and to a jagged gash on one shin that I had no memory of acquiring and that had oozed blood down my stocking and into my shoe.

"Have you other injuries?" she said mildly, as if she heard stranger stories every day of the week.

"No," I said, hoping I was telling the truth. I felt oddly unsettled in my body, and nothing seemed to hurt, even things that clearly should.

The look she gave me said that she shared my doubts, but she did not press me. She gave me my trousers back and told me to come into the kitchen where I could wash the blood out of my stocking and dry it in front of the banked fire while she examined Balaro and Ziniän.

I protested my need for haste, and she gave me a stern look. "Do you want them to accompany you?"

"Yes," I said, for I needed them as witnesses. "But—"

"Then you will have to wait at least long enough for me to clean their hands as I did yours," she said. "But if you prefer dried blood to a damp stocking, that is up to you. Also, I suspect that you need to eat something." She pointed me to a seat at the broad kitchen table and produced the heel of that day's bread. Then she took Ziniän and Balaro into her consulting room.

I washed the blood out of my stocking. I tried to eat the bread she had given me and tried not to wonder what she was asking them (Could they confirm my outlandish story? Had either of them seen the revethavar I claimed had killed their teacher?), but my mind would not quiet, and the bread tasted like nothing and was chokingly hard to swallow, like ashes or hair. I put the heel of bread down on the table and reminded myself that I needed Balaro and Ziniän to confirm to Azhanharad that Osmin Temin really had done what I said she had.

And in truth, it was not very long before the door opened and Othalo Galinin came back in with Ziniän and Balaro and said, "They are very sturdy young women and they insist that they must go with you."

"Very good," I said, as if I had been coherent enough to wonder what I would do if one or both of them refused to come. "Let us be off."

"Othala Celehar," said Othalo Galinin, "you should be going to bed."

"I can't," I said, "for I do not know if my friend will still be alive in the morning if I do."

Othalo Galinin told us how to reach the nearest ostro, and the girls and I went back out into the night. I still felt strange, disconnected, as if my body did not quite belong to me, but I focused on the danger Tomasaran and Sukelo and Nileän were in, and that steadied me.

The tram was lively with operagoers; the three of us made a strange silent blot, like ink on a clean sheet, in a corner of the carriage. We changed lines at the Dachenostro, then again where the Zulnicho line met the Habaro line, and rode as far as we could before getting off and walking the rest of the way to General Parzhadar Square and the imposing face of the Chapterhouse. In the moonlight, the stained glass was unreadable, but the carvings stood out starkly.

The Chapterhouse was always open, it being a truism that the Vigilant Brotherhood never slept, and the novices on duty at the main doors were inclined to be suspicious. I thought again that I must look like a madman, but persevered, finally convincing one of them to go wake Azhanharad, although the prospect was unnerving.

But when Azhanharad appeared, he was neither irritated nor inclined to tell me it could wait until morning. He took us into a side room, where he listened with great intensity while I tried, yet again, to explain the situation. When I was done, he did not demand immediate confirmation from Balaro and Ziniän, as I had expected him to do; instead he gave me an assessing look and said, "Are you injured, Othala Celehar? You look unwell."

Concern from Azhanharad was the last thing I had expected or wanted. I said, "We are fine, we assure you. Merely, at this point, rather tired."

He looked unconvinced, but said, "We regret that we cannot let you go home immediately. We will send a squad to the school to take into custody everyone that they find there, but in the meantime we must get sworn depositions from all three of you."

I felt dizzy for a moment with the relief that Azhanharad had believed me, that he was going to take the necessary steps to ensure Tomasaran's safety. "Thank you," I said.

Azhanharad looked puzzled for a moment, then actually smiled. "We trust your probity, Othala Celehar. Now, if you will pardon us a moment, there are orders we must give." He closed the door firmly behind him.

Ziniän said nervously, "I've never given a deposition before."

"It isn't difficult," I said. "You just tell the truth." Guessing part of the reason for her discomfiture, I said, "No one is going to blame you for what Osmin Temin made you do."

"Maybe they should," Balaro said. "We knew that what she was doing was wrong."

"But if you tried to say anything," Ziniän said, "she'd send *you* to be photographed with no clothes on, and it was just . . ."

"I understand," I said. The othas'ala of Aveio had done and said things I disagreed with weekly—if not daily—and I had said nothing because I knew I would be censured by the townsfolk for speaking against him. "And the truth is, you didn't knife anyone, and we need not speculate about what you *might* have done in different circumstances."

They nodded. Balaro said suddenly, "Ziniän, your knife? What did you do with it?" and their eyes widened almost comically as they both realized they had left their knives at the iron grille without a second thought.

X

At some point, after the sun had come up but before I was allowed to leave the Chapterhouse, Anora appeared, a comforting presence even in the formal coat of office he wore only for funerals.

"Thara," he said when a novice ushered him into the room where I was sitting, alone now and waiting. "I received a most peculiar message from Subpraeceptor Azhanharad. Art thou all right?"

"I hardly know how to answer that question," I said. "I have encountered a revethavar and am still alive to tell of it. I could be much worse."

"Thou dost alarm me," said Anora. "For surely the implication is that thou couldst be much better. And I have heard tales of the revethavarsin, and they are terrifying. Thara, art thou well?"

I said, although I could barely get the words out of my mouth, "No. I am not. I fear the revethavar has torn my calling from me."

Anora said, "Art thou sure?"

"Not entirely," I said. "But I could not speak to—to my companion's body."

"Thy companion? Thou dost not mean that Othalo Tomasaran—"

"No," I said hastily. "I beg thy pardon that I should have made thee think so. Othalo Tomasaran is currently in the Cemchelarna watchhouse, but she is unharmed."

"Perhaps," said Anora, "if thou mightst tell me the tale from the beginning."

I had given a deposition, so the facts were well ordered in my mind. I told Anora the whole, and he sat and listened carefully, without interrupting, as all prelates of Ulis were trained to listen.

When I had finished, he said, "That is a most distressing story, Thara. I am pleased that thou hast come out of it alive."

"Yes," I said. "I also."

"I have never heard of a Witness *vel ama* for the Dead being robbed of their calling," he said. "Perhaps it is temporary."

"Perhaps," I said, although I doubted it. The terrible nothing I had encountered when I had touched Osmin Temin's corpse had not felt temporary. But I did not want to argue with Anora.

"I know thou wilt not argue, even though thou disagreest," he said, startling me. "And I have no wish to argue, either. Therefore, let us hope, but not expect, that you will heal from this wound as you would from a physical one."

I thought about amputation but held my tongue.

The door opened, and Azhanharad said, "Oh good, Othala Chanavar, we are glad you are here. We feel that we can trust you to see that Othala Celehar gets home without encountering any more mythological creatures."

That stung, as I was sure he meant it to.

Anora said, "Yes, we will take care of him."

I wanted to protest that I did not need to be taken care of, but the truth was that I felt ill and exhausted and uncomfortably grateful to Anora for appearing like a zhev in a Barizheise wonder-tale. I was even, and even more uncomfortably, grateful to Azhanharad for summoning him.

We left through the echoing atrium of the Chapterhouse's main entrance and, though it was not what either of us wanted, spent the entire journey to my apartment arguing. Anora felt strongly that I needed to eat, and while in principle I agreed with him, in practice the idea made my stomach spasm with nausea. I said no and no again, and finally, as we stood in my barren room, I said, "Anora, I beg of thee, *leave me alone.*"

"All right, Thara," he said, although the look he gave me was both hurt and skeptical. "But I will return in the evening. Thou *must* eat, whether thou wishest it or not."

"All right," I said—anything to make him leave. Then, finally, his footsteps dwindled to nothing down the stairs. I was alone and could drop onto my bed and weep like a heartbroken child.

)(

Eventually, I slept, and when Anora returned, just as the lamp-lighters were starting their rounds, I was at least able to face the idea of food. We went to the Hanevo Tree, where the server led us to a back corner table without my having to ask.

We sat in silence for a long time after the server had taken our order for a four-cup pot of aikanaro and a plate of steamed buns. I was trying wearily to decide if I owed Anora an apology when he said, "Thou lookst better. Didst thou sleep?"

"Some," I said. I'd also spent hours just lying in the dark with a cold compress over my eyes.

He nodded as if it was the answer he expected. "I have talked to Othalo Rasaltezhen at the Sanctuary."

"Thou hast been very busy on my behalf," I said guiltily. "Anora—"

"Hush, Thara," he said fondly. "I am an adult and can make my own choices. Othalo Rasaltezhen says she will speak to thee if thou wouldst like. She specializes in injuries of the spirit and spends most of her time with the mazei."

"I am no maza," I said.

"No, but Dach'othala Ulzhavar said that Othalo Rasaltezhen was the most likely to be able to help thee."

"Thou hast talked to Dach'othala Ulzhavar?"

"He, too, is thy friend," Anora said, almost reprovingly, "and wishes to help thee."

"But—" I started, and the server appeared with our tea and steamed buns. When she left again, I said, "Anora, this is distressing, yes, but it is not important enough that—"

"No," Anora said. "It *is* important enough. Let me remind thee that thou art essentially the only Witness for the Dead for the city of Amalo, Vernezar having bullied the rest away, and if thou canst not speak to the dead, thou canst not do thy work."

He made me flinch as I was pouring tea, and some splashed on the table. I said, knowing it was a feeble answer, "Tomasaran is—"

"Not ready," said Anora. "Also, it grieves me to see thee hurt."

I flinched again, although this time I had nothing in my hands to spill or drop. "Thou hast not been to speak to Prince Orchenis, I hope," I said, not sure whether I was joking.

"Not yet," said Anora. "But thou wilt be obliged to speak to him soon."

"I know," I said. "Just . . . not yet."

"Not until thou hast spoken to Othalo Rasaltezhen."

We were silent for a while, eating. At least now I was able to manage food, although I took no pleasure in it.

Eventually, Anora said, "Thou also needst to speak to Prince Orchenis to let him know that there is a tomb and a treasure beneath the Hill of Werewolves."

"Thou'rt right," I said. "And that *cannot* wait, for it will not take long for looters to find it."

"The Brotherhood has put a guard at the grille. Subpraeceptor Azhanharad seems to have thought of everything."

"He is very thorough. But still I must speak to Prince Orchenis. I would go to the Amal'theileian tonight if I thought it would do any good, but they will never let me in at this hour."

"I would have thee sleep instead. Thou look'st *better,* but thou dost not look *well.*"

"No," I said, grateful for the ginger bite of the aikanaro. "I would be lying if I told thee I felt well."

"I am glad thou hast decided not to lie, for I would never have believed thee," Anora said gravely, but with a twinkle in his eye.

"I am a very bad liar," I agreed. "Dost thou know what is going to become of the girls from Osmin Temin's school?"

Anora shook his head. "I have heard nothing. But the man who killed the girl—Tedoro?—has told the Brotherhood all about the terrible photography scheme, and two other men have been arrested."

"Good," I said. "It is a vile thing to use children for."

"Yes," said Anora. "I will suggest to the Amal'othala that we should find positions for as many of them as we can. He is always complaining that the Amalomeire cannot keep servants."

"That is a good idea. I will ask Mer Pel-Thenhior if the Opera needs any apprentices in their Wardrobe Department."

"Perhaps the other operas might be asked as well. The city certainly has enough of them."

"True," I said. "I will ask Mer Pel-Thenhior about that, too."

We fell silent again but more comfortably this time. When we had finished the buns and the teapot was empty, we had a reassuringly familiar argument over who should pay the bill, which we settled, as we always did, by each of us paying half. We walked back to my room, and Anora said, "Wilt thou go back to the Prince Zhaicava Building tomorrow?"

"Yes," I said. "I have to. I can only hope that Tomasaran is free of the Cemchelarna watchhouse and has not given up on being a Witness entirely. I would not blame her if she had."

"I think she is made of stronger spirit than that. I am sure thou wilt see her tomorrow."

"I must hope," I said. "Good night, Anora."

He hesitated, and I said, "I promise thee, I am well."

"Thou'rt a terrible liar," he said. "Good night, Thara."

I closed the door and listened to his heavy tread descending the stairs, grateful that he had left me alone, despite his accurate assessment that I was not well. I felt too aware of the silence in my head, as if a whisper to which I was so accustomed that I did not notice it had ceased. But there was nothing Anora or anyone else (Save perhaps Othalo Rasaltezhen? She was still an unknown quantity.) could do.

I undressed, hanging my clothes carefully, and lay down on the bed where, somewhat to my own surprise, I almost immediately fell asleep.

I was awake again long before dawn. I made my poor rent and begrimed coat of office into a neat parcel with a note to my laundress, Merrem Aichenaran, asking her to do what she could. I waited only for the first glimmer of light to go to the public baths for a prolonged soak in the hot pool. I combed out my hair and washed it thoroughly, then washed my body with the same care. I could not wash away the damage the revethavar had done, but it felt good for a moment to pretend that it was possible. It was with regret that I dried off and got dressed again—in the rusty black frock coat, for it was the closest I could come to a coat of office—and with even greater regret that I caught the tram for the Veren'malo and the Prince Zhaicava Building. My momentary pretense was hollow and foolish.

Tomasaran was waiting at the door of my office. She at least looked none the worse for her experience, but her eyes widened and her ears dropped when she saw me. "Celehar! Are you all right?"

The question was unanswerable. I said, "I have to petition for an audience with Prince Orchenis, but then we will talk."

"All right," she said worriedly, and she watched while I got out pen and ink and paper and wax. I knew the formal phrasing of a petition; the only problem came when I had to describe the *reason*

I needed to speak to the prince. I finally left it at "about the Hill of Werewolves," signed the petition, sealed it, melting the wax with my lighter, and took it down the hall to the pneumatic tube drop.

Then back to my office, where Tomasaran was waiting. "Tell me first," I said, "what happened to you. Azhanharad said that he was going to have everyone arrested until he knew better what was going on."

"That's exactly what he did," said Tomasaran. "We didn't even mind, much, because they caught Renthalar—that's the man's name, Horthena Renthalar—absolutely by surprise, and no one was hurt. But it was a very long night, and the girls were terrified—all thirty-five of them in the building."

"I cannot blame them. Were the Brothers at least polite?"

Tomasaran made a face. "They could have been much worse."

The same thing I had said to Anora. "They didn't hurt anyone?"

"No, nothing like that. They just treated all of us as if we were criminals, and it was . . ." She shook her head. "Never mind. Tell me what happened to you. I can see that it must have been terrible."

"It was," I said, and I told her the story.

She was horrified. "Is there nothing that can be done?"

"Anora has found a cleric who specializes in injuries of the spirit, and I will have to go talk to her. But my guess is that she will not be able to help."

"You are a melancholic," she said, "and you see only the worst option."

I knew my ears twitched. "Sometimes the worst option is all there is. At least I'm still alive. I almost wasn't."

"Yes, I am glad of that," she said, "but—"

There was an impatient knock at the door. A part-goblin courier, wearing Prince Orchenis's colors. "Othala Celehar?"

"Yes?"

"The prince bids you attend on him at once."

"Of course," I said, surprised. "Come, Tomasaran. You need to be introduced to the prince in any case."

"I do?" she said, her voice almost squeaking.

"Until or unless my ability returns, you are the city's Witness for the Dead." Her stricken face reminded me, belatedly, that I still needed to learn to be tactful. We followed the courier in silence.

The Amal'theileian was both very ancient and very modern, having received a major renovation in the reign of Prince Orchenis's father. Prince Orchena had added a long jutting wing to the south side of the original building, at the far end of which was the Amal'theileianeise ostro (generally shortened to Amal'ostro), the tram stop used by hundreds of civil servants every day, including me. It had been a stunningly effective boost to the popularity of the Clunethada, and the prince's residence was in the north wing, where the clamor of a busy tram station would not reach him. The throne room was in the great and ancient central octagon, but Prince Orchenis did not use it except on the most formal state occasions. He preferred the more modern Azalea Room in the east wing and the Cinnabar Room in the north wing for private audiences. I was both relieved and unnerved when the courier led us to the Cinnabar Room. It meant that I would not have to discuss the revethavar in open court, but it also meant that Prince Orchenis intended to scrutinize my story with particular attention and care.

The prince was a tall, thin elven man with a permanent frown line between his eyebrows. His secretary, Peris Alcharanar, was also elven, quiet and unobtrusive, known mostly in the court for his resolute refusal to gossip about anything, related to the prince's business or not.

Prince Orchenis was wearing dark gray embroidered in orange and red and had dressed his hair with amber and garnet. He said, "Othala Celehar, we have been hearing the most troubling and dramatic rumors, and it is our hope that you can clarify what seems to be a most confusing situation."

"We can try, Your Highness," I said, "but we cannot promise the confusion will lessen."

"*Try*," said Prince Orchenis, and I began my story once again.

The prince was a demanding listener, and I found myself having to loop back to explain why I had been investigating Osmin Temin before Tedoro's death and then again to explain how I had become interested in the matter of photography to begin with. The prince listened with great intensity and forgot nothing, so that for all the loops, my narrative never lost its way.

He wanted to know more about Osmin Temin and her father than I was able to tell him, and he did a horrified calculation of how many people in Amalo must have known of the entrance to the revethavar's tomb and said nothing.

"There were stories," I said.

"Stories." His ears flicked and he dismissed the entire notion of stories with an impatient gesture. "We mean people who *knew.*"

"Most of them died exploring the tomb," I said. "For the revethavar is also not merely a story."

"We are listening," he said, and I continued my narrative, emphasizing that Balaro and Ziniän had not harmed me and doing my best to describe the tomb and then the bodies with their trapped spirits and then the revethavar. I explained how it had killed Osmin Temin and almost killed me. I still had not found a way to describe what it had done to me that was both clear and simple, and the prince had a number of questions, ending with the same one Anora and Tomasaran—and I myself—had asked: "And you think it is permanent?"

"We do not know," I said, "but we have no reason to assume it is not."

"That is most distressing and we will pray that you are wrong. Is that why you have brought another prelate with you?"

"Yes," I said. "This is Othalo Velhiro Tomasaran. We have been teaching her to be a Witness for the Dead."

The prince nodded to Tomasaran, who made a nervous but graceful bow. "Yours is a most honorable calling," the prince said. "We regret that you are coming to it under these circumstances."

"We have no wish to supplant Othala Celehar," said Tomasaran.

I said, "'Supplant' is hardly the right word. We consider it a great relief to have someone who is able to take our place."

"That is a piece of good fortune amidst the bad," said Prince

Orchenis. He sighed. "We see that we must send someone to be a Witness for the Tomb of Hasthemis Brulnemar. We would ask that both of you go as well, Othala Celehar as the only person we know of who has both gone into and come out of the tomb, and Othalo Tomasaran in order to do whatever it may be possible to do for the trapped spirits of the revethavar's victims."

"Of course, Your Highness," I said, and tried not to sound reluctant.

"It had best be done quickly," said Prince Orchenis, and ordered his secretary to send a courier for a Witness.

"Now?" I said, which I could only blame on lack of sleep.

The prince looked at me. "Have you a reason it should wait?"

"No, Your Highness."

The courier returned very quickly, bringing with him an elven man who would have been quite tall if he had not been wry-backed. I knew who he was from reading the newspapers; he had been the Witness for the Unborn Child in a particularly scandalous and long-running litigation over a soldier's estate. His eyes, a startlingly clear, dark-ringed blue, were sharp, and I saw that he was old-fashioned and wore flat wooden beads in his hair, as all Witnesses did in the days of Prince Orchenis's grandfather's grandfather. He wore a dark green coat that was shabby only if you knew exactly where to look and gold earrings. He made a somewhat lopsided bow and said, "We are Ulthora Csathamar, at Your Highness's service."

Prince Orchenis nodded in return and gave a crisply accurate summary of the situation regarding the tomb of Hasthemis Brulnemar. "We are appointing you Witness for the Tomb. We would ask that you examine it immediately and that you take these two prelates with you—Othala Thara Celehar and Othalo Velhiro Tomasaran."

"Celehar," said Csathamar, placing the name. "The Witness for the Dead."

"Yes," I said. Hopefully no more explanation would be needed.

"We are pleased to obey Your Highness," Csathamar said to the prince. "If it is quite convenient for the prelates?"

"Yes, of course," I said. He looked at me sharply, but said nothing.

"Celehar can guide you," said Prince Orchenis, which all three of us took as a dismissal.

Outside the Cinnabar Room, Csathamar said, "Let's take the north exit instead of walking all the way around the Amal'theileian."

"The north exit?" I said.

"It's a servants' door," said Csathamar. "Those are generally the most efficient ways around this great pile of marble." Tomasaran and I followed him through a discreetly invisible door in a side hall, and then through a series of narrow, clean, and well-lit passageways, which eventually brought us to an outer door and the beautifully tended paths of the Princess Orcheveän Gardens. Fortunately for Tomasaran and me, Csathamar knew the Veren'malo as well as he knew the Amal'theileian and was able to lead us to the Hill of Werewolves, where we found a pair of Brothers guarding the gate.

Csathamar showed them his signet—which, it being quite a bit larger than a personal signet, he wore on a long chain around his neck. They bowed and let us in.

"From here," Csathamar said to me, "you must lead."

"Yes," I said without any eagerness and began to work my way through the Werewolf Gardens around the Hill of Werewolves to its north face. It was not difficult to find the drop-off and the disturbance Balaro, Ziniän, and I had made in clawing our way up it, and at the bottom of the drop-off, there was already starting to be a path worn through the scrub trees and tall grass. That took us to the dry waterway, and from there to the grille was not as far as I remembered it being.

There were two Brothers on duty there. Csathamar showed them his signet and commandeered their big lantern. "We'll be back long before dark," he said, and then the three of us squeezed one at a time through the gap between the grille and the stone. I was worried that Csathamar might not be able to make it, but he proved both determined and adept at maneuvering the odd geometry of his spine.

He lit the lantern, which threw a strong beam of light up the waterway, showing that there were branching paths I had been utterly unaware of. "We go straight," I said, and we proceeded in silence to the bridge, where the lantern revealed the great vaulted vastness of the revethavar's tomb.

"Gracious," Csathamar said mildly. "I feel very small."

With better light, I could see the way the long-ago sculptors had mingled wolves and jackals, and it made me profoundly uneasy. Csathamar did not like it, either. He said, "Well, we knew that the mysteries of Anmura became heretical in their last days. I suppose this is proof."

We came to the first body. I touched it, to prove to myself that I would feel nothing, and indeed, I might have been touching the wall. Tomasaran watched me intently, and when I shook my head, her ears drooped.

"Your turn," I said, and I could not fault her, for she stepped up immediately.

"What must I do?" she said as she crouched beside me.

"You have to find their name," I said. "Find their name and tell them to rest."

"That sounds simple," she said wryly.

"Yes," I said. "Very simple. Just not easy."

She touched the corpse and was frozen for a long moment before she jerked back, nearly falling. "Was he killed by the revethavar?" she said shakily.

"Yes. But it cannot hurt you. All you're seeing is a memory."

"It is a very powerful memory," she said, as if she was not sure she believed me.

"Yes," I said. "It is unnaturally so, because of the revethavar. I was hoping his destruction would change something, but I think that it has not."

"It is hard to imagine it being *more* vivid."

"Did you find any hint of his name?"

"I don't know how you can talk of finding anything in something like that."

It was something that I had learned only with a great deal of practice, which was certainly how I had intended for Tomasaran to learn. I said, "The spirit is an onion."

"An *onion*?" said Tomasaran.

"Hardly the most flattering comparison," said Csathamar, who was watching us with great interest.

"Layers," I said. "What you see—the memory of death—is the top layer. You want to peel it away and find the layer underneath. You may have to do that several times to find his name."

"What you're describing doesn't even sound possible," said Tomasaran. "But I don't see that I have any choice except to try."

She touched the corpse again, and this time did not jerk away. Csathamar and I waited; I was close enough to Tomasaran that I saw sweat beginning to bead on her forehead.

After a long silence, Csathamar said, "What if she cannot find the name?"

His voice had no effect on Tomasaran's concentration. I said, "Then we cannot help the spirit rest."

His eyebrows went up sharply. "You cannot do it yourself?"

"I was . . . injured in destroying the revethavar," I said. "No, I cannot."

"I am sorry. I did not mean for that to be a prying question."

"It was a most reasonable question, and you will not be the last person to ask it."

"I suppose not," Csathamar said, although he still looked troubled.

Tomasaran drew a great heaving breath, like a woman reaching air after a long time underwater, and said, "Echira Branavar! His name is Echira Branavar!"

"Well done," I said. "The prayer is also simple. Echira Branavar, you have been wrongly kept from your slumber. You must rest. Echira Branavar, let the darkness take you." As I repeated the prayer, she began to say it with me, hesitantly at first, but with steadily increasing confidence. It did not take very many repetitions before she lifted her hand from the corpse and said, "It worked. He is gone."

"Excellent," I said, catching myself before I insulted her by asking if she was sure.

"I am exhausted," she said. "How many more bodies did you say are down here?"

"I saw at least a dozen," I said, "and who knows how many I *didn't* see."

Tomasaran made a noise of dismay.

"It does get easier with practice," I said.

"I will have to hope so. All right." She and I stood up, and Csathamar looked up from the notebook he was writing in.

"Ready? I am attempting to draw a map, so we will proceed slowly."

We did indeed proceed slowly, from body to body, as Csathamar drew each intersection and made notes about the friezes and the mosaics, while Tomasaran released the trapped spirits. She became more efficient with practice; she said it helped, terrible though it was to say it, that they had all died in the same way. "It's dreadful, but it's *familiar,* and that makes it easier to reach past it."

"Yes," I said, for offering encouragement was the most I could do to help. "It's like a nightmare that has recurred often enough to become predictable."

"Yes," said Tomasaran. "Very like that. It is *awful.*"

And then, with the tenth body, she touched it and jerked back again, almost as if it had burned her. After a moment, she said, "It is different."

"Different how?"

"This man wasn't killed by the revethavar. His lantern got broken and he . . . he starved to death."

We stared at each other.

"He got this far," I said, "and he *starved* to death?"

"The revethavar must have . . ." She trailed off.

"The revethavar must have watched him die," I said. "It must have found it more enjoyable than killing him outright."

"Oh, how horrible!" said Tomasaran, and made a violent warding gesture with both hands.

"Everything about the revethavar is horrible," I said. "Let us release this poor man's spirit and keep moving."

She was kind. She did not remark on my use of "us," even though I was merely an observer.

When we reached Osmin Temin's body, Tomasaran took several moments to nerve herself to approach, for she had known Osmin Temin, however briefly and however unfondly, and that always made things more difficult. Csathamar continued working on his map; it had grown an elaborate numbered commentary about the symbolism of the friezes, which by now were a strange, upsetting mixture of Anmureise and Ulineise iconography, with wolves predominating everywhere. He said, "There are many things that bother me about these friezes, but one of them is how much time they must have taken. The way I have always heard the story—which I admit I have always taken to be a wonder-tale and nothing more—it was only the last praeceptor of the Wolves of Anmura who led them into heresy and that was why the Archprelate turned against them. As if the two things had happened very close together. But these funerary decorations clearly weren't slapped together in a day. They must have taken years, if not decades. Just how long did the Wolves of Anmura practice their heresies before they were caught?"

"Yes," I said, for no one could miss the care taken by the sculptors over their realistically rendered wolves. "The story must be incorrect, at least in part."

"I must talk to a scholar of the period," said Csathamar, as though it irritated him that one was not immediately available.

I remembered the letter from Aäthis Rohethar and the free afternoon I had yet to have. "I know of one."

"Really?" Csathamar said. "I can find one, but it will take some time. The University is like a hen who doesn't know what her chicks are doing."

"Yes. I, ah, he wants to talk to me about the Hill of Werewolves."

"Does he?" said Csathamar, eyes glinting with amusement. "Just think of all you have to tell him."

I could not quite smile, but I said, "He has asked me to come talk to him on my first free afternoon."

"If I might come with you?"

"Of course."

"Perhaps we will have time today," said Csathamar. "I suppose it depends on what else we find down here."

"We haven't yet come to the actual crypt."

"I know. The scholar may have to wait until tomorrow."

Tomasaran, at the far edge of the lantern light, shoved suddenly to her feet and said, "It is done. Unless you think there are more?"

"It is entirely possible that there are," Csathamar said apologetically. "If the sense I'm making of my map is correct, there is a good deal of this complex we have not found yet—including, as Othala Celehar was just pointing out, the actual crypt."

Tomasaran grimaced but said nothing. I felt a sharp flash of guilt; if I had not been crippled, we could at least have taken turns.

Csathamar and I came past Osmin Temin's corpse, Tomasaran joining us, and continued down the hall to the doorway flanked by snarling wolves.

"These are different," Csathamar said, examining the wolves with great interest. "They're much older than the friezes—at a guess, the complex was built around them and they mark the entrance to the crypt proper. Which means the crypt wasn't built for the revethavar. At least not to begin with." He made a note and drew two tiny wolves on his map, and we proceeded through the doorway.

It was immediately obvious that Csathamar was correct: this was the crypt of Hasthemis Brulnemar, and—it appeared—a number of other people. The floor and walls were punctuated with rectangular name plaques, but what drew our attention most sharply was the circle of skeletons in the middle of the room—seven skeletons, with an eighth alone in the middle.

"Do you think . . ." Csathamar started.

"I strongly suspect that's Hasthemis Brulnemar in the center," said Tomasaran. "Well, there's one way to find out." She approached the body nearest us, reciting the prayer of compassion for the dead, and knelt to touch it. She was there only a moment before she stood and said, "He murdered them all. After they completed the ritual to turn him into a revethavar. That was the first thing he did. These and the two prelates," and she pointed to the corner behind me, where a jumble of shadows resolved into two skulls atop a pile of clothes.

"Ingratitude," murmured Csathamar.

"They knew what they were making," I said. "Tomasaran, did you get any sense of why they did it?"

"So that their enemies wouldn't get their treasure," she said and pointed. "There." At the far end of the tomb was another doorway, this one sealed with a slab of rock. In front of it stood a metal chest, large enough that it might have taken four men to carry it down here.

Tomasaran and I followed Csathamar to the chest, which was not locked. He said, "I suppose with a revethavar, locks become a little superfluous." He opened the chest.

All three of us stared at the contents.

"Books," said Csathamar, as if he could not quite believe what he was seeing. "I shan't touch them—they're crumbling to dust as it is, and they need a scholar to assess them, not a judicial Witness. But . . . they made a revethavar to protect their *books*."

It struck me how disappointed Osmin Temin would have been, and I had to turn away, biting my lip savagely against a burst of hiccupping, hysterical laughter.

"Othala Celehar?" said Csathamar.

"Celehar?" said Tomasaran. "Are you all right?"

"I'm fine," I said, although I was probably lying. "I . . . I suppose they felt they had nothing to lose. Everyone else was massacred anyway."

"Are you *sure* you're all right?" said Tomasaran.

"Yes," I said, more convincingly. "You should release these spirits—I don't know what we're going to do about all the bodies."

"They will have to be given decent burial somewhere," said Csathamar, replacing the lid of the chest, "but it need not be your problem, othala. Prince Orchenis can request someone from the Ulistheileian."

"That is a relief," I said.

Tomasaran knelt first by the two prelates, then in turn by each of the seven—carefully not stepping inside their circle—while Csathamar and I examined the blocked doorway, which was indeed impassable.

Tomasaran said, "Celehar?"

"Yes?"

"Do you think I need to—" She gestured at Hasthemis Brulnemar's skeleton. "Do you think he's still *there*?"

"The revethavar is destroyed," I said.

"Yes, but what if there was something of the man left?"

"I don't think there was."

"Are you *sure*?"

"No, of course not, I've never destroyed a revethavar before." I caught myself. "I'm sorry. If you put it like that, then no, I'm not sure."

"I was afraid of that," she said dismally.

"The revethavar *is* destroyed," I said. "Whether there's anything left of Hasthemis Brulnemar or not, there's nothing there to fear."

"It's not that so much as the circle," said Tomasaran. "I don't like to step across it."

"You've freed all seven of them?"

"Yes."

"Then it's nothing but a circle of cloth and bones and dust."

"All right," she said and stepped resolutely over an outflung assemblage of bone that had once been an arm.

She knelt quickly by Brulnemar's skeleton and stood up just as quickly. "No, you're right. There's nothing here." She came out of the circle and shook herself, almost like a dog coming out of the water.

Then we went out and finished Csathamar's map, finding two more bodies in the corridors. When we came back, blinking, to the grille, it was well past noon, and the two Brothers we had taken the lantern from had been replaced by two more, who gladly accepted the lantern back.

It was easier to climb up the drop-off in the daylight. We were approaching the gate when Csathamar stopped suddenly. "There are people waiting," he said. Then, realizing: "Oh blessed goddesses. The *newspapers*."

We looked at each other in horror.

"Is there another way out of the gardens?" Csathamar said.

"No," I said. "Only the one gate."

"There's nothing for it, then," he said grimly.

"They were sure to find us sooner or later," I said. "I could wish it had been later."

"*Much* later," said Csathamar. "Well, there's no point lurking back here and hoping they go away."

"No," I said and started toward the gate.

Thurizar from the *Evening Standard* saw me first, and his yelp of surprise made both Goronezh from the *Arbiter* and Vicenalar from the *Herald* turn around.

"Othala Celehar?" said Thurizar. "What are you doing here?"

I took a deep breath, pulling myself together as best I could, and said, "We cannot answer questions until the Witness has made his report to Prince Orchenis."

"Ooh, it's Csathamar," said Goronezh.

Vicenalar said, "Mer Csathamar, what can you tell us about the tomb beneath the Hill of Werewolves?"

"You already know more than you should," Csathamar said, scowling.

"Othala Celehar, who's the lady?" said Thurizar.

"This is Othalo Velhiro Tomasaran, a Witness for the Dead."

"A Witness *vel ama,* like yourself?"

It seemed increasingly unlikely that I was still a Witness *vel ama,* but that was not something I intended to discuss with the newspapermen, now or ever. I simply said, "Yes."

Goronezh said, "Are you all right, Othala Celehar? You look haggard."

I could not tell if he was asking out of genuine concern or a newspaperman's prying curiosity—or perhaps some mixture of both. I said, "We are well, thank you."

Goronezh gave me a disbelieving look. Thurizar said, "Two Ulineise prelates. It *must* be a tomb."

"Two Witnesses for the Dead," said Goronezh. "A tomb may not be all it is."

"We cannot answer questions, gentlemen," I said.

Csathamar said, "We must make haste to the Amal'theileian." He did not push past them only because they fell back. Tomasaran and I hastened to keep up.

"We'll find you later," Goronezh said cheerfully, yielding the battle.

"Of course you will," Csathamar said, but under his breath.

When we had some blocks between us and the three of them, I said, "You do not like the newspapers?"

"I dislike the newspapermen's habit of asking me questions they know I cannot answer," Csathamar said. "And I dislike their habit of always referring to me in their stories as 'the wry-backed Witness.' My name should be sufficient."

"Yes," I said, a trifle guiltily, for it was his wry back that had told me instantly who he was when he came into the Cinnabar Room.

"Perhaps it is mere vanity," he said. "But, no, I do not like the newspapers. Also, they are as persistent and maddening as flies."

"They will be waiting when we leave the audience with Prince Orchenis," I said.

"Oh, undoubtedly," said Csathamar. "Something to look forward to."

Csathamar led us back to the Amal'theileian as confidently as he had led us to the Hill of Werewolves, and once there, he knew the correct people to find in order to get Prince Orchenis's attention without also getting the attention of the entire court. Very shortly, a solemn, liveried part-goblin servant was showing us into the Cinnabar Room, and surprisingly soon thereafter, Prince Orchenis joined us there and bade us be seated.

"That took longer than we expected," he said mildly.

"The funerary complex is larger than we thought," said Csathamar, and launched into his report, which was thorough and well organized, as one would expect from a practicing judicial Witness.

At the end, he said, "Othala Celehar says he knows of a scholar of the time period, and we would request that the tomb remain untouched until we have been able to confer with him."

"What is this scholar's name?" Prince Orchenis asked.

"Aäthis Rohethar," I said. "He is a scholar of the first rank at the University."

"Unexceptionable," said Prince Orchenis. "The Brotherhood may not be best pleased to have the duty of guarding the ingress for an indeterminate span of time, but your request seems reasonable and logical."

"We hope to meet Osmer Rohethar tomorrow," Csathamar added.

"Excellent," said Prince Orchenis. "Return when you have his opinion, and we will make a decision about what should be done with this tomb."

The three of us bowed; I was grateful to leave without having had to say more than twelve words.

⋊

I persuaded Tomasaran to go home. I wanted to go home myself, but I needed to talk to Pel-Thenhior about the foundling girls and—as he was the petitioner—tell him the outcome of my witnessing for Tedoro. The Vermilion Opera was performing tonight, so I knew where he was. Neither of my other two coats was any less shabby, so there was no point in going home to change, which meant I was attending the Opera in the rusty black coat.

I ate dinner at a zhoän near the Amal'theileian, and arrived at the Opera early, but not unbearably so. The elven man on duty in the ticket office waved to me. I pushed through the double doors and followed the passage around to Pel-Thenhior's box. There I took a seat and was relieved that none of the people on stage did more than glance at me. It was all stagehands this evening, doing arcane last-minute checks of the scenery for *General Olethazh*.

It was not very long before Pel-Thenhior joined me. He said immediately, "Blessed goddesses, you look terrible. What has happened to you?"

My eyes stung for a moment, and I pinched the bridge of my nose. "It is a long story."

Pel-Thenhior consulted his pocket-watch. "I have time to listen."

I told him the whole of it. As he listened, his ears got flatter and flatter, but he did not interrupt.

"To sum up," he said when, finally, I had finished, "Osmin Temin is dead, her pornography enterprise stopped, and Tedoro's murderer in custody. You have destroyed a revethavar—which I must tell you is a thing I had not believed possible—your apprentice has freed twenty-three spirits, and you are no longer a Witness for the Dead. Am I correct?"

"Yes," I said.

"Is that a relief or a crushing blow?"

"It is a blow." The words were hard to say. "Witnesses for the Dead do burn out, but I had probably four or five more years before that happened. And it would not have been like this."

"I cannot imagine that *anything* could be like 'this.'"

"No, probably not," I said and was glad my voice did not waver.

The audience began to come in, a stream of laughing, chattering people, elves and goblins, and all of them gorgeously dressed and lavishly jeweled. I felt the rusty black coat even more keenly.

"We will talk more later," said Pel-Thenhior. But he continued to watch me in a way I found unnerving until he was distracted by a young elven woman who came up to the outside of the box and said, "Iäna, aren't you even going to wave at me?"

"Hestheno, my pearl! I didn't see you. A thousand apologies! You look delightful."

"Thank you," she said. She was quite pretty, with limpid blue eyes that helped distinguish her from the porcelain-doll sameness that so many elven women seemed deliberately to cultivate. She was wearing a smoky green gown and had dressed her hair with cabochon emeralds to match. I wondered if she was in one of the photographs on his walls.

They began to exchange the pleasant small talk of two people with a large circle of mutual friends. I leaned back in my chair and hoped the curtain would rise soon.

X

*General Olethazh* was a beautiful opera. It was in every way possible the opposite of *Zhelsu*, and it occurred to me that Pel-Thenhior must have planned that, at once reassurance to the more conservative members of his audience that he wasn't going to run mad and fill the schedule with jarring experimental operas, but at the same time, along with *The Siege of Tekharee* (an old warhorse as he had called it), it provided the best possible contrast for an opera that was designed to shock.

What *General Olethazh* was not was attention grabbing. I only half watched that evening's performance, most of my mind too busy to accept the solace the opera offered. After the opera was finished, after the audience's endless applause had finally ended, Pel-Thenhior came back to the box and said, without preamble, "What will you do?"

"I know not," I said and swallowed hard. "I have not yet spoken to the Amal'othala, and much will depend on his judgment."

"Can he send you away?"

"He can . . . that is, it isn't clear what the limits of his authority are. He can certainly make things very unpleasant if he wishes to."

"Will he, do you think?"

"Probably," I said, and my voice cracked like a dead stick.

Pel-Thenhior let me compose myself and then said defiantly, "I would be of comfort to thee if I could."

I was so startled at being thee'd I could barely speak. "Th . . . thou wouldst?"

"Needst not sound so shocked," he said, rather wryly. "I did not think that my regard for thee was any particular secret."

"I thought," I started, then stopped myself. "No. It is no matter what I thought. I thank thee for thy kindness."

"That is not a word I hear about myself very often. My singers complain of my harshness—though less so now that Arveneän is gone. And Tura."

The comparison was ridiculous. "Even before the sessiva, I could never have been one of thy singers."

"Sessiva? Is that what happened?"

"It swept Lohaiso when I was a prelate there. It was a bad year for it. Most people who caught it died, so I am lucky."

"Good fortune can sometimes seem like the opposite," he said, and I remembered him telling me he had been a singer before his voice changed.

"Sometimes, yes," I said. "Dost thou find thyself lucky or unlucky?"

"Ha," he said. "Thou turnest my question back upon me very neatly. But, no, I know that I am lucky. I would never have been happy with someone else telling me what to do, which would make me a very bad choice as a singer. And I find the making of an opera as a whole an endlessly absorbing pastime. So that in truth, no, I do not want to be a singer. But I could not have imagined that when I was thirteen." He looked me over critically. "Thou needst sleep, not my yammering."

I hesitated, then told him a truth I would not even have told Anora: "I dream."

"Oh," he said, and proved himself worthy of the confidence by not making light of it. "Is there anything that helps?"

"I once made myself drunk enough that I did not dream, but it is not an experiment I will be repeating."

"I understand completely. I've tried that once or twice myself."

"But otherwise the only cure I've found is not sleeping."

"That's not a cure," Iäna objected. "That's escaping pirates to be eaten by sharks."

"It is easier," I said, and his ears dipped in a wince.

He was silent for a few moments, then said hesitantly, "Would it help to have company?"

I tried to imagine him in my barren room and failed. "I doubt it. But the dreams will get easier with time."

"I dislike how confidently thou sayest that. Hast thou that much experience with bad dreams?"

I was not going to tell him about Evru. "I have enough," I said.

He drew back a little, like a cat that had been tapped on the nose. "Still," he said. "I would be of comfort if I could."

"Thy willingness is a great comfort," I said truthfully. "And I have another matter wherein I hope thou *canst* help."

"Thou hast been very busy," he said; he sounded impressed. "But tell me of this other matter."

I told him about the thirty-seven foundling girls. "All of them can sew," I finished, "and I remember thou saidst the Wardrobe Department took foundlings as apprentices."

"We do, true enough. But we cannot take thirty-seven."

"No, of course not," I said, and scraped together a smile. "But I wondered if thou wouldst talk to the other operas."

His eyebrows went up. "A cooperative venture among the operas of Amalo? Such a thing has never been done before."

"Is it impossible?"

"No, not impossible," he said, beginning now to look thoughtful. "And the Orchen'opera is in dire need of seamstresses. I think I myself am not the correct person, but I know Ulsheän talks to the other wardrobe masters. They meet at the Silkmarket every week to gossip and look for bargains."

"Then she could ask very easily," I said and felt my heart lighten again.

"Yes," said Iäna. "If thou wouldst like, I can probably catch her now. She stays down there until all hours of the night."

"Wouldst thou?"

"Of course. But thou shouldst go home and sleep. Even if there are dreams. Lack of sleep will hurt thee, too."

"Thou wilt talk to thy wardrobe master?"

"Yes, I promise. Good night, Thara."

"Good night, Iäna," I said and went home.

Cats began appearing as I unlocked my door: the marmalade tom, the half-blind sable queen, the shy brown tabby. I shared the sardines out among them and sat to watch them eat, grateful for their uncomplicated company, their straightforward desires.

I still did not know what Iäna wanted—simple friendship or something more. For that matter, I didn't know what *I* wanted. I didn't know if, after Evru, I was even capable of "more." The idea did not terrify me as it had when I first met Iäna, but I felt like the gutted husk of a burnt-out building.

The sable queen butted my shin imperiously with her head, and I obediently began petting her. Her purr was extravagant, a tremendous noise from such a small and delicate-looking creature. It changed nothing, but, for that long moment, until she turned her head and caught my hand gently between her teeth, it made me feel better, as if all problems were inherently solvable, as if no answer I chose would be wrong.

⟪

In the morning, no better rested than I had been the night before, I went to the Prince Zhaicava Building. I got there before Tomasaran, but only by a matter of minutes. She said as she came in, "Merrem Nadaran and Min Nadin want you to come visit."

"Do they?"

She was blushing. "They feel that you are my family in Amalo and that therefore they should welcome you to their house as they welcome all of their lodgers' families."

"That's . . ."

"Exceptionally hospitable of them," Tomasaran finished. "I understand that in practice, many of their lodgers have no family in Amalo they wish to speak to, but Merrem Nadaran was very earnest in asking that I invite you. She said something about a previous lodger?"

"Arveneän Shelsin," I said. "I witnessed for her and found her murderer."

"Oh," said Tomasaran. "That explains it better. Merrem Nadaran seems to feel that they owe you something on Min Shelsin's behalf."

"Which is nonsense. I am a Witness for the Dead—" And then I caught myself. "Or I was."

"You should go talk to the cleric whose name I have forgotten."

"Othalo Rasaltezhen," I said. "I can't today. We are talking to Osmer Rohethar this afternoon."

"No, I meant you should go *now*."

"I can't. I have to be here."

"I'm here," she said.

"Do you feel prepared to deal with a petition on your own?" I said skeptically.

"No, but I'll have to learn sooner or later. Besides, odds are good there won't be any. You should go, Celehar. What if it's like a bone and has to be set before it starts to heal crooked?"

"It's not like a bone," I said, "but I take your meaning. If you're quite sure?"

"Quite sure," she said, and I had no real choice except to believe her.

I took the tram back down the Zulnicho line to the Ulzhav'ostro, whence I walked to the Sanctuary. The novice on duty at the main doors was glad to escort me to Othalo Rasaltezhen's workroom.

Othalo Rasaltezhen was part goblin, with pale gray skin and pale yellow eyes. She was younger than I had expected, younger than I was. She was also taller than I was. She knew who I was when I introduced myself, and she said at once, "I don't know if there's anything I can do to help, but I'll be glad to try."

"'Try' is all I can ask for," I said. "I don't think there's anyone else who can even get as far as 'try.'"

"Then come in and sit down," she said, waving me to the two chairs wedged in one of the oddly shaped corners of her workroom, "and tell me what happened."

I sat down and said—blurted, really, for it was not how I'd intended to start—"It was a revethavar."

"A *revethavar*?" Othalo Rasaltezhen said, and she certainly believed me enough to be alarmed. "What became of it?"

"I found its name and quieted it," I said. "But it was . . . it was like knives, like being ripped to pieces. And afterward . . . I do not hear the dead anymore." Saying it straight out like that made my eyes sting. I blinked hard.

Othalo Rasaltezhen said, "You are very lucky—we are all very lucky, I think, that you defeated it."

"It was trapped," I said. "In a tomb under the Hill of Werewolves. But anyone going in there became its victim."

"Still," she said. "It is horrible to think of there being a revethavar in Amalo. But now let us find out if I can do anything. It depends on whether hearing the dead is anything like the mazei's powers."

"I have no idea," I said.

"Nor do I," she said cheerfully. "This is very simple, although most people find it uncomfortable. I need to look into your eyes."

"All right," I said, meeting her gaze, and a second later I understood why she said people found it uncomfortable. She was not merely meeting my gaze; she was looking inside my head through my eyes just as I, inside my head, looked out through them.

"Well," she said after a long silence. "The damage is certainly extensive. To be perfectly honest, I'm surprised you're sane." She sat back, releasing me from her gaze.

"There's nothing you can do."

"I don't know. There's nothing I know how to do *today*. With the mazei, it's generally a matter of a single broken thread, and it's easy enough to knot it back together. But this is . . ."

"I know," I said, for I did know. "I didn't expect you to be able to help, but my . . . my friends were very insistent that I talk to you."

"Don't give up on me yet," she said. "With time to consider the problem, I may well come up with something. And I will consult with my maza friend. I admit that right now I do not know how to help you, but I do not despair of figuring it out."

"Thank you. I appreciate your willingness to try."

"If you can defeat a revethavar, the least I can do is give you more than five minutes' thought."

"It was mostly luck, I think." Luck that it wanted to toy with me rather than kill me outright.

"I don't know that I would call it luck," she said. "Finding a revethavar's name strikes me as something very few people would have the presence of mind to try."

"I have quieted several ghouls," I said. "This was the same thing, only much worse."

We stood up. She said, "I will think further on your problem and see if I cannot come up with a solution. And you never know. Perhaps you will heal on your own, with no help from me."

"Perhaps," I said, without much hope.

"May I write to you, if I think of something?"

"Of course. A letter to the Prince Zhaicava Building will find me. Thank you for your time, Othalo Rasaltezhen." I bowed to her and she bowed in return.

"Good luck, Othala Celehar," she said, and I did not ask her what she meant.

)(

Tomasaran and I had agreed to meet Csathamar in the Prince Zhaicava Building at noon, so I returned to my office, where Tomasaran took one look at my face and said, "She couldn't help."

"No."

"I'm sorry, Celehar."

"I wasn't expecting her to be able to."

"I know you weren't, but I'm sorry all the same."

"Were there any petitioners?"

"No. Nothing of any interest happened."

"It was a good morning then," I said wryly.

She laughed, and a tap on the door heralded Csathamar, who was wearing a dark blue coat and sapphire earrings, though still the wooden beads in his hair and a dull brown overcoat. The dark blue made his already startling eyes almost unearthly. "My wife insisted that if I was going to the University, I had to wear my best coat," he said apologetically. "Her father was a scholar of the first rank, and she has strong feelings about the University. She would have become a scholar herself, if they would let women in."

I was wearing the rusty black secondhand coat, off which, long ago, all the seed pearls had been snipped to be used for some other garment, except for a couple of lonely holdouts on the left sleeve. Next to Tomasaran's canon's coat, I looked moderately shabby. Next to Csathamar, I looked like a bundle of rags. I said, "My coat of office was torn in the initial exploration of Brulnemar's tomb. I am hopeful that my laundress can get it repaired."

Csathamar nodded. "I have always been grateful that Witnesses do not have coats of office or other dress requirements."

"You are lucky," Tomasaran said feelingly. "It is terrible to have your most costly garment be the one you wear every day."

"It is," I said. I was still trying to figure out how I was going to afford buying a new one, if Merrem Aichenaran could not help me. I doubted the Amal'othala would be sympathetic to any request for financial assistance. He was grudging enough about my stipend. . . .

My thoughts ground to a jarring halt. My stipend depended on my being a Witness for the Dead. If I was not, if I could no longer speak to the dead at all, I would have to tell the Amal'othala and I would be . . . The Ulistheileian had washed their hands of me, so I could hardly seek a benefice. And what was I to tell the Archprelate?

I followed Tomasaran and Csathamar almost without noticing as Csathamar led the way to the zhoän he favored. It was true that we had to eat, but I could not have told anyone what I ordered or what it tasted like. Csathamar, being a good Witness, was drawing Tomasaran out to talk about her husband and her husband's horrible family, and my thoughts went round and round in helpless, useless wheels.

It was not until we had boarded the Cevoro-line tram for the University that I took a deep breath and told myself sternly that, as there was nothing I could do about any of it right now, there was no point in panicking over it. I asked Csathamar, "Have you been sent to the University before?"

"Once or twice," said Csathamar. "There was a terrible dispute a few years ago when one of the scholars of the third rank accused one of the scholars of the first rank of stealing his work. All of the scholars took sides, and the two of them very nearly fought a duel. I was the Witness for the Scholar of the Third Rank."

"Was it true?" Tomasaran asked. "Had the other scholar really stolen his work?"

"Not that we could ever determine," Csathamar said. "The Witness for the Scholar of the First Rank and I spent hours with their notebooks, and it was true that they were studying the same thing and had come to similar conclusions, but it could not be proved that the scholar of the first rank even *knew* that the scholar of the third rank was working on the same material."

"What were they studying?" I asked.

"I used to be able to explain it," Csathamar said ruefully. "Something about the philosophers at the court of the Emperor Edrevechelar V and their influence on imperial policy. Another scholar of the first rank I talked to said that the conclusions were not particularly original and said less about lack of probity than lack of imagination."

"That's a stinging judgment," I said.

"All scholars have venomous tongues," said Csathamar. "It is one of the reasons I chose to become a judicial Witness after I completed my course of study."

"What did you study?" Tomasaran said. She sounded envious.

"Military history," said Csathamar. "I wrote a thesis on the building of the Anmur'theileian."

"Does that make you a ranked scholar?" she asked.

"No. It means I'm eligible for the *next* round of thesis-writing. If I passed that, I would be a scholar of the third rank. But I have the right to be called a scholar of the University of Amalo, if I want to get particular about it."

The University ostro was enormous, with great peaked arches and elaborate murals on the walls. It was also nearly as busy as the Dachenostro or the Amal'ostro. I was grateful again for Csathamar, for he set off at once, confidently, and Tomasaran and I had only to keep up with him in the crowds. He stopped to wait for us in front of a giant frescoed map, marked with the sigil of the Cartographers' Guild, that showed the whole University with a delicate eight-pointed star where the station was.

"Do you know where you're going?" I asked Csathamar.

"I know where the historians are," he said, and tapped a cluster of buildings directly north of the ostro. "At that point we'll have to start asking people for Osmer Rohethar."

The station's main doors were directly beside the map. We went out, and Csathamar continued to lead the way, now through clusters of students and ranked scholars. The wind was bitter, and I wished for a better overcoat than the threadbare one I had.

Yet another thing I could not even scrape zashanei for if the Amal'othala revoked my stipend.

The University was like an architect's sampler, buildings from every period going back a millennium—it was a latecomer to Amalo. No one had made any effort to harmonize the buildings, as had been done at the great University in Cetho; here they were just jumbled bewilderingly together.

Csathamar led us to a fountain, already turned off and drained for the winter, and said, "This is the Historians' Memorial. The buildings around it are the Department of History. Now we just have to find Aäthis Rohethar." He must have seen something of my feelings—lost and tired and still trying not to panic—in my face or my ears, for he said, "It shouldn't be hard. Scholars of the first rank aren't so common as all that."

He picked at random an elven scholar of the third rank who was passing the fountain, his robes billowing in the wind, and said, "I beg your pardon, but we are looking for Osmer Rohethar. Do you know where we can find him?"

Catching his cap before it could blow away, the scholar said, "His workroom is in Mavelar House," and pointed at a low rambling building to the east of the fountain. "Anyone you ask will be able to show you to it." He gave us a brusquely polite nod and continued on his way.

"Mavelar House it is," said Csathamar.

If nothing else, we would be out of the wind.

But the scholar had told us truthfully; the first person we

encountered in Mavelar House, a half-goblin student with Barizheise braids, said, "Yes, of course," and very obligingly led us
down one corridor, around a corner, down seven steps, and down
an even longer corridor to a door with a crisply engraved brass
plaque: AÄTHIS ROHETHAR, SCHOLAR OF THE FIRST RANK, HISTORY.

The student bowed and disappeared down a different corridor.
Csathamar knocked on the door and said, "Osmer Rohethar?"

"Come in!" The voice sounded surprised.

The workroom was crowded with books, more books than I'd
ever seen in one place in my entire life. There were shelves on all the
walls and books crammed on them, stacks of books on both long
tables, and more stacks of books on the floor. Some of the books
were clearly very old; one or two were tied in parcels with long blue
ribbons. Probably half the books were in Barizhin, and I saw a few
that were in languages I did not recognize.

At the far end of the room was a desk, with more piles of books, but
a clear space down the middle (which, probably not coincidentally,
was lined up with the door), so that we could see the man sitting behind it, his pen poised in the middle of a word.

He was elven, with a narrow, rabbity face and eyes of a color
somewhere between green and blue. He wore his hair in the two long
scholar's braids, plaited with red ribbons to show he was a scholar
of the first rank, and he had gold rings with red beads in his ears.
He was not wearing his robe, which was lying on a pile of books beside the desk, but wore a respectable tea-green frock coat. His silver
scholar's key was well-polished. It was obvious that what he had said
about his health was true, as I did not think the flush on his face was
from exertion.

He looked at us in blank puzzlement. I said, "We are Thara Celehar, a Witness for the Dead. You wrote to us—"

"Yes, of course!" said Osmer Rohethar, his face lighting up. "Come
in, please. Forgive us if we do not stand—we contracted borlaän when
we were a child, and it makes us abominably awkward. We wrote to
you with a question about the Hill of Werewolves."

"Yes," said Csathamar, shutting the door behind us, "but the question has become more complicated. We are Ulthora Csath-amar, the Witness for the Tomb of Hasthemis Brulnemar."

"A tomb?" said Osmer Rohethar. "We do not understand."

"We will explain," said Csathamar, and did, carefully and in detail. After a few sentences, Osmer Rohethar began jotting notes across whatever he had been working on.

When Csathamar had finished, Osmer Rohethar said, "This is all fascinating, and we thank you very much for the account of the tomb. But you cannot have come here simply to tell us this."

"No," said Csathamar. "We need someone with the knowledge to assess the tomb and its contents before Prince Orchenis decides what to do about it."

"You want *us* to . . ."

"Or to suggest someone," Csathamar said. "We knew your name because you wrote to Othala Celehar, so we started with you."

"It is the chance of a lifetime," Osmer Rohethar said, mostly to himself, "but that is farther than we have traveled in years. And from what you describe, we doubt that we will be able to *reach* the tomb, much less get inside it."

"That is a problem, yes," Csathamar said.

"We had best recommend you to someone else," Osmer Rohethar said, although it obviously pained him. "Our colleague Osmer Lisava Ormevar is nearly as knowledgeable about the reign of the Warlord Tobaris Clunethar as we are. He will be able to assess the historical value of the tomb—although we can tell you, without even seeing it, we have so little remaining from the Wolves of Anmura that it is almost certainly priceless."

"Thank you," Csathamar said.

"We will come introduce you to Ormevar," said Osmer Rohe-thar, and got to his feet, which was clearly a difficult, possibly pain-ful, effort. He took a pair of walking sticks from the stand beside his desk and limped slowly across the room. He was right; it was obvi-ous that he would not be able to manage the rough ground between the manicured paths of the Werewolf Gardens and the entrance to the tomb.

"Ormevar is just along here," said Osmer Rohethar, and led us slowly three doors down, where he stopped and knocked on a partially open door. "Ormevar?"

"What am I wrong about this time, Rohethar?" called a voice as deep and rich as any opera singer's.

Osmer Rohethar pushed the door open and said, "Nothing like that. This is Ulthora Csathamar, Witness for the Tomb of Hasthemis Brulnemar. He has offered us an opportunity we cannot make use of, and we think you are probably his next best choice."

"You slay us with your praise, Rohethar," the deep voice said dryly. "Well, come in, then, Mer Csathamar, and whoever that is with you."

Osmer Ormevar's workroom had fewer books in it than Osmer Rohethar's, although it had a tailor's dummy wearing armor that I recognized from seeing the ghosts on the Hill of Werewolves.

"And don't clump by the door like sheep," said Osmer Ormevar. "Or students. Come in properly. I even have enough chairs for everyone." He was elven, not much taller than I was, and wore his hair as Osmer Rohethar did, though he had ruby studs in both ears. His coat was a soft blue, and his scholar's key gleamed against it. His eyes were gray and very sharp. "Why in the world do you have two prelates with you?"

Csathamar stepped forward unhesitatingly and took the chair nearest Osmer Ormevar's desk. He said, "This is Othala Celehar and Othalo Tomasaran. They are Witnesses for the Dead." Tomasaran and I bowed and found chairs. Osmer Rohethar took the chair nearest the door. I noticed it had a walking stick stand beside it.

Osmer Ormevar sat down again, propped one elbow on the desk and his chin on his hand. "Your story is obviously a beauty," he said. "Tell us, please."

Csathamar told the story again. Osmer Ormevar went from mock-interested to genuinely interested very quickly; like Osmer Rohethar he took notes. When Csathamar had finished, Osmer Ormevar consulted his pocket-watch and said, "We have time to go today, if we do not dawdle. Will that suit you, Mer Csathamar?"

"Admirably," said Csathamar. "In fact, it would be of great benefit, as Prince Orchenis wants to make a decision as quickly as possible."

"Of course," said Osmer Ormevar, bounding to his feet. He took his robes from the back of his chair and shrugged into them, then picked up his cap from his desk and put it on. "We are ready when you are." He swept us all out into the hall before him, locked the door, and said, "We are sorry you cannot come, Rohethar."

"Ah well," said Osmer Rohethar. "We will count on you to tell us everything."

"Of course," said Osmer Ormevar.

We walked back through the University's strange collection of buildings to the tram station and boarded the next southbound tram. Osmer Ormevar—who proved to be as inveterate a talker as Iäna—told us a great deal about the Warlord Tobaris Clunethar and the Wolves of Anmura. Csathamar listened intently, Tomasaran politely. I tried to listen as well, but had trouble keeping my attention focused until Osmer Ormevar started talking about what little was known of Hasthemis Brulnemar. Much of it was cruelty and corruption and fit well with the revethavar as I had encountered it. But he had also apparently been a very learned man and had founded several schools, none of which outlasted the Wolves of Anmura.

"They could hardly be expected to," said Osmer Ormevar. "But if he were not remembered mostly for being the *last*, he might have been known as Hasthemis the Educator—which would have been a markedly better legacy."

He turned suddenly to me and said, "You must be the Witness Rohethar has been going on about. You've seen the ghosts of the Hill of Werewolves?"

"Yes," I said, a little taken aback that he had noticed me at all, much less connected me with the Hill of Werewolves.

"Tell me about them," said Osmer Ormevar. "How were they dressed?"

"All alike," I said, "with armor such as you have in your workroom."

He continued to pepper me with questions as we got off the tram at the nearest stop to the Hill of Werewolves and as we walked the rest of the way, which was only a matter of blocks. There were still two Brothers on duty at the gate, who let us in after due consideration of Csathamar's signet, and we walked briskly through the Werewolf Gardens, slithered down the drop-off, and followed the now very clear path to the waterway and then to the grille, where there were two more Brothers; they were singing to pass the time, and their voices broke off guiltily when we came into sight.

Csathamar showed his signet again. Osmer Ormevar considered the narrowness of the space between the grille and the stone and took off his robes and cap. "I'd best leave these here," he said, and handed them to a startled Brother. "Kindly put them somewhere they won't get dirty."

The Brothers had two big lanterns; we took them both.

※

Osmer Ormevar was fascinated by everything about the tomb: the mosaics, the friezes, the pattern of the corridors. He took notes in a tiny, precise hand; we often stopped for several minutes while he wrote. He was particularly taken with the standing wolves, crouching down between them and wishing aloud for a measuring tape.

"Wait a moment," Csathamar said, digging in his pockets. "Ha! I thought so." He pulled out a looped and tied measuring tape and tossed it to Osmer Ormevar, who caught it neatly.

"Why . . . ?" said Tomasaran.

"It's often useful," said Csathamar, "and I grew tired of never having one when I wanted it. It's an easy thing to carry about, as long as I remember to move it from one coat to another."

"What else do you have in your pockets?" Tomasaran asked.

"Notebook, pen, piece of chalk in a jeweler's bag, since it often does no good to measure things if you can't mark them, extra hairpins, a small folding knife . . ."

Osmer Ormevar measured and jotted notes for another few minutes, then stood up and returned the measuring tape to Csathamar. "I'll never manage your trick of looping it," he said.

"Don't worry about that," said Csathamar, and his agile fingers quickly had the flopping tape restored to its tidy bundle. He smiled. "I've had practice."

"Thank you for the loan," said Osmer Ormevar. "Now, I take it these wolves are guarding the entrance to the crypt, because why else would they be here?"

"Correct," said Csathamar. "The crypt is just through there."

The crypt seemed to strike Osmer Ormevar speechless for several moments. When he recovered, he paced the full circumference of the room, stopping to read occasional plaques aloud. They were the revethmerai of the praeceptors of Anmura of the Wolves. "These alone make this crypt an invaluable find," he said. He examined the skeletons, although he did not step inside their ring, and then came to the chest. "I assume you've opened this."

"We have," Csathamar said.

"I would have, too," said Osmer Ormevar, "though as a scholar I should have liked to see it in its undisturbed state. However." He opened the chest and looked inside. "Oh dear."

"That was the point at which we realized we needed a scholar," said Csathamar. "We haven't touched anything."

"Well done," said Osmer Ormevar. "These are probably very valuable, but it's a good question whether they can be salvaged. I will have to consult with my friend who works in the municipal library in the Csonena district. He knows a great deal more about the habits of paper than I do."

"This is starting to seem like that wonder-tale," said Tomasaran. "The one that ends 'the pig jumped over the stile and the old woman got home that night.'"

Csathamar laughed and said, "I don't think we need another expert before Prince Orchenis makes his decision. If he decides he wishes to make the tomb into a museum, I imagine there will be any number of experts called upon for their opinions."

"And it's all or nothing, isn't it?" said Osmer Ormevar. "We can't get the chest out of here without doing something about that grille, and I'm very dubious about the wisdom of trying to carry these books out one at a time. Although I suppose that if it came down to that, I would try it."

"You might have to work fast," Csathamar said. "The Brotherhood isn't going to post men out here indefinitely, and I imagine the head gardener would like to open the Werewolf Gardens again."

"I'm sure that's true," said Ormevar, and muttered a curse under his breath. "Well, in that case, I must take the risk of opening one—I cannot give a good opinion about what to do with the books if I don't know what they are." Very gingerly, he reached into the chest and opened one of the books on the top layer. "In ancient Amalin, as to be expected. Picks up in the middle of a sentence, so it's one in a series." He read for a few moments. "It's the chronicle of the Amaleise Wolves of Anmura. Blessed goddesses, Rohethar would give his eyeteeth to see this."

"Valuable, then," said Csathamar.

"Priceless, actually," said Osmer Ormevar, who looked a little stunned. "If Prince Orchenis decides to wall up the tomb, the entire Department of History will have to come here and try to save these books. But if possible, it would be far better to leave them here and let the scholars come to the books rather than the other way around."

"It is Prince Orchenis's decision," said Csathamar.

"But he will ask you for your opinion in making it," said Osmer Ormevar, who was watching Csathamar like a hawk watching a rabbit.

Csathamar smiled, a shade ruefully. "I will tell him I think the tomb should be preserved for study, but there is no knowing whether he will take my advice or discard it."

"Of course not," said Osmer Ormevar, but he looked satisfied.

We left the tomb just as the sun was beginning to set, returning the lanterns to the Brothers guarding the grille as we went. The journey was becoming familiar; I'd learned the trick of getting up the embankment without ruining my clothes. Equally familiar were the newspapermen waiting outside the gate. Csathamar and I both winced.

"What is it?" said Osmer Ormevar.

"Men from the newspapers," said Tomasaran. "They ask a lot of questions."

"And we *still* cannot tell them anything," said Csathamar. "Not until Prince Orchenis makes his decision. Otherwise, they'll try to make the decision for him in what they publish, which he finds extremely irritating."

"I can see that," said Osmer Ormevar. "Very well. We say nothing to the newspapermen." I thought he looked a little disappointed.

But he held his tongue, even when Vicenalar said, "A first-ranked scholar? Perhaps if you'd just tell us your specialty?"

"Mer Vicenalar," said Csathamar, "you know better than that."

"There's no harm in asking, Mer Csathamar," Vicenalar said with a flash of a smile.

"But harm in answering," said Csathamar. "Prince Orchenis would *not* be pleased."

"Afterward?" Vicenalar said hopefully.

"Afterward," said Csathamar, "with Prince Orchenis's permission, we will tell you the story."

"The *whole* story?" said Thurizar.

"As much as we can," Csathamar said prudently.

It occurred to me, as we walked back to the Amal'theileian, that there was no possibility the revethavar would stay a secret—if for no other reason than that Osmin Temin's relatives would demand an explanation of her death. I would have to tell people *something*, some story of how I defeated it.

Some story of why I was no longer a Witness for the Dead.

We did burn out, although I was young for that, and the newspapermen, at least, would find the timing suspicious. But there wasn't anything they could do to prove me wrong, and if I was no longer a Witness for the Dead, there was nothing to keep me from lying about it.

Some of the weight on my heart lifted with that thought, although surely it was wrong to be relieved at the prospect of telling lies.

We followed the winding path through the Princess Orchevëan

Gardens and into the Amal'theileian's east wing through a public entrance rather than a servant's door. I supposed Csathamar did not want to share that secret with Osmer Ormevar. Again, Csathamar knew the right person to speak to, and we were soon ushered into the Cinnabar Room, where Prince Orchenis was writing letters. He looked tired.

He said as we came in, "We hope that you have good news for us, Mer Csathamar."

"We are able to complete our report," Csathamar said.

"That is good news," Prince Orchenis said. "What is your determination?"

"Based on the assessment of Osmer Ormevar," Csathamar said with a gesture at Osmer Ormevar, who bowed, "it is our recommendation that the tomb be secured as a place of study. Osmer Ormevar says that the books are priceless."

Prince Orchenis raised his eyebrows.

"Not that they would be worth stealing," Osmer Ormevar interjected. "Even if it were possible to get them out of the tomb without damaging them, we can't imagine who would buy them. But their value to historians is immense."

"Ah," said Prince Orchenis. "Then you agree with Mer Csathamar's recommendation. What about you, Othala Celehar?"

"We know nothing of the tomb's historical value, Your Highness."

"Not that. How do you feel about leaving the tomb open?"

"The revethavar is gone," I said. "There is no danger."

Prince Orchenis held my gaze a moment, as if giving me the chance to say something, but I had nothing else to say.

Tomasaran said, "Forgive us, Your Highness, but there is also the matter of the bodies."

"The bodies," said Prince Orchenis. "Yes, of course. What about the bodies, Othalo Tomasaran?"

Tomasaran was blushing a hard red, but she said doggedly, "They must be given proper burial."

"How many of them are there?"

"Twenty-three, counting the ten in the crypt."

"We don't know if they might rise as revenants," I said. "We don't think it likely, but it is not a matter to leave uncertain."

"No, it is not," said Prince Orchenis. He considered a moment, the frown line deepening between his eyebrows, then said, "Othala Celehar, will you oblige us as a personal favor by seeing to the proper disposition of these twenty-three bodies? The principate will pay the costs."

"Yes, Your Highness," I said, for there was no way to say anything else.

"Your Highness," said Csathamar, sounding worried. "Should the matter not be given to the Ulistheileian?"

"It should," Prince Orchenis agreed, "but if we do that, it becomes a political kicking ball with all the prelates in the scrimmage, and the bodies get buried, with luck, two years hence. We trust Othala Celehar to take care of the matter quietly and expeditiously."

"We thank you for your good opinion," I said. "We will do our best to live up to it."

Prince Orchenis nodded and said, "But that still leaves us with the question of the tomb itself. Against Mer Csathamar's recommendation, we must weigh the question of cost. Leaving it open will require that it be guarded, and that cannot be left to the Brotherhood, nor have we so many personal guards that we can spare two of them daily. Thus it becomes necessary to hire guards, and it is not clear to us whence the money for that is to come."

"The University could pay for guards," Osmer Ormevar said.

Prince Orchenis's eyebrows went up. "Are you authorized to speak for the University, Osmer Ormevar?"

"No," said Osmer Ormevar, "but it is the University that would primarily benefit from the tomb being available for study. It only makes sense that the University should bear the cost."

"We do not know that the University Senate will agree with you," Prince Orchenis said dryly.

"If the Department of History votes in a block, they will," said Osmer Ormevar, "and that we *can* guarantee."

"Indeed," said Prince Orchenis. "But that is not a thing that can happen quickly."

"No," Osmer Ormevar said reluctantly. "The Faculty Senate meets only once a month, and it is generally more work than it is worth to try to call a special session."

"When did they meet last?"

"Last week," Osmer Ormevar said even more reluctantly.

"Of course," said Prince Orchenis. "Well, for three weeks, we can rearrange our guards' schedules, although our guard captain will not be pleased with us. We will not order the tomb sealed until after Osmer Ormevar has had a chance to persuade the University to take on the expense of leaving it open."

"Thank you, Your Highness," said Osmer Ormevar.

"Mer Csathamar," said Prince Orchenis. "You have discharged your duty as a Witness most honorably. And quickly. We are grateful and will remember your name in the future."

"Thank you, Your Highness," Csathamar said.

"Othala Celehar, a word with you before you go?"

"Of course, Your Highness," I said, as the others, recognizing their cue, left the room.

"Will it be a great burden on you to deal with these twenty-three bodies?" Prince Orchenis said. "The truth, please."

"It is not an easy task, Your Highness," I said.

"No. Which is another reason we do not want to hand it to the Ulistheileian. Vernezar will only botch it."

"We will consult with the prelate of Ulvanensee," I said, "for Ulvanensee may very well be able to take twenty-three bodies at once. Then the question only becomes their transportation."

"There," said Prince Orchenis. "Already you have the problem half solved." He paused, then said, "And you? Are you well?"

I understood what he meant. "No, there is no change."

"We regret to hear it," said Prince Orchenis. "Is Othalo Tomasaran prepared to take up your duties?"

"Maybe," I said.. "Those twenty-three bodies did give her a great deal of practice."

"We suppose that is true." He paused again, this time giving me a thoughtful look. "Have you spoken to the Amal'othala yet?"

I knew my ears dipped, even if I was able to keep my feelings off my face. "Not yet."

"You will have to soon."

"We must request an audience, and the Amalomeire is not as efficient as the Amal'theileian. It will take several days."

"What do you think he will do?"

"What *can* he do?" I said. "He will write to the Archprelate."

"And what will the Archprelate do?"

"We have no idea."

"Then you had best make sure Othalo Tomasaran is ready to take over your responsibilities before then." He gave me a stern stare. "Go home and sleep, Othala Celehar. You look dreadful."

"Thank you, Your Highness," I said and startled him into a smile.

"We are better at truth than at politics. But we stand by our advice. Good night, Othala Celehar."

"Good night, Your Highness," I said, and left, grateful to get out of the Cinnabar Room relatively unscathed.

Tomasaran and Csathamar were waiting for me.

"Are you all right?" said Tomasaran.

"What did the prince want?" Csathamar asked.

"To make sure that Othalo Tomasaran is ready to take up my duties."

Tomasaran said, "But I'm not!"

"No," I said, "really you are. There's very little about being a Witness for the Dead that can be taught. Most of it you have to learn as you go."

"My father was a master in the Woodworkers' Guild," said Csathamar. "He was an avid proponent of the idea that the best way to learn something was by doing it. Disregarding my miserable skills at woodworking, it is good advice. Isn't that what you've been doing all day?"

"I suppose it is," Tomasaran said after a moment's reflection. "But I'm not worried about the dead people."

I laughed, although it was a harsh sound like a dog's bark. "Any prelate of Ulis will tell you that the living are the difficult part."

They both looked at me with some concern. "*Are* you all right?" said Tomasaran. "I don't think I've ever heard you laugh before."

"I am very tired," I admitted.

"And so your guard is down," said Csathamar. "You must spend your life on guard, Othala Celehar."

A Witness's insights could often be uncomfortable. "I suppose," I said.

"Oh dear," said Csathamar. "I'm sorry. I didn't mean for that to sting."

"It's all right," I said.

Csathamar seemed unconvinced. "In any event, I should have learned by now not to attack people with my observations. I apologize."

"No harm has been done," I said.

## Ж

The cats were waiting for me when I got home, blue eyes bright with hope. I obliged them and sat for a long time petting the half-blind queen; she was in an unusually complaisant mood and purred throatily for much longer than she normally had patience with.

Then I went inside to read my post, a letter from Anora encouraging me to see Othalo Rasaltezhen as soon as possible and providing a dryly funny account of his audience with the Amal'othala, who seemed as frightened of thirty-seven adolescent girls as he was rumored to be of mice. *No immediate success,* Anora concluded philosophically, *but I will try again. Sometimes he is more receptive to an idea the second time he hears it; sometimes he gives in because he knows I am more persistent than he is. But do thou ask thy friend at the Opera, for of course the girls may not want to become servants to the clergy, and it would be best to provide them with a choice— which is more than they would have had at Osmin Temin's school, from what Balaro and Ziniän have told me.*

How had Anora met Balaro and Ziniän? It must have been at the Chapterhouse, but . . . had Azhanharad introduced them? Why would he have done such a thing?

For the obvious reason, I answered myself almost as soon as I'd asked the question. To get Anora to do exactly what Anora had done, which was interest himself in finding a good solution to the problem of thirty-seven adolescent girls with neither homes nor prospects. It was very canny of Azhanharad—more canny than I would have given him credit for. But, of course, he and Anora had known each other for years, as a subpraeceptor of the Vigilant Brotherhood in the Airmen's Quarter would have to know the prelate of Ulvanensee. Perhaps it was not a canny move so much as the relief of sharing a burden. Perhaps he felt, as I did, thankful that Anora could be trusted to find the right thing to do.

I was growing maudlin. I hung my clothes up and went to bed.

Where I dreamed of the revethavar, over and over again.

☀

In the morning, I assembled the best approximation of Othala Thara Celehar that I could and took the tram to the Amal'theileian.

Tomasaran appeared as I was unlocking my office door. "Good morning, Celehar."

"Good morning, Tomasaran. Shall we hope for a boring morning?"

"It would be a nice change."

"And I must request an audience with the Amal'othala," I said, finding paper, pen, ink, and wax.

"Oh dear. Must you?"

"He will have to know eventually. I can't fraudulently claim that stipend forever."

"But it isn't fraudulent. Just because you can't hear the dead anymore doesn't mean you aren't a Witness for the Dead."

"Doesn't it? I thought that was exactly what it meant."

"You work with the living as much as with the dead. And I can do the speaking to the dead part."

"The Amalomeire still ends up paying two people to do one person's work."

"I can't do this by myself," she said, her voice flat with incipient panic.

"Of course you can. You're a well-spoken woman. The rest of it, as Csathamar's father said, you learn by doing it."

"I'd rather learn by watching you—at least for a few more days!"

"It will take the Amalomeire two or three days to respond to my letter," I said, "and probably a week after that before the Amal'othala can see me. So in reality you still have plenty of time."

"All right," she said. "And I do understand. I just dread the thought of having to do this entirely by myself."

"The important thing is to *listen,*" I said. "To the dead *and* the living."

"You make it sound simple."

"Because it is. You know the only trick to it there is. And—oh! If you ever have to quiet a ghoul, you do it the same way you freed those spirits."

Her eyes widened with horror. "Quiet a ghoul?"

"It's unlikely to happen if you stay in Amalo—although Prince Orchenis did send me to Tanvero, so it's best to be prepared."

"Prepared to quiet a *ghoul*?"

"Better than being unprepared," I said, a little more sharply than I had intended.

"I didn't know Witnesses for the Dead had to quiet ghouls."

"Not very often." Unless one's prelacy was in Aveio, but there was no need to tell Tomasaran about Aveio. No one would send a woman there.

I dipped my pen and wrote a formal request for an audience with the Amal'othala. I did not specify the reason, knowing that the Amal'othala's post was read by several other people before it got to him.

I was reading the letter over again, trying to find anything the Amal'othala might take offense at, when there was a hesitant tap at the door. "Are you the Witness for the Dead?"

The question seemed impossible to answer with either a *yes* or a
*no*. I settled on, "You have come to the correct office. I am Othala
Celehar; this is Othalo Tomasaran. How can we help you?"

The petitioner was a young goblin woman, black-skinned with
vividly orange eyes, a manufactory worker by the look of her clothes,
which immediately raised the question of why she wasn't at work. "I
don't know that you can," she said nervously. "But my father won't
do anything but drink, and my brother's funeral is tonight."

"And your mother?"

"Died five years ago. She wouldn't put up with Poppa behaving
like this, but he won't listen to me. I'm just his daughter." She rolled
her eyes in a kind of grief-soaked frustration and then sighed so
heavily her shoulders dropped.

"Sit down," Tomasaran said kindly. The goblin woman sat down
and put her face in her hands. We waited while she composed herself.

"I'm sorry," she said. "Let me start over. My name is Danavo
Tozharharad. My oldest brother, Molinis, was murdered two days
ago, and even though we all know who did it, the Brotherhood
won't arrest him without some kind of proof."

"And you think your brother's spirit will know his murderer?"

"Of course he will," she said with a laugh that was like ashes and
salt. "It's my second brother, Mandara."

)(

The story was excruciating in its simplicity. Molinis and Mandara had hated each other from infancy, the one jealous and
the other envious, not helped by the fact that each parent had a favorite son. For Mer Tozharharad, it was his firstborn. For his wife, it
was Mandara. Always Mandara. The seven other Tozharharad children had grown up making do with what scraps of parental affec-
tion they could get, and none of them (said Min Tozharharad) could
understand why Molinis and Mandara kept perpetuating their feud,
each seeming to delight in finding new ways to infuriate the other.

"It got worse when they got old enough to be interested in girls," said Min Tozharharad, "and it got worse again when Mama died. I've known for years that one of them was going to go too far and kill the other, but I thought it was Mandara who would end up dead, not Molinis."

"And you're certain Mandara killed him," I said.

"No one else had any reason to harm Molinis," said Min Tozharharad. "No one."

"What does Mandara say?"

"That he didn't do it."

"But you don't believe him."

"He is a liar," she said flatly. "He has always been a liar."

"But it isn't proof," Tomasaran said softly.

"No, it isn't proof. Which is why I'm here."

"It is a reasonable petition," I said to Tomasaran. "Do you want to accept it?"

Tomasaran looked alarmed; Min Tozharharad looked puzzled. "Are you not the Witness for the Dead, then?"

"We are both Witnesses for the Dead," I said, deciding that it was still not quite a lie. "I am training Othalo Tomasaran as my replacement. We will both come."

"Yes," Tomasaran said. "It is a reasonable petition, and I accept it."

"Good," I said and remembered to smile at her. "Let us go talk to Molinis Tozharharad."

)(

The Tozharharad family lived in Penchelivor in a compound improvised by buying three row houses and knocking connecting doors in the walls at several crucial points. Min Tozharharad's father was, as she had said, drunk and barely grunted when we came in through the kitchen door. A goblin girl who was manifestly Min Tozharharad's younger sister said, "Mandara's locked himself in his room and refuses to speak to any of us."

"At least we know where he is," said Min Tozharharad. She gestured to us. "This way—we have Molinis in the main room."

The main room, with load-bearing pillars where one wall had been, was big enough for eleven people to be in at the same time, which the kitchen was not. Another younger sister was keeping vigil by Molinis Tozharharad's body, which lay on a long table, carefully dressed in what must have been his best clothes.

"You know how to do this," I murmured to Tomasaran, who looked perfectly composed except for her ears being down. "It's easier than trying to find a name. All you need to look for is the face of the person who killed him."

"Yes," said Tomasaran. She said the prayer of compassion for the dead and stepped forward, laying her hand gently on Molinis's cheek. She stood that way for several moments, the Tozharharad sisters watching her anxiously, then stepped back and said, "It is Mandara. Molinis saw his face clearly, and his last thoughts were of his brother."

One of the younger sisters bit back a sob. Min Tozharharad said, "Then we must take Mandara to the watchhouse. Othalo Tomasaran, will you come with us? The subpraeceptor won't believe us otherwise."

"Of course," said Tomasaran, and she and I and Min Tozharharad went up the main stairs, three flights to the attic, which had been parceled out into individual rooms for the nine children. That was a remarkable luxury, and I wondered if the Tozharharad parents had had aspirations, or if the enmity between their two eldest sons had made separate bedrooms a necessity. Min Tozharharad proceeded down the narrow hallway to the east end of the building, where sunlight was coming in through a dormered window, which had been turned ingeniously into a child's play nook. A battered pair of wooden horses showed that it was still in use.

"Mandara?" Min Tozharharad said, knocking on the door nearest the window. "Mandara? It's Danavo."

There was no answer—no noise at all—and I had a sudden horrible suspicion. "Is the door locked?"

She tried it. "Yes."

"Is there a key? Can we get in?"

She heard the urgency in my voice and said, "Yes, there's a key, but—"

"Never mind 'but,'" I said. "Where's the key?"

"In Poppa's room. I'll have to go get it."

*"Hurry,"* I said, and she took her skirts in both hands and ran back down the hall to the stairs.

"What in the world . . . ?" said Tomasaran.

"I fear I know why Mandara is so quiet," I said. "Let us pray that I am wrong."

Tomasaran's eyes widened as she grasped my meaning. *"Is* there a prayer? I mean . . ."

"No," I said. "There is no prayer that asks for the truth not to be the truth, and Ulis is not a god for hopeful prayers in any event. Pray to Csaivo that we are in time, although I doubt it."

We were both praying silently when Min Tozharharad returned, out of breath, but with a small brass key, which she used in the door of Mandara's room.

I saw at once that I was correct. We were too late.

He had hanged himself from the gas bracket—had probably done so as soon as Min Tozharharad left the house. The chair he'd used to reach it was lying on its side, kicked over either deliberately or in his last strangling agony. There was a note, left in plain view on his perfectly made bed. I picked it up and read, in a strong, jagged hand, *I do not care to wait for the Witness for the Dead to find the truth. I killed him. I am not sorry.* I gave the note to Min Tozharharad, who read it and shuddered.

"That is how much they hated each other," she said in a soft, flat voice. "What do I do now? Can we even *have* a funeral for a suicide?"

The way they'd laid out the body had told me they followed one of the cults the gold miners had brought from Barizhan more than a century ago. I said, "Yes, but make sure you bury the two of them as far apart as possible. Otherwise, there's a strong possibility they will haunt the cemetery."

"How horrible," Min Tozharharad said, and wept.

※

On our return journey from Penchelivor to the Prince Zhai-cava Building, once we were sure we were on the right tram, Tomasaran asked me, "How did you know that they could have a funeral for a suicide? I didn't think that was allowed."

"It isn't in Ploraneise custom," I said. "But they follow a Barizheise cult that is a little more forgiving."

"But how did you know *that*?"

"He was laid out in their main room, rather than at the ulimeire, and they had dressed him in his best clothes. Those aren't Ploraneise rites."

"You could tell all that just by looking at the corpse? How can you possibly say I'm ready to take your place?"

"You can do what I did and ask Othala Chanavar. And I'll teach you as much as I can."

"You keep saying being a Witness for the Dead is simple," Tomasaran said. "Do you really believe that or have you been lying to keep my spirits up?"

"It *is* simple, far simpler than the responsibilities of having a benefice. I'm sorry. I forget that you haven't really had any training."

"I really haven't," said Tomasaran.

"Go to Ulvanensee this afternoon," I said. "Othala Chanavar will be happy to help you, and he's a better teacher than I am."

"I think you do very well," she said, smiling, "but I will take any help I can find."

※

When we returned to my office—Tomasaran's office—there was a part-goblin courier waiting for us. The Amalomeire's colors. "Othala Celehar?" she said. "The Amal'othala wants to see you at once."

"At once?" I said disbelievingly. The Amal'othala never wanted to see me "at once," even when he'd summoned me.

"Those are my instructions," said the courier.

"But I can't," I said in horror. "My coat of office is still being mended."

"You can borrow mine," said Tomasaran.

"That is very kind of you," I said. "But you have a canon's coat, not a prelate's."

"It's better than your frock coat," Tomasaran said, undiplomatically but accurately.

"Will it fit?"

"Let's try," she said. She unbuttoned her coat and took it off. She was wearing an unimpeachably correct shirtwaist, with the faintest possible white-on-white pinstripe, and a plain black waistcoat with her sweeping black skirt.

I took off my rusty black frock coat and laid it carefully on the desk. Just because it was old and shabby did not mean I could afford to treat it carelessly. Then I tried on Tomasaran's coat.

It was not a terrible fit. The sleeves were a little too long and the shoulders a fraction of an inch too narrow, but I could wear it.

"Are you sure?" I said to Tomasaran.

"Yes. Don't fret about it. I can wear yours and we can trade back tomorrow. You need that coat far more than I do today."

"Thank you," I said.

The courier, who had watched all this with some sympathy, said, "If you are ready? The carriage is waiting outside."

"The Amal'othala sent a carriage?" I asked weakly and followed her out of my office and along the hall to the main staircase, which I never ordinarily used. Too many people and all of them avid for gossip.

I reminded myself that there was nothing unusual or worthy of comment in the Amal'othala summoning a prelate to the Amalomeire. That was all this was.

It wasn't, of course, but I didn't think anyone could tell. I climbed into the carriage after the courier and tried not to look nervous.

It was a long drive, almost three-quarters of the length of the city.

The courier and I did not speak. I had to make a deliberate effort not to let my hands fidget, and although I stared out the window of the carriage, I could have told an inquirer nothing about what I saw. It was almost a relief when we reached Osreian's Spur, because as nerve-wracking and physically exhausting as the stairs were, at least climbing them was an action, and they required enough careful attention that I would not have much to spare for, as Tomasaran had said, fretting.

The courier climbed with me, and we stopped about halfway up in one of the copper-roofed turrets that marked the hairpin turns. Someone, probably centuries ago, had put a bench there, and I sat down on it gratefully. The courier sat beside me, and although we still did not speak, I was nonetheless heartened not to be treated like a plague-carrier.

At the top of the stairs, an elven canon was waiting. The courier and the canon bowed to each other, and the canon said, "Othala Celehar?"

"Yes," I said.

"This way, please," said the canon. "The Amal'othala is waiting."

My heart sank even lower as I followed him down a spiral staircase into the Amalomeire. The stairs were narrow enough that I could put both hands on the walls without extending my arms, and the steps were treacherously slick. It was a relief that we did not descend very far. The Amal'othala had chosen, of the numerous audience rooms available to him, the one nearest the top. Another elven canon was standing at the entrance. The two canons bowed to each other, and both followed me into the room.

The Amal'othala was indeed waiting, seated at a lavishly carved secretary-desk that had been inset into the rock wall. As always, he was dressed in his formal robes, and his wig was elaborately wound with gold ribbon and blue lacquer beads, the same kind of beads that hung from his ears.

"There you are," he said peevishly. "What have you been doing, Celehar, that you are permitted to see Prince Orchenis at all hours of the day?"

His informants in the Amal'theileian apparently couldn't tell him everything, and I thought the word "permitted" was less accurate than the word "ordered," but rather than saying either of those things, I said cautiously, "It is a very long story."

"Then you had best start telling it," said the Amal'othala.

I told him the whole, grateful for the practice the deposition and Prince Orchenis had given me. The Amal'othala listened without interrupting, his expression growing more and more sour. When I had finished, he said, "We will have to remind Prince Orchenis that a discovered tomb falls into the Amalomeire's jurisdiction, not the principate's and certainly not the University's."

I said nothing.

"And you have lost your ability to hear the dead." He looked at me in pinch-faced exasperation. "What are we supposed to do with you?"

It was a rhetorical question, but it was also an opening. "Well, we were hoping that until Othalo Tomasaran is ready—"

"Until who?" said the Amal'othala.

"Othalo Tomasaran. The new Witness for the Dead?"

"*What* new Witness for the Dead?"

The Amal'othala and I stared at each other.

"Dach'othala Vernezar sent her to us with a letter," I said.

"*Vernezar* did? Lumanar, send someone to fetch Vernezar *at once.*"

One of the canons bowed and left the room, not quite running.

"Vernezar," said the Amal'othala, "does not have the authority to assign a prelate to a benefice, and *he* knows that, even if you don't."

"Witnessing is not a benefice," I said.

"It comes to the same thing," said the Amal'othala. "The Prelacy of Amalo is paying you exactly as we pay Othala Chanavar." I said nothing, which seemed by far safer than any answer I could think of.

"Hestamar," the Amal'othala said to the remaining canon, "find somewhere for Othala Celehar to wait. We will want to speak to him and Dach'othala Vernezar together."

"Yes, Holiness," the canon said and gestured to me. I followed him along the hall and down a short flight of stairs that dead-ended in a door. This the canon unlocked, and ushered me into a small room, starkly carved out of the rock, which contained five chairs and nothing else. We bowed to each other, and he left, shutting the door behind him.

*At least there are chairs,* I pointed out to myself and sat down. Nothing now to do but wait and hope the Amal'othala did not forget I was here.

Ж

I meditated. There had been little time and much need for it lately; although I could not quite bring myself to be grateful to the Amal'othala for the opportunity, I was not fool enough to waste it. I chose a simple prayer to Ulis in his moon aspect, which was his mildest face, and tried to sink into myself. I persevered through the Amal'othala's scowl, Tomasaran's anxiety, my own fatigue and uncertainty, but the next mental obstacle was the revethavar, and I jolted back to the reality of the barren room with five chairs.

It was destroyed. It could not hurt me. But my body was still reacting as if it could. I calmed my breathing and my heart. I tried to resume meditating, but found myself flinching away from the memory of the revethavar. *It is destroyed,* I said to myself. *It cannot hurt thee again.* But it had hurt me so grievously in that one encounter that I could not persuade myself that the memory of it was harmless.

I got up and paced the length of the room, which was no great distance, and applied a technique I had learned as a novice, imagining that each step I took wore away the fear of the revethavar a little more.

I was still pacing when the door opened and Canon Hestamar said, "The Amal'othala bids you return."

I was glad to go, to get away from my circling, endlessly twining thoughts, even though it meant an audience with both the Amal'othala and Dach'othala Vernezar.

They were shouting at each other when Canon Hestamar and I came in. Canon Lumanar looked like he wanted to cover his ears.

"You are not the only one with eyes in his head!" the Amal'othala finished furiously.

Vernezar saw me and tried to shift the tone of the argument. "It seemed too trivial to bother you with."

"A new Witness for the Dead is hardly *trivial*, given our current circumstances, which you *must* know I know."

"She begged me to help her!"

The Amal'othala's eyebrows went up. "Did she?"

"She was terrified of being sent away from Amalo for training, and I certainly couldn't promise her she wouldn't be."

"Better that she have no training at all?" said the Amal'othala.

Vernezar shot me a resentful look. "I knew Othala Celehar could be trusted to teach her what she needed to know."

I wasn't sure his confidence was well placed. The Amal'othala said, "Othala Celehar is not certified to train novices."

"Well, she isn't exactly a novice, is she?" said Vernezar. "She's an adult woman."

"A widow," I said.

"Yes, a widow," Vernezar said eagerly. "I can't put her in with a bunch of adolescents!"

"Once again," the Amal'othala said dryly, "you seem to forget that 'putting' Othalo Tomasaran anywhere was not your prerogative." He sighed heavily. "Well, what's done is done. Othala Celehar, how is Othalo Tomasaran's training proceeding?"

I wasn't sure what the Amal'othala wanted from me, so I fell back on the simple truth. "She is a Witness *vel ama* for the Dead." She had been that the first day she appeared in the Prince Zhaicava Building, but it was safer than going into what I had seen fit to call her training.

"And we need a new Witness for the Dead?" said the Amal'othala.

It was a petty piece of revenge. He already knew the answer; he was just making me say it in front of Vernezar. "Yes," I said. "We are no longer a Witness." The words felt like chains.

Vernezar said, "You aren't?"

"We have burnt out," I said, because it was basically the truth and the revethavar took too much explaining.

"Othala Celehar is too modest," said the Amal'othala, as if he was enjoying jabbing pins into me. "He defeated a revethavar."

"A *revethavar*? Those are just in wonder-tales."

"This one was quite real," I said. "It was trapped in a tomb beneath the Hill of Werewolves."

"We would say you were joking, but that seems an even more implausible tale," said Vernezar. "What will you do?"

"We know not," I said.

"*That*," said the Amal'othala with obvious satisfaction, "is a question for the Archprelate."

✕

It was well into the afternoon before I was able to escape from the Amalomeire. The first thing I did was find a zhoän and eat a bowl of split-pea soup. The second thing was find Anora. He and his prelates were involved with the registers, but he saw the expression on my face. It must have been dire, for he at once said, "You three know your work," and came over to the doorway where I was standing.

"What is amiss?" he asked, waving me into his office.

"What isn't?" I said. "The Amal'othala is writing to the Archprelate."

"Is this not a good thing?" Anora sat down behind his desk, which was a massive norezhin-wood thing that would probably still be standing here when Ulvanensee was nothing but hauntings and cobwebs. I took the other chair.

"I don't know what he's going to say. And I don't know how the Archprelate will answer, but he will probably call me back to Cetho to find something useful I can do."

"Thou canst be useful here," Anora said.

"Can I? I am no longer a Witness for the Dead. What else can I do?"

"I am sure we can think of something," Anora said. "For it is immediately obvious that thou must also write to the Archprelate."

"I must? Why?"

"Thou didst say it. We don't know what the Amal'othala was going to say. Was he very angry?"

"Infuriated," I said and told him about Tomasaran.

"Why in the world did Vernezar do such a foolish thing?" Anora said.

"*He* says she begged him to help her. *I* suspect that he saw a chance to get Amalo's Witness for the Dead—if there must be one, and Prince Orchenis's actions suggest there must—in his pocket."

"He couldn't know thou wouldst encounter a revethavar."

"No, but he knows, as we all do, that this is a temporary assignment, and it would only make sense for the Archprelate to recall me when Amalo turned up a spare Witness. And she would both owe him a favor and be easily blackmailed. Nothing binds two people closer than a secret shared."

"Yes," said Anora, "that sounds like Vernezar."

"The Amal'othala has given him penance, though I don't know what."

"*That* gossip will reach me, never fear," Anora said. "But we have wandered from the point. Thou must write to the Archprelate."

"But what's the use?"

Anora gave me a disbelieving look over his glasses. "Dost *not* want the Archprelate to hear thy version of the story the Amal'othala tells? And if thou wishest to stay in Amalo, he will not know it unless thou tellst him. *Dost* thou wish to stay in Amalo?"

"Not without some kind of purpose," I said.

"Thou art ducking the question, Thara," Anora said dryly.

I thought guiltily of Iäna. "I am comfortable here," I said. "Perhaps I should welcome change instead of fearing it."

"Perhaps thou shouldst write the Archprelate and tell him thou wishest to stay. And tell him about the revethavar and the tomb."

"That was another thing the Amal'othala was angry about," I said. "That the Amalomeire had not been consulted."

"I think the Archprelate needs to hear the story from thee," Anora said. "If thou dost not wish to plead thy case, that is thy choice. But I do not trust the Amal'othala to tell the story straight."

"I concede thy point," I said. "I do not trust the Amal'othala either."

"Wilt tell him thou wishest to stay?"

"Thou art insistent."

"Thara. I am thy friend. Of course I want thee to stay. But not if thou dost not wish to."

"I don't know," I said. "And in any event, I cannot stay if the Archprelate does not assign me something to do, for the Amal'othala is not going to keep paying my stipend."

"A good point," said Anora. "But it still does not hurt to make thy wishes known."

"I wish I knew what they were," I said ruefully. "But you are correct. I will write to the Archprelate and tell him of the revethavar. And, yes, I promise I will tell him I am comfortable here."

"Good," said Anora. "I have pen and paper here if thou likest."

"Dost fear I will not do it?"

"No, no, I trust thee. I just want to get the letter to the Archprelate as fast as we can. I know the Amal'othala's will get there first, but I would rather thine were panting on its heels than lost in the dust."

"Yes," I said. "I hadn't thought that far. I will write the letter now."

"Good," said Anora. "Use my desk. I will go hire a courier."

"A *courier*?" I stared at him. "Anora, I can't afford to pay for a courier."

"I can."

"But I can't let thee—"

"Of course thou canst."

"But why?"

"I want the Archprelate to receive the truth of how thou wert injured before he makes any decisions about what to do with thee now."

"The Archprelate would hardly—"

"We don't know what the Amal'othala will tell him, but he will almost certainly suggest that thou be called back from Amalo."

"Oh," I said and thought again of Iäna. "Well, if I cannot stop thee—"

"Thou canst not."

"I will write the letter," I said.

)(

The letter took me eight drafts, and I was not entirely satisfied even with the eighth, but Anora knocked on the door and said, "Must I wrench it from thy hands?"

"It's not . . ." But I wasn't sure what it was that the letter was not, and Anora's courier was waiting. "All right." I folded and sealed the letter and handed it to Anora.

"Good," Anora said, quite sternly, as if he expected me to argue. I said nothing.

When Anora came back, I said, "I had quite intended to ask thee about something else."

"Oh?" said Anora, and I explained about the twenty-three bodies, one of which was Osmin Temin and one of which was the last remnants of a revethavar.

"Well, the Temada must want Osmin Temin's body," Anora said.

"I don't think they've been notified," I said. "At least, I have not done so."

"Azhanharad took care of that," Anora said.

"He did?"

"I thought he told thee."

"Maybe he did," I said. "My memory of that morning is . . . not clear."

"Thou wert badly injured, even though thy body shows it not. But thou dost not need to worry about notifying the Temada."

"I must be thankful to Azhanharad," I said.

"It is his duty," said Anora.

)(

Over dinner at the Chrysanthemum with Anora and his junior prelates, Anora told me that he had managed to find suitable housing for the thirty-seven foundling girls. The fifteen thirteen-year-olds and ten fourteen-year-olds had been taken in by another foundling school, this one in Tenemora. Three of the twelve fifteen-year-olds had been able to go to the jobs they had secured for when they turned sixteen and had to leave the school. Thus, the problem was now reduced from thirty-seven girls to nine, which was, as Anora said, much more manageable, and they could be made comfortable, temporarily, in Othalo Prenevin's ulimeire. I told him Iäna had agreed to ask his wardrobe master to ask the other wardrobe masters of Amalo if they could use an apprentice, and Anora said, "I think in truth that may be our best chance. The Amal'othala is so exercised with other matters that he refused my request for a second audience."

"Oh dear," I said.

Anora shrugged. "He has thought I am a nuisance for years. This changes nothing."

Othalo Vidrezhen said, "Many of the girls do not want to work for a prelate."

"Oh?" said Anora. "They tell you what they won't tell me?"

"I'm a woman," Vidrezhen said, as if that were explanation enough. Then she smiled suddenly. "Othala Celehar, one of them wants to work for you."

"For *me*?"

"She said she doesn't know how to be a secretary, but she's sure she can learn."

"I hope you told her I have no staff," I said. "I couldn't afford staff even if I had anything for them to do."

"I did," said Vidrezhen. "She was very disappointed."

I wondered which of the girls it was, but decided asking would be foolish.

After dinner, I took the tram to the Amal'theileian and walked from there to the Torivontaram, where I was lucky enough to find Iäna at a table full of rowdy opera singers. He got up when he saw me and met me in the doorway. "Thara? What's going on? I did not think to see thee tonight."

I said, "Let us take a walk."

He assented readily and retrieved his greatcoat.

The streets of the Veren'malo were largely deserted. Iäna said, "We can walk to the Opera and admire the lights."

"What's playing there tonight?"

"Oh, I forget. Music of some kind. But tell me why thou'rt here— aside from the joy of my company, which we may take for granted."

I felt myself smiling. "I wanted to ask if thou hast had the chance to talk to your wardrobe master."

"I have, in fact," said Iäna. "Ulsheän says that our Wardrobe De-partment can take two apprentices. She says she will ask the other operas. How many girls are in need of jobs?"

"Nine," I said. "And they apparently don't favor having a prelate as their employer."

"Well, it leads to all sorts of things," Iäna said. "I can name five comic operas in which the greatest obstacle to young love is the ingenue's prelate employer. And that's without stopping to think. There are *dozens*. And then there's *Civulano*, where the prelate rapes the poor girl and then kicks her out for being pregnant."

I thought with a pang of Isreän, who had probably only pre-empted being fired by throwing herself in the Mich'maika. "Does she commit suicide at the end?"

"She does," said Iäna. "It's a brilliant opera, but no one ever per-forms it because the lead is a servant girl."

"Like a manufactory worker?"

"Quite, only a little less scandalous because of course *comic* operas have servant girls all over them. Ebrezhanar just switched genres. Many people actually object quite strongly to *Civulano*— we've never performed it, but I can't think why."

"Something for next year?"

"Yes, perhaps." He gave me a sidelong look. "But thy nine found-ling girls cannot be the only reason thou hast sought me out."

"No," I said and explained about my audience with the Amal'othala and the likelihood that I would be recalled to Cetho.

"Is it a certainty?"

"No, but only because I can't predict what the Archprelate will do. It *is* a certainty that the Amal'othala will tell him there's no use for me here if I'm not a Witness for the Dead."

"The Amal'othala does not like thee?" Iäna hazarded.

"No, he does not. He has always disliked the fact that, technically, I work for the Archprelate, not the Amalomeire, but it is the Amalomeire that has to pay me."

"I can see his point."

"Oh, yes, so can I. But the Archprelate was very firm that the Archprelacy of Cetho could not pay me to work in the Prelacy of Amalo. Apparently there are all sorts of precedent cases in which things became so muddled that the prelate never got paid. Thus, although I regret that I have never been able to improve the Amal'othala's opinion of me, I am quite grateful for the decision."

"But what wilt thou do?"

"Whatever the Archprelate decides," I said helplessly. "I am a prelate. I must go where he tells me."

"Needst thou be a prelate?" said Iäna.

It was lucky the street was deserted, for I stopped in the middle of the sidewalk and stared at him.

"I put that badly," said Iäna. "But if thou art no longer a Witness *vel ama* for the Dead, art thou necessarily still a prelate? Art thou necessarily *not* a Witness, for that matter? Most Witnesses cannot speak to the dead, either."

"I am not a judicial Witness," I said. "I'm not qualified." I started walking again. "And if I have no ability to speak for the speechless, I am no use as a clerical Witness, either."

"Most clerical Witnesses are not Witnesses *vel ama*."

"They're also sorely out of fashion. Even here in Amalo. People came to me because I am—was—a Witness *vel ama*, not because I was a clerical Witness."

"All right," said Iäna. "I will trust your knowledge on that point. But thou art still qualified to be a prelate."

"I don't want a benefice," I said, and admitting it aloud was a surprising relief. "I have tried that, and it did not go well. But thou art correct; there are still many ways in which I can be useful as a prelate, and I cannot think of any way I can be useful if I am not."

"Is that your criterion? Usefulness?"

"I must do *something*," I said. "I spent some months at the Untheileneise Court doing nothing and I cannot face that again."

"Thou couldst work for the Opera."

"It is a kind thought, but I do not think I could bear to work with so many *people*."

He laughed. "Thou art honest."

I said, "My friend Anora has browbeaten me into writing to the Archprelate myself, and I did tell him that I would like to stay in Amalo."

"Good."

"But it may not be possible."

"No, I understand. Thou must do as thy patron tells thee."

I started to object that the Archprelate was not my patron, but on second thought, I saw Iäna's analogy. "I am sorry," I said.

"Why art thou sorry? It is no doing of thine."

"There's no one else alive to blame," I said wryly.

"Then let the blame rest with Osmin Temin, where it belongs."

"I keep thinking that there must have been something else I could have done. Something better."

"Sometimes there isn't," Iäna said simply.

We started walking again, but we were silent the rest of the way to the Vermilion Opera.

ᚷ

In the middle of that mostly sleepless night, I realized I had forgotten to give Tomasaran the keys to her own office.

X

I n the morning I went back to the Prince Zhaicava Building, beat-
ing Tomasaran there by almost two minutes. We traded back
coats, and I handed her the office key.

"That's yours," she said.

"You're the Witness for the Dead. It will do no one any good if a
petitioner comes and finds you waiting in the hall."

"I suppose not."

"And I must warn you that you will probably be summoned before the Amal'othala. He is unhappy."

Her ears dropped in obvious dismay. "I thought . . ."

"Dach'othala Vernezar is in more trouble than you are," I said,
wondering if that was a comfort or not. "But why were you so desperate not to leave Amalo?"

"This is already farther from home than I've ever been," said Tomasaran. "And at least here I *can* go back and see my child and my
sisters occasionally. Dach'othala Vernezar said I might be sent to
Cetho for training."

How cunning of Vernezar. I said, "You'd probably be sent to
Ezho, but you could be sent anywhere to serve as a junior prelate."

"And it just seemed . . . you were here, and I'm only a prelate because I'm a Witness for the Dead anyway."

"A situation which would change if you had proper training," I
said. "I'm sorry, I should have inquired more deeply into how you
ended up in my office, but I assumed Vernezar had consulted with
the Amal'othala before sending you to me."

"I didn't think the Amal'othala would care."

"Oh, he doesn't. Except about the fact that Vernezar didn't have
the right to decide what you should do. He's jealous of his preroga-
tives, not interested in his prelates."

"I don't think I have ever heard you say something that harsh
about anyone."

"I am . . ." I sighed. "I am out of charity with the Amal'othala. But I should not have said that."

"Do you think I'll be sent to Ezho?"

"Not now," I said. "If Amalo is to have an unbeneficed Witness for the Dead, it has to be you."

"I still think you should stay Witness for the Dead."

"I can't," I said. "Besides, the Amal'othala has already written to the Archprelate."

"Oh no!" said Tomasaran. "What will happen to you?"

"I don't know. It depends on what use the Archprelate has for me."

"But you could be sent *anywhere*."

"Yes," I said. "I could."

After that, we did not speak for a long time, until one of the building clerks came by with the messages from the pneumatic tube system that linked all the government buildings to the Amal'theileian. There was only occasionally something for me; today, there was word that Lord Judiciar Erimar had decided in the case of Esmeän Tativin.

The story had been clear, both from my deposition and from Witness Parmorin's; thus, the judiciar found her guilty and sentenced her to die. She could afford no lawyer to speak for her, but it most probably would not have made a difference. She confessed to the murder, and her reasons were not such that they could be claimed as mitigation, as sometimes happened in the cases of blackmail victims who killed their blackmailers. (Tura Olora might have gotten a lesser sentence than death, if he had tried.) Osmin Tativin would be executed in one week.

Tomasaran said, "Does it bother you when your witnessing leads to an execution?"

"Yes," I said, "but it is not preferable that a guilty person should escape punishment."

"No," she said, although she sounded a little uncertain.

"Osmin Tativin should not be allowed to get away with murder—and a selfish, pointless murder at that."

"Oh, no, I didn't mean that at all," said Tomasaran. "I was just wondering."

"It is not an easy thing to live with," I said, thinking as always of Evru, "but justice is important, or else why have a government?"

"Is that the purpose of government? Justice?"

"It is *a* purpose of government, but without it, no government can function honestly."

"And so Osmin Tativin must die."

"She is not a sacrificial animal," I said impatiently. "She is a murderer." As Evru was, and I had not spoken out for him.

"Yes, but . . ."

"But what?"

"Nothing, although I do think the marquise might have tried to help her."

"She might have," I said, "if Osmin Tativin hadn't murdered her first."

"You are harsh," Tomasaran said, surprised.

I was a little surprised myself, but also trying not to look at the door for fear I would see Evru smiling at me from the hallway. I said, "I cannot disavow what I have said. Osmin Tativin is a murderer and deserves death."

"You are *very* harsh," Tomasaran said, now almost disapproving.

"The case is a straightforward one." As Evru's had been.

"Yes, but—"

"What bothers you? Is it that she's a woman?"

"No," said Tomasaran. "I don't disagree with you. I suppose I just wish it could be different."

"Yes," I said. The hallway was empty. "So do I."

※

That afternoon, I took the tram out to the University and found Osmer Rohethar's workroom. He was surprised to see me. I said, "We never told you about the ghosts."

"The ghosts! Of course! Please just stack books on the floor until you find a seat. It's the only way."

I moved a five-volume set of books in Barizhin off the chair in front of Osmer Rohethar's desk and sat down. Osmer Rohethar meanwhile dug through his desk drawers until he found a notebook with some blank pages remaining in it, then said, "Please tell me everything you remember."

I pretended I was giving a deposition, perhaps witnessing for the stones of the Hill of Werewolves, and did my best. Osmer Rohethar listened with great care. He did not ask questions until I was done, but then had a dozen he'd written down while I spoke. We were still involved in discussing the ghost I'd seen of the Ulineise prelate being dragged to his death when there was a perfunctory knock at the door and Osmer Ormevar burst in and strode up to the desk.

"Rohethar! We did it!"

"Did what?" said Osmer Rohethar.

"The tomb!" crowed Osmer Ormevar. "The prince is going to let us study it."

"I thought that had to wait for the University Senate to meet," said Osmer Rohethar.

"Well," said Osmer Ormevar. "I may have gotten around that by talking to Udrichalar."

"Udrichalar can't agree to that sort of thing unilaterally."

"No, but he can talk to Trivonezh and secure funding."

"It still has to go to a vote."

"By the time the Senate meets, the vote will be in favor."

"You have been very busy," said Osmer Rohethar.

"And it's one in the eye for the Amalomeire," said Osmer Ormevar with great satisfaction. "Orchenis refused to believe that they had more right to the tomb than we did, especially since they weren't willing to pay for guards. Oh, hello, Othala Celehar! Sorry. I didn't mean to sound so gratified by the discomfiture of the prelacy."

I said, "Are you just going to have the entrance guarded forever?"

"Not ideally," said Osmer Ormevar. "We just need to design something that can make that grille impassable—but that can be removed to allow entry."

"Like a door?" Osmer Rohethar asked dryly.

"Well, yes, essentially. Oh, bother you, Rohethar. You know what I mean."

"Not at all," said Osmer Rohethar, and they both laughed.

"Othala Celehar must think we are madmen," said Osmer Ormevar. "But that reminds me. The bodies. Have you worked out what is to become of them?"

"They will be buried properly in Ulvanensee," I said. "The junior prelates will transport them once they have permission to enter the tomb. But we were not sure whom to ask."

"That *is* a good question," said Osmer Ormevar. "But as of today, the answer is me. Rohethar, have you a blank half sheet?"

Osmer Rohethar wordlessly tore a sheet out of his notebook and handed it and his pen to Osmer Ormevar.

"You are kindness itself. You must have a stick of wax somewhere."

"Of course," said Osmer Rohethar.

Osmer Ormevar cleared a space on Osmer Rohethar's desk and bent to write a paragraph-worth of words in a lovely, lyrical hand. He took the wax Osmer Rohethar offered, heated it with his lighter, and then planted his signet firmly at the bottom of the page.

"There," he said, folding the paper in half, and gave it to me. "They can show that to anyone they need to."

"Thank you," I said. "I will give this to Othala Chanavar tonight."

"Good," said Osmer Ormevar. "And I still need to talk to my friend at the municipal library. I'll see you at dinner, Rohethar." And he strode out as abruptly as he had stridden in.

✕

On the way from the University to Ulvanensee, I bought copies of all three of Amalo's newspapers and read them carefully. It had been difficult, when Goronezh and the other newspapermen had cornered me, not to tell them too much, but while the papers had a great deal of speculation about the contents and history of the tomb, they did not mention there being a revethavar at all, and I was referred to only as the Witness for the Dead—they had been more interested in Tomasaran than in me, and she had gotten a good, swift lesson in how to fend the newspapermen off one's private life.

In Ulvanensee, I found Anora alone, engaged in weeding the flagstoned courtyard. "Thara!" he said, getting to his feet. "I was hoping to see thee today."

"Hast thou news, then?"

"I do. I have spoken to Osmin Temin's uncle."

"And?"

"They want nothing to do with her."

"Even in burial?"

"Her uncle said he had disowned her ten years ago and saw no reason to change his mind."

"That is very harsh."

"From what you have told me of the woman, it is entirely warranted," said Anora. "In any event, it relieves us of one problem: she can be buried with the other twenty-two bodies and no one will object."

"Yes, and I have a paper from Osmer Ormevar so that your junior prelates can go collect the bodies." I handed Anora the paper; he glanced at it and nodded approval.

"I'll have them start tomorrow morning. And we'll have to see about coffins."

"They could go straight to the revethmerai, I think. There wasn't much left but bones and cloth. Except for Osmin Temin, of course."

"They should spend at least a season in reveth'osrel," said Anora. "At least, if it were one of *my* relatives, I would want that."

"Prince Orchenis would probably pay for the coffins," I said.

"Oh, I'll be submitting a list of all our expenses," Anora said. "The principate may not agree to all of them, but at least I will have asked. In general, Prince Orchenis is very reasonable about paying incidental costs. *Unlike* his father. You had to fight for every zashan with Prince Orchena." He gave me an assessing glance and said, "Thou lookst tired and sad. Come with me and have koshvolot."

Koshvolot was a kind of dumpling soup, made only by the goblins of the Mervarnens, and Anora knew I had a weakness for it. "Thy argument is a compelling one," I said. "Koshvolot it is."

)(

When I got home, there was a letter from Azhanharad in the post. I opened it warily and reluctantly, but it said only: *We have some information that might be of interest to you about the murder of the foundling Tedoro. You will find us at the River-Cat tonight.*

I was aware of a desire to curse him, aware also that this reaction was inappropriate and uncharacteristic. He was offering me a favor which he was in no wise obligated to offer, but it felt like he was hounding me.

I stared at the letter for a long time before I was able to admit why. Azhanharad had seen me in the aftermath of the revethavar, when I had been weakened and hurt. Azhanharad knew the whole story. Azhanharad *knew,* and I cringed away from the thought of facing him.

I didn't have to face him, a sly and wheedling voice pointed out. I was no longer a Witness for the Dead. My business with Azhanharad was finished. But that was pure cowardice, and he was right. I *was* interested in information about Tedoro's murder. I heaved a sigh and set out for the River-Cat.

)(

I found Azhanharad in a back corner booth, frowning at a copy of the *Arbiter*. He transferred the frown to me as I came up to the table and stood up. "Othala Celehar."

"Subpraeceptor."

"This is a good place to meet, but a bad place to talk. Will you walk with us?"

"Of course," I said.

We walked in silence for several blocks, until we came to one of the tiny cemeteries that dotted the Airmen's Quarter. Here, surrounded by the silent dead, Azhanharad stopped. "We have had some very enlightening conversations with Horthena Renthalar."

"The murderer."

"Yes. His desire seems to be to get as many people in as much trouble as possible. If Osmin Temin weren't already dead, she would be executed."

"Yes." That had been a given since the moment she told me she had ordered Tedoro's murder.

"But what Horthena Renthalar has told us about the arrangement is very interesting. The photographer is his brother, Anvina Renthalar."

That part made sense, but . . . "How did he become involved with the school?"

"He—the photographer—was Osmin Temin's lover."

"He was *what*?"

"He was her lover first, and they came up with this terrible scheme together," said Azhanharad.

I said, "She didn't seem like the kind of woman who would do that." She had seemed much more like the kind of woman who would have an illicit relationship with one of the teachers at her school.

"Renthalar has no reason to lie."

"She must not have objected very much to Mer Renthalar's plans for her students."

"No, she didn't. From what Renthalar tells us she didn't object to anything that promised to bring in money."

"Why did it take so long for one of the girls to seek help?"

"Firstly, they were told that they would go to prison if anyone found out. Secondly, who were they to tell? Osmin Temin suborned their teachers, and we believe there were bribes paid to the othas'ala, although as of yet we cannot prove it."

"They had no one to turn to."

"No," said Azhanharad. "And they knew that all Osmin Temin had to do was deny the accusation. Subpraeceptor Mobrasar would certainly believe her word over the claims of a bunch of foundlings."

"Yes," I said, for that was true. "And thus Tedoro took a chance."

"Yes. One of the other girls said that Tedoro thought any Witness was better than none. Which turned out to be correct."

"Too late for Tedoro, though. We suppose that now we will never find out why Osmin Temin wanted her murdered."

"From what the other girls told us, Tedoro was unwise enough to say aloud that once she was free of the school, she would go to a judicial Witness, and she was due to leave in a matter of weeks. Someone told Osmin Temin what Tedoro had said, and Osmin Temin decided it was a risk she was unwilling to take."

"What a horrible person," I said.

"Yes," said Azhanharad.

"What will happen to the other teachers?"

"Merrem Caltavezharan will be dealt with leniently, for it is clear that, although she knew the truth, she was intimidated and bullied into silence—threatened with the loss of her job, and she is a widow with two small children. Min Tesavin, on the other hand, swears, through floods of tears, that she had no idea what was going on."

"Do you believe her?"

"No," said Azhanharad. "We think she found it more convenient to be blind and therefore did not see. But it is, of course, very difficult to prove, and she will probably be let off with a fine."

"And Min Orbelin?"

"Min Orbelin was taking her share of the proceeds. She is as guilty as Osmin Temin and the Renthalar brothers, and will be sent to Esdravee. How long will depend on how Prince Orchenis feels about the matter. He is unlikely to be sympathetic."

"Good," I said.

Azhanharad raised his eyebrows.

"We have our own feelings on the subject," I said.

"Of course."

"We are witnessing for Tedoro," I said. "Is there anything else we should know before we make our deposition?"

"She was murdered by Horthena Renthalar," said Azhanharad. "He has confessed it to his Witness, and also that he was ordered to kill her by Osmin Temin. The circumstances of her murder are very clear."

"Justice will be done," I agreed.

"As best we can. Osmin Temin escaped us."

I shuddered at the memory of Osmin Temin's death. "You need not worry," I said. "Her death was ugly enough to satisfy the most bloodthirsty of judiciars."

"It was an ugly murder."

"Yes."

He scowled at me suddenly and demanded, "Are you well?"

"We are quite well, thank you," I said.

His scowl deepened, and he said stiffly, as if I had offended him, "You were not, the last time we saw you."

My face heated. I said, equally stiffly, "We assure you, we are well."

He gave me an uncomfortably sharp look. "Are you a Witness for the Dead?"

"Tedoro is the last," I said reluctantly.

"And you are well?"

"We are as well as we can be."

"It is all any of us can do," Azhanharad said, almost sounding sympathetic.

"Is there anything else, Subpraeceptor?" I said briskly.

"No, we do not . . . Wait. There was one thing. We found Isreän's employer."

"You did? How?"

"He came asking about bodies pulled out of the Mich'maika. Quite a bit too late, as it happens."

"But why? He did not care for her."

"Apparently," said Azhanharad, "he had begun having dreams. He went to his prelate, and his prelate told him he owed it to her to find out what had happened to her, and advised him to ask us. So now he knows that he drove the poor girl to suicide." Anticipating my next question, he added, "There was nothing we could do. He had done nothing illegal—or at least nothing illegal we could prove, although we are *not* convinced he is innocent of rape."

"She did not remember it as rape," I said, "but we doubt she had much choice in the matter."

"Nothing we could prove," Azhanharad repeated. "But he'll be seeking help at Ulvanensee soon enough, for we cannot rid him of his dreams."

"No," I said. "There may not be anything Othala Chanavar can do, either. Dreams do not come and go at anyone's bidding."

"No," said Azhanharad with grim satisfaction. "They do not."

)(

In the morning, after making my deposition concerning Tedoro's murder, I went to the Prince Zhaicava Building and talked about funeral practices with Tomasaran. No petitioners interrupted us, and at noon she said, "Come to lunch at the boardinghouse. Vinsu and Aunt Rhadeän keep asking after you."

I couldn't pretend I had other business—Tomasaran would know I was lying. I consented, and we made the long journey from the Prince Zhaicava Building to the boardinghouse. It was getting too cold for Min Nadin to sit on the porch, but she saw us from the front window and waved.

The front rooms on the house's ground floor were a pair of sitting rooms, each with double doors opening onto the hall. Min Nadin had taken over one room with the quilt she was piecing. In the other, an elderly elven man was gravely reading the *Arbiter* front to back.

Merrem Nadaran emerged from the kitchen to say, "Lunch is almost ready. Oh, hello, Othala Celehar. I'm so pleased you could come. Velhiro, wilt thou help Aunt Rhadeän with the quilt? It really shouldn't be left lying on the floor."

"Of course," said Tomasaran. I went with her and between the two of us we managed to get the quilt confined to one sofa. It was a beautiful thing, a pinwheel-like swirl of tiny triangles all the colors one could dye a piece of cloth.

"I only do this one once every five years or so," said Min Nadin. "That's long enough that I forget how fiddly it is."

"It is very beautiful," I said.

"That's why I do it once every five years," said Min Nadin.

We went in to lunch together, in the long dining room where three tables had been pushed together to make one.

"At dinner, when everyone's here, we need this much space," said Merrem Nadaran, "although it looks a little silly now. Come sit down at this end and I'll cut the tart." She had made an egg tart big enough to feed an army. As she was carving slices and handing them around, a part-goblin woman, middle-aged and plain, came in and said, "Hello, my darlings! I have the good gossip today."

"Hello, Camilo," said Min Nadin. "What hast thou heard?"

"The Marquess Ulzhavel has committed suicide."

Tomasaran and I both startled. "Are you sure, Lethormin?" said Tomasaran.

"Oh, yes," said Min Lethormin. "It's his heir who brought the news to the Amal'theileian, trying to find out how to get probate expedited. The poor old man made hezhelta tea and drank a toast to his wife's portrait. He was dead before any of the servants even knew what was going on."

"How horrible," said Merrem Nadaran.

"But why?" said Tomasaran.

"He left a letter," said Min Lethormin. "The new marquess was waving it at everyone he talked to. The old marquess said that without his wife, he found nothing worthwhile in living. He waited long enough to be sure that her murderer would be executed, but he saw no reason to wait any longer."

"Grief," said Tomasaran.

"Grief," agreed Min Lethormin. She sat down beside me and said, "I don't think we've met. I'm Camilo Lethormin. I'm a clerk in the Amal'theileian and hear everything."

I thought of Min Talenin and Merrem Bechevaran in the cartographers' office and did not doubt her. "I am Thara Celehar," I said and stopped the reflexive, *a Witness for the Dead.* "A . . . a prelate of Ulis."

"You must be a friend of Tomasaran's," said Min Lethormin. "No, wait. I do recognize that name. You're the Witness for the Dead."

I froze for a moment, and Tomasaran said, "Othala Celehar is taking a sabbatical."

"Leaving you in charge?" said Min Lethormin.

Tomasaran hesitated, but then said, "Yes," firmly.

Merrem Nadaran's egg tart was excellent, and lunch turned out to be quite pleasant. Min Lethormin was a vividly engaging story-teller and did most of the talking. I was grateful to escape question-ing about my "sabbatical." I thought Min Nadin had guessed there was something more to the story, but she was kind enough not to ask in Min Lethormin's presence.

From the boardinghouse, I returned to the Veren'malo and walked to the Vermilion Opera. Iäna would be in rehearsal, of course, but I was hopeful that he could spare me a minute.

The goblin woman sweeping the lobby smiled at me and I nodded back. In the auditorium, I heard Iäna's voice before I saw him. He was explaining to the chorus how he wanted them to stand—this had to be a rehearsal for *The Dream of the Empress Corivero,* for there seemed to be some confusion between the Chorus of Roses and the Chorus of Rooks.

I came down the aisle, and one of the chorus members said alertly, "There's Othala Celehar."

"Celehar?" Iäna said, emerging from the wings. "Oh, hello! Here to see me?"

"If you have a moment," I said.

"I do," he said, "for I think perhaps all of us could use a break. You stay there—I'll come to you." He came downstage and crossed the plank that acted as a bridge between the stage and the audi-torium.

"We can go elsewhere," he said as he reached me. "The third-floor boxes are private enough—it's frequently a consideration when one works with people as temperamentally nosy as opera singers."

"All right," I said. We went out to the foyer and started climbing stairs.

Iäna said, "Thy foundling girls have all been snapped up by the city's wardrobe masters."

"I am pleased to hear it," I said. It was one less thing to worry about in the middle of the night.

"Ulsheän is delighted. She took two girls. One of them she says should be apprenticed to an embroiderist and the other one does invisible mending that is truly invisible."

"A rare talent," I said.

"*Horribly* rare," said Iäna. "She'll have work to keep her busy, considering some of the graceless oxen in my chorus." He sighed and opened the door of the nearest box. "This is as good as any of them."

The box was dark except for the distant glow of the footlights. Iäna said, "I apologize for the accommodations, but I thought thou wouldst prefer to be private."

"I would, yes," I said. "Will there be any trouble with the Opera taking on the two girls?"

"Trouble?"

"With the Marquess Parzhadel."

"I see thy point. Yes, I'll have to explain the new expenditures to him. I can never tell whether he views the Opera as a business venture or a very expensive hobby, but he is stringent about knowing where each zashan goes."

"The marquess seems rather terrifying," I said.

"Oh, he is!" said Iäna. "Decorous and very calm and utterly ruthless. I find him baffling, to tell the truth. He seems the *last* person who would support an opera company, especially when he can't attend himself. But he's never *actually* balked when we needed money."

"Does he never attend?"

"I have been told he cannot leave his bed," said Iäna, "and certainly I have never seen him anywhere else. It must be profoundly boring."

"Perhaps that's why he supports the Opera," I said. "Vicarious excitement is better than none at all."

"Perhaps," said Iäna. "But here I've been nattering on and haven't even asked thee the reason for thy visit. Is there something I can do for thee?"

"Thou didst wish to hear the rest of the story of the murder of the Marquise Ulzhavel," I said, "and I have just heard that the marquess has committed suicide."

"*Suicide?*"

"For grief," I said. "I think he could not bear knowing that she had been killed for such a petty reason."

"Thara," said Iäna. "Stop and tell the story the right way around."

"Yes, of course." I explained about the photographs and the marquise's discomfiture and the terrible price she paid for learning Min Tativin's secret.

"But she achieved nothing by killing the marquise," said Iäna. "She was still out of a job."

"I don't think she thought the matter through. I think she panicked, and maybe it was revenge as well. She did not *seem* angry, but she very well may have been at the time."

"And so the marquise is dead, the marquess is dead, and Min Tativin will be executed within the week. What's become of the pictures?"

"I have them," I said. "I know where they came from, for Mer Nathomar could identify the photographer, but I have no idea how they reached the marquise. Well, no, that's not quite accurate. They reached the marquise via a steward of the Amal'theileian, but I don't know who purchased them from Mer Renthalar."

"Renthalar!" said Iäna. "Isn't that the name of the man who murdered the foundling girl?"

"His brother. Dost think the two are connected?"

"I think it unlikely that they are not. Thou wert seeking Osmin Temin originally because of the murder of the marquise, wert thou not?"

"Well, yes, but—"

"And thou knowest that she knew the Renthalada."

"She was having an affair with Anvina Renthalar," I said, remembering what Azhanharad had told me.

"And somehow a woman she bore a grudge against was embarrassed in public by some of Mer Renthalar's photographs? I think it unlikely that this is a coincidence."

The jagged edges suddenly meshed together. "The photographs were sent to the marquise by a well-dressed elven woman. Which could probably describe half Amalo, but *does* describe Osmin Temin. And she's the thing the two stories have in common. I can't at this point prove she was ever in Mer Renthalar's studio, but she could have been, and she was certainly the sort of person who would send distressing and pornographic pictures to an elderly lady purely in order to cause trouble."

"May we all be so successful in our endeavors as Osmin Temin was in causing trouble," Iäna said dryly. He hesitated. "Art thou any better?"

"Can I hear the dead, dost mean? No. There is no change."

"What wilt thou do?"

"That is for the Archprelate to decide. I have written to him, but I do not know when I will hear back."

"And yet thou'rt still sane! I'm not sure I would be."

"Sometimes insanity is tempting," I admitted.

In the dark, Iäna's hand found mine, and we sat for a while in silence, until I dredged together enough fortitude to say, "I am keeping thee from thy rehearsal. I should go."

"As long as thou com'st back," said Iäna.

X

I walked to the Dachenostro and took the Zulnicho line to Ulvanensee, where Anora and his prelates were organizing the burials of twenty-three people. The headstones weren't ready, of course, but Vidrezhen and Erlenar had made temporary ones out of wood, and there was little chance of a ghoul rising in Ulvanensee. Anora kept the grounds too carefully, and the cemetery was surrounded on all sides by the city, with living people coming and going almost constantly. Bad territory for ghouls, which liked solitude and disrepair.

Anora stopped what he was doing and said, "Thara! An answer to thy letter has come!"

"It hasn't been long enough," I protested.

"I had him go by airship," said Anora.

"*Airship?* Anora, that must have cost—"

"Hush, Thara. It cost no more than I can afford. And it was well worth the money, for the Amal'othala's courier and mine traveled together."

"So the Archprelate got both letters—"

"Essentially at the same time, yes. But here. Open it!"

I eyed the letter Anora was holding out. I did not want to read it, because whatever it said was the end. I would *officially* no longer be a Witness for the Dead.

"Thara," said Anora.

"I know," I said and took the letter. I broke the seal and opened it, my eyes already skimming past the greeting. *We are saddened to learn of your wounding,* wrote the Archprelate, *and will hope that your ability will return to you with time. In the meantime, we have an assignment in Amalo that is uniquely suited to your abilities. It is one about which we feel a certain amount of impatience and thus would be most grateful for your assistance in resolving. The courier is waiting for this letter, so we will send you the details under separate cover, but please do not fear. You are a loyal servant to the prelacy and the empire, and we will not reward your loyalty with abandonment. Have courage.* And then the elaborate near-sigil he made of his signature.

I stared blankly at the letter for a moment, but Anora was waiting impatiently and I could see that his junior prelates were all listening.

"Well?" Anora said.

"It's all right," I said, and finally let myself smile. "I can stay."

※

The Orshaneisei seemed mildly surprised that I had come out to walk their corn maze in the absence of corn—again—but they did not mind. One of the sisters guided me through the compound and left me on the back porch with a reminder to be out of the maze by sundown. She added, smiling, "I hope you will stay to share a meal with us," and went back inside; I started along the pebble-outlined path to the maze.

This time I had to remind myself not to hurry. The point was not to finish the maze, but to walk it. I had made only three twists of the maze when I was overcome by a wave of grief so intense that I had to stop walking lest I stumble off the path. At first, I couldn't even tell what I grieved *for*. I pressed my hands to my face and concentrated on breathing deeply and evenly, and eventually, like a swimmer in an alien sea, I managed to get my head above water and to make better sense of what I felt.

I acknowledged the old weight of grief for Evru and set it aside. Grief for the stone-faced Marquess Ulzhavel and for his wife and their love that had lasted fifty years only to be destroyed by a foolish and desperate panic. Grief for Tedoro, who had come so close to freeing herself from Osmin Temin. Grief for Isreän and for Merrem Pel-Venna's stillborn child. Grief weighted upon grief like a pile of stones and at the bottom, a stone with a flaying edge, the unceasing grief for myself, a Witness for the Dead who could no longer witness.

I had thought my calling lost once before and been wrong, but I could not count on being wrong twice. Ulis was not a god of miracles.

*This is rank self-pity,* I said to myself, blinking tears away from my burning eyes. *Really, Celehar.* But the weight of grief would not be denied, self-pity or otherwise, and it was some uncounted length of time before I was able to start walking again.

The *Grief of Stones* was the shipwreck in Iäna's opera, and I felt like a shipwreck, weighted too heavily with grief to stay afloat. Moreover, I knew the old wonder-tale from which the phrase came. To win the hand of the princess, the young man had to do three increasingly impossible things, the last of which was to learn the grief of stones. He went to the castle's great defensive wall at midnight and dripped three drops of his own blood on a stone of the foundation.

The grief of the stones was grief for every man killed in the building of the wall, for every man who died defending or attacking, for every man executed by being thrown off the battlements. "But those are our worst criminals!" the king protests, and the young man says, "That doesn't matter to the stones."

There were different endings to the story. In one, the young man marries the princess and becomes the most just and merciful king in the history of the kingdom. In another, the young man refuses the hand of the princess, for learning the grief of the stones has made him think twice about his ambition, and instead becomes a prelate of Ulis.

*That* was a little too close to the bone. I stopped and evened out my breathing again. It was no use denying the grief I felt for the loss of my ability, an ability I'd thought about no more than I thought about the use of my hands, and it was not a grief I could chide myself out of like a spoilt child denied a treat. The loss was real.

I kept walking and gradually felt a sort of equilibrium returning, as if I'd shed some measure of the weight simply by acknowledging it was there. It was not, after all, so heavy that I could not carry it, and while it was unwise to hope the damage might miraculously be repaired, it was also unwise to forget that I had thought myself destroyed once before and been wrong.

I was surprised to reach the middle of the maze. I took a pebble from the bowl of tokens and put it in my inner waistcoat pocket with the token I'd found in Tedoro's clothes and still did not know the meaning of.

And I probably never *would* know its significance, for I could not ask Tedoro. She was dead and I was deafened.

I walked the second half of the maze more mindfully, aware now of the cold, of the broad sweep of the cornfield around me, of every careful twisting step of my path. Nothing was resolved or changed, and the memory of the revethavar still waited, like the ogre in another old wonder-tale, but acknowledging my grief made it easier to bear, now that I was not wasting strength on denying it.

I stepped out of the maze just as the lower rim of the sun touched the horizon and walked back to the Orshaneisei's main building among the long shadows. They welcomed me placidly, not commenting on my tear-reddened eyes, and I supposed they were accustomed to having pilgrims come out of the maze in all sorts of conditions. A different sister showed me to a washroom, where I washed my face and hands and felt more presentable for it.

Dinner with the Orshaneisei was much as I remembered it, cheerful and noisy and with a plentitude of food: a stew of mutton and root vegetables, bread still warm from the ovens, and a firm yellow cheese that was mild and sharp at the same time. Conversation was general, and I did not know what prompted me to take out Tedoro's pilgrimage token and ask my neighbors if anyone knew the pilgrimage it came from.

My immediate neighbors had no more idea than I did, but they passed it down the table, and at the end nearest the kitchen, an older elven brother took it, frowned at it for a moment, and said, "This is a token from the Pilgrimage of Stairs in Ezho. Where did you find it?"

*A dead girl's pocket.* "A secondhand clothes store in Cemchelarna," I said, since that was most likely where Tedoro had come by it. "What is the Pilgrimage of Stairs?"

"It's also called the Unfinished Pilgrimage," said the brother, "because the man who was carving the stairs died before he reached the top of Mount Kezrinin, and no one has been called to finish it. So it's a staircase that winds about halfway up a small mountain and stops. *Someone* was called to widen out a landing there, and to carve a hollow for tokens in the side of the mountain, but it is not a pilgrimage to take if heights make you at all dizzy."

"I'm out, then," the elven woman next to him said cheerfully. "But is it a pilgrimage to Osreian?"

"No. To Cstheio. The quartz is to symbolize clear seeing."

And it seemed suitable in its own way that an unfinished staircase would be sacred to Cstheio, who was a goddess of the lost and the broken. Like Tedoro. Like me.

They passed the token back along the table to me, and I put it away carefully. Secondhand pilgrimage tokens might be nothing more than pretty bits and bobs, but they could also be useful as reminders, and this one would serve to remind me of the truth I'd found in the corn maze. I could not lay down the grief I carried, but I could name it for what it was, and by naming it ease the burden; clear sight was the gift of the Lady of the Stars.

# ACKNOWLEDGMENTS

My deepest thanks go to my Patreon patrons: Sabine Moehler, KJ Monahan, Elaine Blank, Kate Diamond, Katy Kingston, ScottKF, Gordon Tisher, Paige Morgan, Elizabeth Woodley, Gretchen Schultz, H. E. Wolf, Hilary Krause, E.S.H., Liz Novaski, Sarah Shope, Paul Keelan, Kris Ashley, Megan Lynae, Eleanor Skinner, Bill Ruppert, Jennifer Lundy, Sasha Lydon, Jennifer G Tifft, Margaret Johnston, Emily Richards, Laura E. Price, Cecil I. Roth, Liza Furr, Mariam Kvitsiani, Oliver Barrett, Katie Jones, Ruthanna and Sarah Emrys, Lindsay Kleinmanu, lunarennui, Sarah Ervine, Jesper Stage, Katee V, Clifton Royston, Simone Brick, Teresa Doyle Kovich, and Asia Wolf.

Thanks also go to everyone at Tor, especially Beth Meacham, Claire Eddy, Molly McGhee, Desirae Friesen, Becky Yeager, Renata Sweeney, Christina MacDonald, Greg Collins, Jamie Stafford-Hill, Megan Kiddoo, and Jim Kapp.

Thanks to my agents, Jack Byrne and Cameron McClure.

Many thousands of thanks to my writers' group: Elizabeth Bear, C. L. Polk, Arkady Martine, Jodi Meadows, Ryan Van Loan, Scott Lynch, Celia Marsh, Alex Haist, Devin Singer, Fran Wilde, Fade Manley, Amanda Downum, Jamie Rosen, Tochi Onyebuchi, Clarissa C. S. Ryan, John Wiswell, Liz Bourke, Max Gladstone, Amal El-Mohtar, Stella Evans, and Deanna Hoak.

If I've missed somebody—and I feel morbidly sure that I have—please know that it is not intentional.

# ABOUT THE AUTHOR

K ATHERINE ADDISON's short fiction has been selected by *The Year's Best Fantasy and Horror* and *The Year's Best Science Fiction*. Her novel *The Goblin Emperor* won a Locus Award. As Sarah Monette, she is the author of the Doctrine of Labyrinths series and coauthor, with Elizabeth Bear, of the Iskryne series. She teaches as adjunct faculty for the MFA program at Ashland University, and she lives near Madison, Wisconsin.